MW01027963
что ты особенный!
внез
Alya Sometimes Hides Her Feelings in Russian
тничает

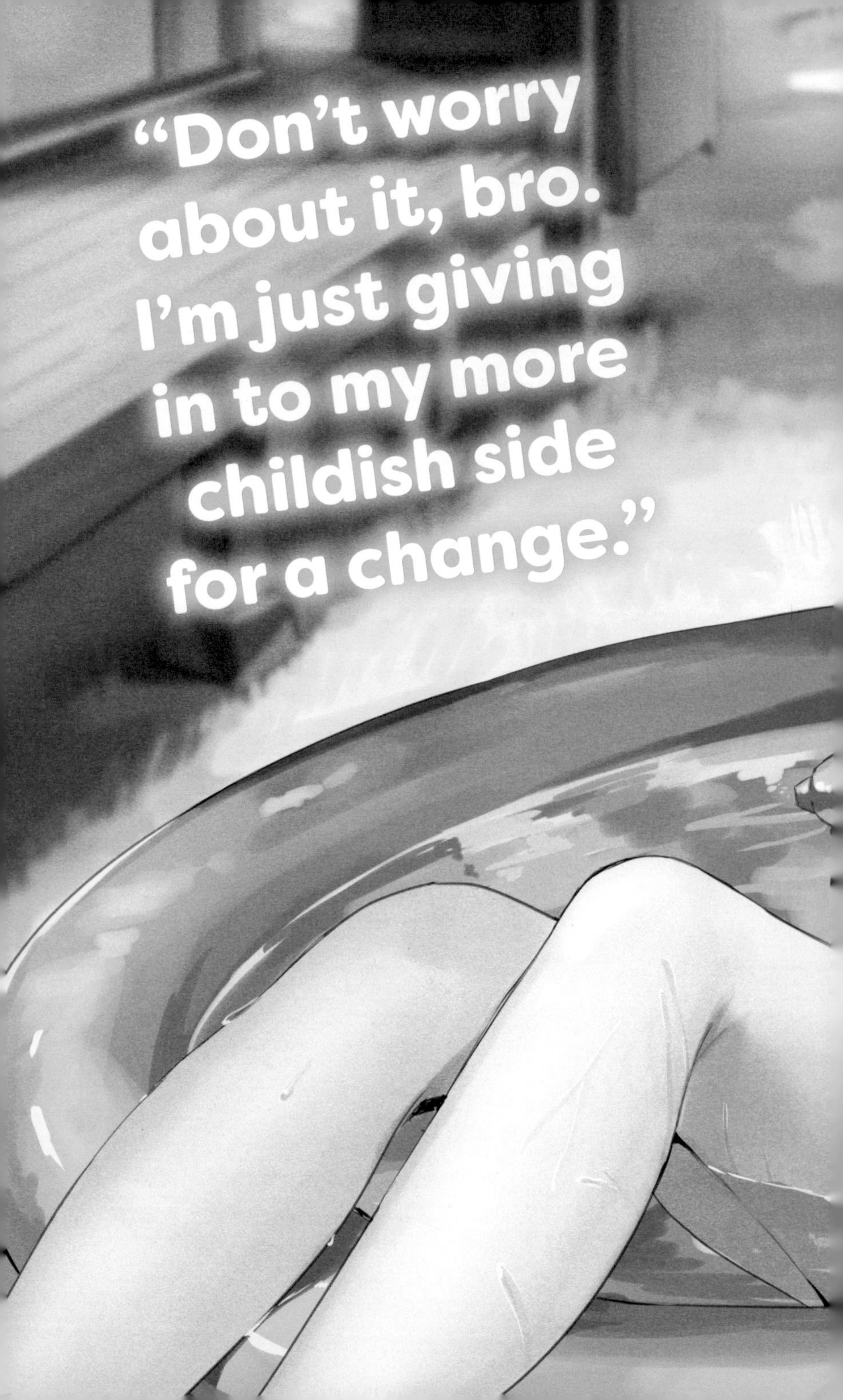
"Don't worry about it, bro. I'm just giving in to my more childish side for a change."

"S-stop staring!"

"K-Kuze?
If you keep
staring like
that, I..."

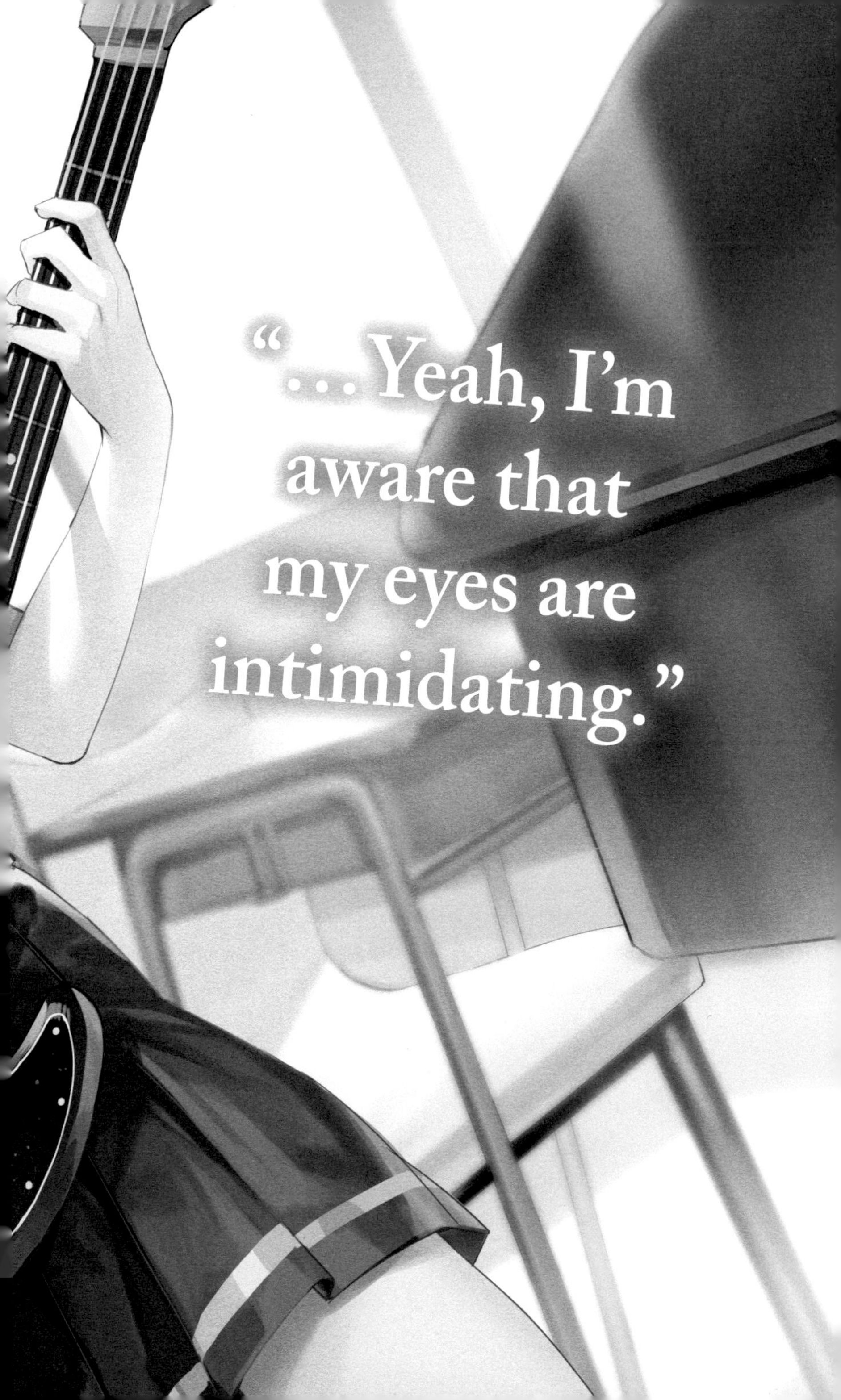
"...Yeah, I'm aware that my eyes are intimidating."

Contents

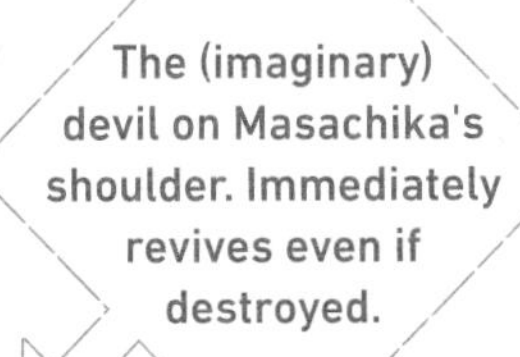

The (imaginary) devil on Masachika's shoulder. Immediately revives even if destroyed.

Alya Sometimes Hides Her Feelings in Russian

5

Sunsunsun
Illustrated by Momoco

New York

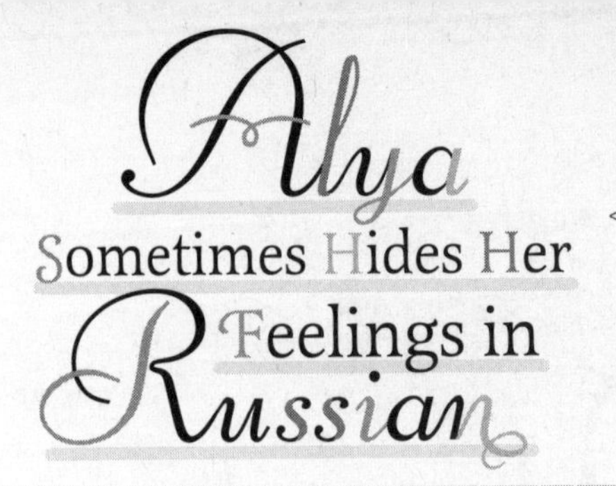

Translation by Matthew Rutsohn
Cover art by Momoco

Yen On
150 West 30th Street, 19th Floor
New York, NY 10001

Visit us at yenpress.com • facebook.com/yenpress • twitter.com/yenpress
yenpress.tumblr.com • instagram.com/yenpress

First Yen On Edition: August 2024
Edited by Yen On Editorial: Leilah Labossiere
Designed by Yen Press Design: Liz Parlett

Yen On is an imprint of Yen Press, LLC.
The Yen On name and logo are trademarks of Yen Press, LLC.

The publisher is not responsible for websites (or their content) that are not owned by the publisher.

Library of Congress Cataloging-in-Publication Data
Names: Sunsunsun, author. | Momoco, illustrator. | Rutsohn, Matt, translator.
Title: Alya Sometimes Hides Her Feelings in Russian / Sunsunsun ; illustration by Momoco ; translation by Matthew Rutsohn.
Other titles: Tokidoki bosotto roshiago de dereru tonari no Arya san. English
Description: First Yen On edition. | New York, NY : Yen On, 2022-
Identifiers: LCCN 2022029973 | ISBN 9781975347840 (v. 1 ; trade paperback) | ISBN 9781975347864 (v. 2 ; trade paperback)
Subjects: CYAC: Language and languages—Fiction. | Friendship—Fiction. | Schools—Fiction. | LCGFT: Humorous fiction. | School fiction. | Light novels.
Classification: LCC PZ7.1.S8676 Ar 2022 | DDC [Fic]—dc23
LC record available at https://lccn.loc.gov/2022029973

ISBNs: 978-1-9753-8950-5 (paperback)
978-1-9753-8951-2 (ebook)

10 9 8 7 6 5 4 3 2 1

LSC-C

Printed in the United States of America

PROLOGUE Encounter

"I thought I had this in the bag..."

"How could this have happened...? I practiced so hard..."

"He got first place again? Tsk. I bet he barely even practiced."

"My dad told me that I'm wasting his time if I don't win... I can't take it... I don't want to play anymore..."

These kinds of comments had always followed Masachika, even from an early age, but he started really noticing it after he began living with his paternal grandparents.

"He gets to be the last performer again? Sounds like the teacher's playing favorites."

"I heard his family is well-off, so the teacher probably *has* to."

"Why was my child not chosen?! This is rigged!"

"Come on. Can't we put that kid in some kind of hall of fame so he can retire? We need to give other kids a chance to win, too..."

It was a maelstrom of despair—the cries of the unrewarded. There were people around Masachika who did not hide their hostility. They shunned him. After leaving the Suou residence, he no longer had to desperately attempt to please his family, which meant he could focus on other activities. However, that came at the cost of noticing how much others despised him.

"*Sigh*. It's not fair. It must be nice being a piano prodigy."

Those were the words of another performer after yet another piano competition ended with Masachika in first place.

"It's not fair." Perhaps it wasn't. Masachika had always practiced for a decent amount of time, and then he would get results that exceeded the amount of time he spent on it. Never had he felt distressed or defeated. He had never hit a wall, and he never felt as if there were any obstacles in his way, either. Furthermore, he was able to accomplish what most people couldn't—no matter how hard they tried—with one hand tied behind his back. Ever since he was a small child, he had participated in far more after-school activities than his peers, and he always ended up being the best among them.

When he took swimming lessons, he was the fastest swimmer, and when he did karate, he got his black belt far sooner than kids who trained every day. Whenever there was a piano competition, he had the privilege of being the last to perform, and in calligraphy class, his work was always displayed on the wall where it could be seen by everyone. However, none of these activities were actually things he enjoyed. There was never any passion. He simply wished to meet his grandfather's expectations. He wanted his mother to praise him. He needed to reassure his sister. That was it. That was it…

Wait… Then why am I still doing this?

He would never be praised by his mother again. His grandfather would forever be disappointed in him. Plus, there was no way he was going to give his sister any relief after he'd lashed out at school. So what was the point of using this "unfair" prodigy mind of his to trample on the hard work of others? He pondered this question…until it eventually hit him.

"If it's pointless…then I should just quit."

There were most likely countless people who had to choke back their tears in the shadows of Masachika's radiant success. These were people who were passionate about what they did and went through soul-draining hardships to reach that point. Masachika, however, ignorantly crushed their dreams without even noticing the noble sacrifices they'd made to get to where they were.

"…I feel empty."

All these activities felt meaningless, and having no passion for anything he did left him feeling empty. Every victory he ever had was hollow.

"Masachika, you have to get moving. It's time for swim practice."

Even when his grandmother came to his room to get him, he felt nothing.

"...I'm not going."

"What? Oh... Okay. You're taking the day off? Then—"

"I'm never going back. I'm quitting. I'm quitting everything."

"...Oh. Well, if that's what you want, then maybe it's a good thing," said his grandmother, seeming to have picked up on his apathetic mood. She neither forbade nor questioned him. She simply agreed, and that kindness she showed made him extremely uncomfortable.

After sneaking out of the house, Masachika walked aimlessly around town until he eventually heard something loud and exciting coming from the shopping district: an arcade.

Video games, huh?

He thought back to conversations he'd heard his classmates having at school. Apparently, most elementary school kids around his age were obsessed with video games. Meanwhile, Masachika had never even touched one, since Gensei claimed they were evil.

"..."

His urge to rebel against his grandfather suddenly began to swell in the pit of his stomach, and he slowly drifted toward the arcade. The first thing that caught his eye was a zombie game, which he promptly decided to try. At first, he didn't understand how to play and immediately died, but he started to get the hang of it on his fourth try, and by his seventh attempt, he already managed to beat the last boss. The final cutscene was followed by a screen displaying his score: a B rank.

"...Interesting. So the less damage I take and the fewer bullets I use, the higher my score."

He was surprised that he beat the game so easily, but then he realized that this was where the true fun began. On a test, all he did was answer the questions, but now he needed to focus on fixing his mistakes and improving his overall grade. That was the real challenge here.

"Well, I guess I might as well go for a perfect score."

Since there was no one behind him waiting to play, he decided to continue until he was satisfied with his score, and once he finally got that perfect score, he saw his name beautifully displayed at the top of the high score list.

"...I guess that's it."

His interest instantly faded. He walked over to the claw-machine corner, but it only took a few tries before he got the hang of it, and he ended up mindlessly emptying the machines of their prizes. Plus, it wasn't like he wanted any of the prizes, so after grabbing as many as he could, he started passing them out to the people who had gathered around to watch. This continued for days and days, until he was eventually banned from all the arcades in the neighborhood.

"Well, I guess I shouldn't be surprised with all the rumors going around..."

That's what he told himself to feel better, but the frustration in his heart didn't fade. It was as if being exceptional excluded him from having fun, and no matter how hard he tried, he couldn't dispel that dreary thought.

"*Sigh*... What should I do with *this* now?"

Masachika gazed at the giant teddy bear in his arms and sighed. It was a prize from one of the claw machines that he happened to be holding when he was kicked out of the arcade. Returning the prize would be a pain in the ass, so he decided to hang on to it...but this was obviously a prize made for little girls. Yuki couldn't have any stuffed animals because of her asthma, so the only person he could give it to would be Ayano. That said, he wasn't planning on returning to the Suou residence anytime soon, so he had no idea when he would see her next. He didn't know how he would even go about giving it to her, either.

"...Maybe I'll just give it to Grandma," he muttered to himself. That was when he realized he was standing in front of a park with lots of playground equipment. His eyes naturally wandered around until he noticed a group of five girls around his age, but his gaze was especially drawn to one of them.

I-is that an angel...?

Masachika briefly lost himself in a trance. That was a testament to how ethereally beautiful this girl was. Her snow-white skin reflected light. Her soft, long golden locks complemented her twinkling blue eyes. Her charm almost took his breath away. However, that adorable face was currently clouded with confusion and sorrow as she seemed to be desperately pleading.

"No...that...uh, to...do?"

"I have no idea what you're trying to say."

"Come on, Maria. Speak Japanese."

The little girl was desperately trying to speak in halting Japanese with a heavy accent while the others stood around her and watched with malicious grins. Nevertheless, she continued to try her hardest to convey her feelings. Regardless, they continued to pick on her, deliberately trying to make her panic, even though they probably already had a good idea of what she wanted to say.

"I have no idea what you're saying."

"Your Japanese is terrible."

As Masachika watched them harass her, he suddenly got a sense of déjà vu, and he frowned at the mean-spirited grins of the four monsters laughing at the little girl. These were the venomous expressions of people who were trying to hurt someone far more exceptional than them. They despised this anomaly, just like Masachika's persistent classmates who wouldn't leave him alone until he ended up having to resort to violence.

"<I hate this... They don't understand me at all...>"

The little girl eventually began to sob, murmuring in Russian through her tears, but that only made it worse. It was as if these four vultures had been waiting for this moment.

"Whoooa! I seriously have no idea what she's saying."

"Has she never heard the phrase, 'When in Rome'? I guess a foreigner like her wouldn't understand."

"*Sigh*... Come on, girls. We tried, but she just doesn't want to talk to us. Come on. Let's go play without her."

"Good idea."

After insulting her to her face, the four spiteful girls ran off, leaving their sobbing peer behind to squeeze her skirt tightly with both hands and tremble in silence.

"..."

The thought of chasing after the four girls and kicking them as hard as he could crossed Masachika's mind after he witnessed the disturbing sight, but he managed to get his anger under control, and he shifted his focus to the lonely little girl instead. She stood there, pressing her light-pink lips together as if bravely suppressing her tears. The sight was far too much for Masachika's heart to bear, prompting him to unconsciously walk over to her and use what limited Russian he knew.

"<Are you…okay?>"

The girl swiftly lifted her chin, and her moist eyes opened wide as she stared at Masachika in disbelief.

"<Wait… Did you…?>"

"<Russian. I speak. A little?>"

Calling his Russian poor would be a compliment, since all he could do was string a few words together. Nevertheless, the little girl's face lit up, and her entire body seemed to vibrate with what had to be excitement and joy.

"<Wait. You can speak Russian? Wow! You're so smart!>"

"…!"

He honestly didn't understand everything she said, but from the words he did know, he could tell that she was complimenting him a lot. The genuine praise and her glittering eyes touched Masachika's heart, and it was something he hadn't been expecting.

"<I'm Masha!>"

"Huh…?"

"<Masha!>"

But in the midst of his uncertainty, the little girl mirthfully introduced herself with a beaming smile. Although he first thought she was saying a Russian word that he didn't know, he soon realized what she was saying when she asked:

“<What’s your name?>”

“Huh…? Oh, your name! Uh… Ma…?”

“<Masha!>”

“Macha?”

“<Ma. Sha.>”

“Oh, Masha?”

After the little girl, Masha, cheerfully nodded back numerous times, she took his hand and began to trace the following words on his palm as she spoke:

“<What’s your name?>”

“Oh… Masachika. Masachika Suou.”

“<Mashachika Shuou?>”

“Masachika. Ma. Sa. Chi. Ka.”

“…! Masaaachika!”

“Y-yeah? Good enough, I guess?”

Masachika nodded, though he was baffled by how she mispronounced his name. Masha’s smiling gaze lowered, and she asked:

“<Who’s that?>”

“Huh?”

“<What’s his name?>”

“…? Oh!”

After a brief pause, he realized that she was asking for the teddy bear’s name, which made him blush because this *angel* thought that he was a little boy who carried a teddy bear with him wherever he went. That was a misunderstanding far too embarrassing for a kid his age.

“No…! Uh… Arcade! Do you know arcades? Video game arcade.”

Her reaction told him that she had no idea what he was talking about, so he once again tried to utilize what few Russian words he could remember.

“<Present… Game. Present. Don’t want. Present for you.>”

“<…? What? You’re giving this to me?>”

“<For you.>”

When he pushed the teddy bear into her arms, Masha seemed puzzled for a moment, but it wasn’t long before her lips curled.

"<Wow! Really? Thank you so much! He's so cute. ♡>"

Seeing the girl affectionately squeeze the teddy bear as if she had never been happier in her entire life almost made Masachika feel like *he* was being hugged. He promptly looked away while his heart was filled with indescribable embarrassment and joy, and Masha once again asked:

"<So? What's his name?>"

"<No. No name.>"

"<Really? Hmm… Then I'm going to name you Samuel the Third!>"

"…"

Although he couldn't understand much of what she was saying, he somehow knew she was giving the teddy bear a very unique name, so he smiled awkwardly. Masha then took his hand and looked toward the climbing dome.

"<Masaaachika, let's play!>"

"Uh…?"

"<Race you!>"

"Wh-what…? Uh…"

Masachika hurried to keep up as Masha led him by the hand. The little girl he'd thought was an angel turned out to be a simple, innocent child, but it was that cherubic smile of hers that flipped his world upside down. There was no disgust in her eyes, unlike the expressions he was used to seeing. He could feel his dry, cracked heart slowly being healed by playing and talking with Masha, and he wanted to talk with her more. He wanted to show off to her more.

Crossing paths with Masha encouraged Masachika to start watching Russian movies with his grandfather—something he was never really interested in before—and he did so with enthusiasm. He even gradually began participating in after-school activities again despite quitting once already. Perhaps he viewed Masha as a replacement for his mother. Maybe he craved praise, acknowledgment, and acceptance from her—all things that his mother never gave him.

Regardless, there was no question about it: This was love.

"<What's wrong, Masuchika?>"

"<Uh… Do you think you could stop calling me that? It sounds like a Russian boy's name.>"

"<Really? Then what should I call you?>"

"<Maybe we could at least shorten my name to make it sound more Japanese? Like a nickname?>"

"<All right… I'll start calling you Sah, then!>"

"<No, that's— Seriously?>"

That's the part of your pronunciation I'm trying to fix, thought Masachika with a wry smile. Masha leaned in closer with a beaming grin.

"<What about me?>"

"Huh?"

"<What about my nickname?>"

Masha's already your nickname. There was no reason to shorten her nickname and give her a new one…but he swallowed those thoughts the moment he saw her eyes twinkling with excitement.

"Hmm…"

The first idea that popped into his head was simply adding *-chan* to the end of her name to make it sound more Japanese, but it was far too embarrassing for a little boy to do that…

"<Come on. What's my nickname?>"

"Errr…"

Any thought of backing down was purged from his mind the moment he once again saw how excited she was. So he averted his gaze, timidly opened his mouth, and replied:

"<All right. I'll call you—>"

CHAPTER 1 A Reunion and a Farewell

"M-Mah?"

The nickname had risen from the deepest corners of Masachika's memories before naturally falling from his lips. Maria slowly nodded back at him with a melancholic smile.

"Yes… It's me, Sah."

That girl's face slowly emerged from the fog that had been obscuring it all these years until it was perfectly mirroring Maria's face. She completely resembled… She resembled…

She doesn't exactly *resemble her?*

Although he could finally remember what that girl—*Mah*—looked like, there were too many little things about her that didn't match the other woman in front of him. At all. Of course, height and body type were easily explainable, but neither the length nor color of their hair matched, either. Even their eye color was different. The blond-haired, blue-eyed girl had changed into a brunette with brown eyes, which gave her a completely different look. The girl from his memories looked like an angel, while the older woman in front of him seemed more like a loving, affectionate older sister, and no matter how much Masachika thought about it, he couldn't see them as the same person.

No wonder I didn't realize it. Then again…how could I have not noticed even after knowing her for over two months now?!

He reflected on this fault of his while gazing into Maria's eyes in almost disbelief.

"Uh… You're Mah, aren't you? The girl who used to play with me in this park six years ago."

"Yep."

"Oh, uh… Well… That's…"

Not only was this an unexpected reunion, but the girl he once loved was actually someone he knew, so Masachika didn't know how to react. Ambiguous filler words escaped him, and his eyes wandered until Maria eventually smirked faintly and gently took his hand.

"Let's go somewhere where there's shade to sit and talk, okay?"

"Oh. Yes, ma'am."

"Come on. Don't be weird."

"Uh…"

As she led him to a bench under a tree, Masachika thought back and realized he had never spoken to her so formally before. Only after seating themselves did he finally begin to process what was going on, and he finally managed to form a single question.

"So… How long have you known?"

"Hmm… Since I met you in the student council room," replied Maria in a matter-of-fact manner, still facing forward.

"You figured it out the moment we met?!"

"Yep. I was a little confused because your last name was different, so I tried to speak in Russian to check. You didn't answer, though, so I thought, '*Maybe it isn't him, after all?*'" she replied before shifting her gaze to Masachika. The look in her eyes was warm, and she added:

"But when I looked at you, all I could see was Sah, so I knew it had to be you. Plus…I saw this…"

"Huh…?"

Paying no heed to his bewilderment, Maria gently rubbed Masachika's right shoulder…or so he initially thought, but it wasn't his shoulder exactly. She was actually rubbing the old scar he had there.

"This was all the proof I needed. You got this scar when you protected me, right?"

"Uh…"

"*Giggle.* Are you really that surprised?"

"Oh, sorry… You're right…" But even then, to Masachika, this person wasn't Mah. This was Masha. He couldn't simply flip a switch and see her as someone else, and too much time had gone by for him to start acting overly friendly with her again like he used to when they were kids. "But...like... What a coincidence, huh? It's hard to believe this is where we'd meet again. It's almost too perfect to be a coincidence," Masachika said.

"It's no coincidence."

"What...?"

Despite Masachika trying to change the subject due to not knowing how to react, Maria's expression became serious, and she quietly replied:

"I told myself I was going to give up by the end of summer break if you never showed up, but here you are. This...was fate."

"F-fate...? I don't know if I'd go that far. Sounds like something out of a movie..." Though he was disagreeing with a tense half grin, Maria's attitude did not change, and her unclouded eyes made Masachika trail off until the smirk was wiped off his face. "What do you mean...it was fate?" he quietly asked.

Perhaps it was a very unromantic, senseless question, but Maria did not hesitate to answer honestly.

"I told you when we were at the beach, right? I told you how I felt about destiny and about having a soulmate. Do you understand what I'm trying to say?"

Maria was unquestionably confessing her love for Masachika. Immediately, his heart began to race, the irregular beats making it feel like it was going to explode.

"Wait, wait, wait. Hold on. This doesn't make any sense. This isn't right."

He reflexively tried to argue.

"Why?"

"'Why?' Because there's no reason for you to like me, and I'm not even Masachika Suou—Sah—anymore, either. I've never done anything that deserves your attention. If anything, I've only shown you how pathetic I can be..."

The self-deprecating words spilled out of his mouth, and Maria replied with a slightly melancholic smile.

"Yes… You are a lot different from the Sah I knew."

"Right? Looking back, I was a little brat who just bragged all the time. I mean, I had to have been annoying, right?"

"*Giggle.* I never thought you were annoying, but you did brag a lot."

"Ngh… I knew it…"

It was something even he was well aware of, but having her confirm it made him want to run away, and the unbearable embarrassment had him fidgeting restlessly. Maria, on the other hand, was staring off into the distance as if she were reminiscing about old times.

"You were always laughing and smiling, saying things like, 'What do you think of that?! Pretty amazing, huh?'"

"Ugh…"

"And whenever I complimented you, you would smile from ear to ear as if you were the happiest you had ever been… *Giggle.* You were so cute."

"O-oh…"

Masachika hunched over, and he seemed to gradually shrink into himself, feeling as if she were treating him like a little kid. However, Maria's lips curled into a different kind of smile.

"Deep down inside, you were hurting, but you made yourself believe that you didn't deserve to feel hurt, so you always forced yourself to smile…"

"…?!"

Masachika blinked in astonishment at the sudden change of course in the conversation. She gazed right into his eyes and said in the sweetest voice imaginable:

"But there is nothing in the world that I love more than your smile."

"…!"

"You are always unbelievably kind and considerate, and yet you won't admit it. On the other side of that smile are the scars from the wounds you inflict on yourself...and whenever I see you like that, I just want to hug you as hard as I can. I want to hold you, rub your head, kiss you on the cheek, and say, 'You don't need to hate yourself anymore. You have already done more than enough,' as many times as it takes."

Her eyes were brimming with passion and sympathy.

What? So she's into terrible, hopeless guys?

That was the first thought that came to mind, as if he were trying to divorce himself from reality, but he almost immediately shook that tactless assumption out of his head.

Hmm... But maybe this means that she finds guys cute when they try to hide behind acting tough? Or something like that?

After interpreting it in a way that he could vaguely comprehend, Masachika smirked as if he were trying to avoid Maria's intense emotions.

"I'm no dark hero with a troubled past or anything cool like that..."

To him, there was nothing especially tragic about his past. He simply had a fit, ran away from home, and never went back. He was merely someone who refused to forgive and forget. That was it. *And it's pathetic,* he thought.

But in the midst of his self-deprecation...a shudder went through Maria, as if she couldn't take it any longer.

"If you keep making such a cute face like that..."

"Huh?"

Masachika was wondering what she was whispering to herself... when all of a sudden, she wrapped her arms tightly around him.

"Big hug!"

"Whoa?! Why?!"

"This is your fault, Kuze, for tempting me with that cute face of yours!"

"When?!"

He was in utter shock as she squeezed him tightly in her arms while rubbing her cheek against his. Every thought he had left his head, never to be seen again, as this older woman expressed herself with her very direct body language. A flood of information filled Masachika's mind—the curves of Maria's feminine figure against him, her sweet fragrance tickling his nose, him overheating in the blink of an eye.

So soft... Smells good...

His overloaded brain had him thinking like a caveman.

"You really are Sah..."

As her soft voice caressed his earlobe, he suddenly felt a tight pain in his chest, which magically cleared his mind.

Now that I think about it...

Maria said that meeting in the park wasn't a coincidence. In other words, that meant that she had been visiting this park from time to time with hopes of being reunited with an old friend, despite there being absolutely no guarantee that she would ever see him again.

Seriously? That's... That's...

The courage it took to do that made Masachika start to tremble, and tears suddenly welled in his eyes. A fire was burning in the depths of his heart, urging him to hug this person sitting right next to him.

"Masha, I—"

He lifted his arms, giving in to his emotions, when—

"Oooh! Maria's on a date!"

Masachika instinctively turned in the direction of the high-pitched, bold, uniquely childlike shout and discovered a group of seven elementary school kids around ten years old. Maria shyly scooted away from Masachika, leaving his arms to hang in the air momentarily before he returned them to rest on his lap.

"O-oh my... How embarrassing. ♪"

"...Do you know them?"

"Ha-ha... They're friends I sometimes play with when I'm here..."

That was when three girls from the group ran over with sparkles in their eyes. The four remaining boys soon followed, albeit with skeptical gazes.

"Maria, Maria, Maria! Is this the boy you've been telling us about?"

the girl in the lead enthusiastically asked as if the curiosity was killing her.

"Yes… This is the boy I like." Maria, although bashful, nodded firmly.

""""Aaaahhh!""""

The three girls squealed shrilly in excitement, but at the same time—

What was that sound? Did I just hear the sound of hearts tragically shattering? It sounded like a quartet, too…

One look at the faces of the four boys in the background was more than enough to prove that Masachika wasn't simply imagining things. Each of their expressions was frozen, and they seemed to have forgotten how to blink.

"Maria! What do you like about him?!"

"Stop it. She's on a date."

"Yeah. Um… Enjoy your date, you lovebirds!"

"Ha-ha-ha! You're so funny."

The three girls noisily took off into the distance while impressively not forgetting to take the boys with them.

"…Girls are really maturing quickly these days," muttered Masachika in a daze, taken aback by the storm that had suddenly come and gone.

"*Giggle.* You can say that again."

But Maria's voice instantly pulled him back to reality, reminding him of what she had just said.

"Um… So… Like…"

He fidgeted.

"Hmm?"

"Ngh…! That thing… You know, when she asked about who you liked…," he mumbled timidly. Maria nodded, her lips curling into a mature smile that made his heart skip a beat.

"I like you. I've always had feelings for you and only you."

Her confession was the epitome of genuine and direct…and yet Masachika's heart filled only with sorrow.

"Then why…?"

"…?"

"Why did you…abandon me that day?"

"What…?"

As she blinked multiple times in confusion, Masachika continued to bitterly regurgitate those painful memories buried in the back of his mind.

"You told me that day that we couldn't meet anymore. You said that I wasn't your soulmate, so you weren't interested in playing together!"

"Wh-what?!"

Maria's eyes widened, and she leaned back in shock, but after a few moments went by, she shook her head wildly.

"I—I didn't say that! I never said that!"

"But I can remember that day so clearly…"

"I did tell you we had to say good-bye and that we couldn't meet anymore, but what I said after was, '*If you aren't my soulmate, then we will never meet again, but if you are my soulmate, then I know we'll meet again someday!*'"

"…Huh?" Masachika grunted in disbelief as he traced his memories…until he realized that she was right. He had simply been so shocked when he heard that they couldn't meet anymore that he could hardly process anything she said after that. In other words, he'd misheard her.

By the time he had come back to his senses, Maria was already gone. Even after that, he continued to stop by the park as often as he could, believing it had to be some sort of misunderstanding, but he never saw her again. Masachika refused to face reality, refused to think deeply about it, and refused to accept any answer other than his tragic, knee-jerk conclusion that she must have betrayed him like his mother had. And just like that, his recollection of interactions with her had been labeled "bad memories" and were sealed away in the back of his mind. Perhaps if he had never run away, and actually thought hard about it, then he would have realized the truth.

"Ha-ha...ha-ha-ha..." Masachika laughed dryly, as if he had been thrown into a pit of despair. The thought that he'd hurt himself unnecessarily over such an absurd misunderstanding was simply too funny to him. On the other hand, Maria's brow furrowed sympathetically, as though she was feeling genuine guilt.

"I... I'm sorry. I wanted to tell you good-bye in Japanese because it was really important...but it looks like I caused a misunderstanding since I wasn't really that good at Japanese back then..."

"Oh... No. It was my fault for jumping to conclusions, so there's nothing you need to feel bad about..."

Maria could have been correct. After all, it was highly possible that her halting, non-native Japanese was the cause of this misunderstanding, but it was just as likely that Masachika's pessimism negatively distorted his memories. Recollections from one's childhood could easily be twisted to suit one's own bias. Regardless, there was no way to check what had really happened, so any more speculation was a waste of time.

"I'm really sorry...," Maria said once more, and she gently embraced him. Masachika surrendered to her unbelievably comforting touch...until her confession suddenly played back in his head, making his heart race.

"Uh... I..."

Despite his inarticulate delivery, she nodded as if she understood everything he wanted to say.

"It's okay... I'm not expecting an answer immediately."

"...!"

"I mean, you've never thought of me as anything other than a friend, right?"

"Errr..."

It truly was as if she could see right through him, which made Masachika uncomfortable for a different reason from his earlier one. Although he froze with an awkward look on his face, Maria giggled, let go of him, and softly added:

"Besides, I'm sure you've already noticed how Alya feels about you, right?"

"…!"

Her unexpected comment took his breath away. As he tried to come up with a response, she continued:

"*Giggle.* It doesn't look like Alya has even realized it herself, though… Maybe we fell in love with the same guy because we're sisters."

"…"

Although most people might expect a bloodbath if siblings fell in love with the same person, she spoke as if it weren't a big deal, and that made Masachika feel odd.

"How…?"

How can you be so calm about this?

Maria somehow knew exactly what he wanted to say, despite his inability to fully put it into words.

"It makes me really happy that Alya, of all people, has finally found someone she loves, and that person happens to be someone wonderful like you," she replied with her unchanging, soft voice.

"…"

"I'm truly happy…because I care about both you and Alya so much… And that's why…"

She swiftly lifted her chin and gazed into the sky.

"I really don't want to compete with Alya," she muttered as if she were truly taking in this moment. The words echoed what she had said that one day in the hallway illuminated by the evening sun, but this time, they rang with a different meaning.

"Does that mean…?"

Did that mean she was going to give up for her sister's sake…?

Maria smiled softly at Masachika's wide-eyed astonishment.

"And that's why I want you to truly consider how Alya feels about you without running away."

"…?"

"I want you to come to terms with how she feels about you…and then if you still end up choosing me…"

She paused.

"...I want you to ask me out. Could you do that?"

Her endlessly sweet, brave words tied a knot in Masachika's chest.

"Masha... Are you okay with that?"

Maria perfectly understood how both Masachika and Alisa felt, and she'd decided to back down and prioritize their feelings. Masachika couldn't help but think it was an unbelievably self-sacrificing proposal. She easily picked up on that and frowned as if slightly troubled.

"Don't look so sad. I'm doing this for me. Because the last thing I want is to hurt Alya or you."

Her smile was rueful.

"...I'm sorry. I knew that telling you how I felt now would be hard for you, but I couldn't hold back these feelings any longer. Still, I really don't want to hurt either of you. I promise. I want you two to be able to make a choice you won't regret," she confessed somewhat sorrowfully. She then raised her index finger in front of her lips and continued, "And that's why...I want you to keep this a secret from Alya. Please don't tell her what happened here today or about our past, okay? Because if she knew you were Sah...then she would most likely bow out and bottle up her emotions."

Masachika's heart was suddenly overcome with a loneliness he couldn't describe, for it was a feeling he had never known. Despite his bewilderment, he nodded.

"...All right."

"Thanks."

After subtly nodding back, Maria faced forward once more. Silence followed, but there was strangely nothing uncomfortable or awkward about it. However, the indescribable loneliness continued to spread throughout Masachika's heart, and Maria seemed to stare sorrowfully into the distance.

"...Now, then," she abruptly muttered after some time passed. She got to her feet and looked down at Masachika with a cheery expression. "I think we said everything we needed to say...so maybe we should start heading home."

"Yeah… Good idea. Uh… Want me to walk you back?"

"No, it's fine. I'm sure you have a lot on your mind, so let's part ways here."

"Oh. Okay."

Although somewhat deflated by how easily she said good-bye for the night, Masachika stood and realized Maria was holding her arms out to him.

"…? What are you doing?"

As he hesitantly braced himself for another hug, Maria let out a vaguely bitter laugh, then asked:

"Do you think I could kiss you on the cheek just like old times?"

After thinking about it for a moment, Masachika recalled that she had always said good-bye with a kiss on each cheek when they were kids, and that nostalgia pushed him to agree without really putting any more thought into it.

"Yeah, sure."

"Thanks."

Once he turned to face her, Maria swiftly approached him and wrapped her arms around his shoulders before placing her right cheek on his, followed by the left.

This really brings back memories…

The familiar sensation made Masachika relax, but right as her left cheek began to slide away—

"Huh?"

He froze with his eyes opened wide, taken aback by what was now touching his cheek. "I'm sure Alya would forgive a little peck," Maria said impishly, gazing into his eyes.

"Uh…?"

"*Giggle!* Anyway, see you around. Let's just act the same way we always do the next time we see each other!"

With a bashful grin, she waved good-bye to Masachika and began heading to the park entrance.

"Yeah…"

He waved back in an almost trancelike state until Maria left the park and disappeared into the distance. Only then did he finally understand why he felt such loneliness in his heart.

Oh... That's why...

It was the sorrow of a tale that had finally reached its end. The fleeting love story between Sah and Mah, which had been left incomplete for years, had finally come to a close. The great pretender Sah and the exceptionally sweet, innocent Mah no longer existed. Even if Masachika and Maria were to fall in love all over again, they would not be continuing where they'd left off, for that tale from their past was now nothing more than a concluded story and a memory they would tuck away in their hearts.

"..."

He quietly looked back at the park and vividly saw memories of their past play out before his eyes: how they had talked endlessly on the playground equipment, how they used to hold hands and run all over the park with smiles, and how their good-bye had been tainted by a misunderstanding. It was the finale to the tale of his first love, which ended in sadness...

"Good-bye."

After bidding farewell to the two mirages of his past, Masachika exited the park, alone.

Maybe dreams aren't always meant to come true.

Masachika trudged along his weary way home with an indescribable sense of loss. Even though he'd originally stopped by the park for closure, the moment he got a conclusion to his past love, he was overcome with an unbelievable feeling of isolation and didn't know how to deal with it. Despite getting the closure to move forward with his life, he realized that he couldn't stop thinking about the past, even though he had numerous other concerns he needed to sort out involving Alisa and Maria.

"*Sigh...*"

Even the road he was walking down was a path often used by Masachika Suou in the past. It reminded him of the time he had sprinted down this street one day on his way home, propelled by excitement and embarrassment from Mah kissing him good-bye on the cheek. After finally making it home, he had sneaked into his room through the back porch to make sure his grandparents didn't see how giddy he was.

Now Masachika arrived home and reflected on past memories as he opened the gate and went around to the back porch...and that was where he found Yuki wearing a school swimsuit and sitting in an inflatable pool clearly made for children.

"...What are you doing?" he asked, looking at her wearily. More important, he wondered why she was even there in the first place. She'd never said a word to Masachika about stopping by that day. Perhaps she was nothing more than an illusion. But the moment

Masachika placed a hand on his forehead and closed his eyes to consider the possibility, his face was soaked with cold water.

"Pfft?!"

He reflexively wiped his face and opened his eyes to find Yuki pointing a water gun right at his head, her lips curled impishly in a grin.

"...Seriously. What are you doing?" asked Masachika once more. Yuki snorted smugly, shifted her gaze to the summer sky, and spun her water gun around her finger like some sort of hotshot detective.

"Don't worry about it, bro. I'm just giving in to my more childish side for a change."

"Your 'childish' side?"

"Yep. I'm trying to get that adolescent rush. Know what I mean?"

"*Adrenaline* rush. Don't try to make what you're doing sound cool," he growled with a reproachful glare. He then briskly walked over to his sister and immediately began rubbing her head aggressively, messing up her hair.

"There's some bonus serotonin for you."

"Oooh! I can feel the happy hormones oozing from my bodyyy! ...Wait. What in the world am I doing here?"

"How can you ask me that with a straight face? That's what *I'm* trying to figure out."

"What was I doing...? Argh! My head...!"

"Were you brainwashed? Hurry up and remember already."

"Guh...! Hff...! It was at that moment I remembered it all. This world is the world from the otome game I was playing right before I died."

"Nobody asked you to remember your past life."

"Yuki...Suou...? Ngh...! No...! That can't be! I was reincarnated as a villainess?!"

"Oh, wowww. You were a villainess this whole time?"

"I remember everything now... I played the spiteful husband who picked on the heroine with her older brother."

"Oh, is Ayano the main character?"

"Precisely, my dear brother. Ayano Kimishima is the heroine of this world, aka the protagonist of *The Dark Noble's Infatuation: All of the Beautiful Yandere Men Are Obsessed with Me*!"

"Can I get all the names of the male characters she can choose from? I need to kill them."

"Hikaru Kiyomiya."

"Hmm… I surprisingly don't really know how I feel about that."

"Yuushou Kiryuuin."

"He's just evil."

"Ouji Hachioji."

"Isn't that supposed to be a student council president in the next town over? And what kind of name is that?"

"And the secret character…Sakuya Sarashina."

"I don't know who that is, but that sounds like a last boss if you ask me. This is one of those stories where you can play the last boss's route after completing all the other routes, right?"

"Brother, the time to slaughter has come. Start by killing the hidden character."

"I'm sorry. I can't. You should probably just keep that character hidden."

"What? But the world will be destroyed if you don't defeat the secret character…"

"Definitely sounds like the last boss to me."

"Oh, but if we're following the source material, then you're supposed to have a fan-service scene today where you accidentally see some boobs, which causes copious amounts of blood to shoot out of your nose until you die of blood loss. So I guess you're not supposed to be the one saving the world."

"What a disappointing way to go. Today's the day, huh?"

"Yep. Now go dry off your face. You look like a wet dog."

"And whose fault is that?"

After lightly smacking his sister on the head, Masachika took off his shoes, stepped up onto the porch, and walked through the tatami-matted room with slumped shoulders.

Sigh... I'm exhausted already.

Masachika headed to the bathroom while using a handkerchief to dry the water dripping from his hair. The air was still in the hallway past the tatami-matted room, and there was no sign of anyone else being around. It was only natural that his grandfather wouldn't be home, since he was walking the dog, but his grandmother didn't seem to be there, either.

Did Grandma go out today...?

He tilted his head curiously, opening the door to the bathroom... only to find himself standing face-to-face with his completely nude maid, Ayano.

"Sorry."

He promptly closed the door. The entire exchange lasted for one point seven seconds, an impressive display of Masachika's godlike reaction speed.

Why don't you ever make any noise?!

He screamed internally. From the looks of it, Ayano appeared to be in the process of wrapping a towel around her body, so why didn't the fabric at least make a rustling sound? Despite knowing that he was shifting the blame, Masachika still couldn't help but scowl in frustration at the maid who was silent even at times like this.

Wait! Is this the fan-service scene she was talking about?!

Yuki *knew* that Ayano was in the bathroom, which was why she had led him here. It was unfiltered malice. That entire ridiculous conversation about the nosebleed was all foreshadowing for this as well.

In other words, yelling or panicking would be exactly what Yuki wanted, so the smart thing to do would be to casually walk away as if nothing had happened...

But before Masachika could even finish that thought, the door before him silently slid open.

"Good afternoon, Master Masachika. Please come in. Don't mind me."

"Seriously?! I do mind!" shouted Masachika, unable to handle how willingly she invited him in while hardly covering up with her towel.

"If anything, you should be bothered by this more than me!"

"...! Oh, right. You have my sincere apologies."

Ayano promptly began drying Masachika's wet chin and hair with the towel that was wrapped around her body...unsurprisingly, revealing herself to Masachika in the process.

"No, I'm not talking about my hair!"

He immediately leaped back and averted his gaze.

"Are you stupid?! Have you no shame?!"

"Master Masachika, it may not look it, but I am working extremely hard in order to overcome my embarrassment."

"Could you not?!" he pleaded before sprinting back to the tatami-matted room like a scared rabbit. After landing on the floor, he clutched his head tightly and began to groan. His cries were short-lived, as he was soon interrupted by the cackling of a demon, prompting him to lift his head and shift his gaze in the direction of the noise.

"Oh, wow. It looks like you cheated death. I'm impressed."

"..."

Yuki was sitting in the inflatable pool with her legs crossed and a grin on her face, staring into the house. Masachika silently turned his back to her, since it was obvious that she was going to make fun of him, regardless of how he reacted.

"Hey, come on, bro. What's wrong? Can't get the image of Ayano's birthday suit out of your head?"

"..."

"Hello? Can you hear me? Stop ignoring meee."

"..."

"Whoopsie-daisy! Oh no! My boobs popped out of my swimsuit!"

"..."

Why did she think that was going to make me turn around? wondered Masachika. *She understands I'm her brother, right?*

But he fought through the strong urge to point that out and decided to sulk on the floor instead.

"...Tsk! Looks like a little nip slip isn't going to be enough. I guess

seeing me half-naked in a school swimsuit isn't nearly as enticing as seeing Alya braless in a white T-shirt at the beach!"

"..."

"Curse you, Alya! My cute, little lamb, Alya... Before I even realized it, those E cups grew and grew until they were E cups no more..."

"...?!"

"Hey! I just saw your shoulders twitch a little."

Crap, thought Masachika, but right as Yuki's grin became more depraved, Ayano suddenly appeared and slid open the door. This time, she was wearing clothes and carried a clean towel as she swiftly walked to the edge of the porch.

"I am sorry to keep you waiting, Lady Yuki. This way, please."

"Hmm? ...Oh." Yuki grunted while hopping out of the pool reluctantly; she slipped on her sandals. Once she walked over to the porch and Ayano briefly dried her body off, Yuki thoroughly cleaned the bottom of her feet, then wrapped herself in the towel and headed to the bathroom. However, when she stepped into the hallway, she swiftly turned around and casually asked Ayano:

"By the way, Ayano, how much did my brother see?"

"Go take your bath, you freak. Ayano, don't answer her."

Masachika promptly closed the sliding door, shutting Yuki out of their lives (physically). Only after his sister's chuckling and footsteps faded into the distance did he finally face Ayano once more.

"Sorry about not being more careful before opening the door."

"Oh, no. I should be the one apologizing for my unsightly appearance..."

If anything, her delicate yet feminine body was breathtakingly alluring, and her wet, luscious black hair only complemented her charm. Nevertheless, being foolishly honest like this would likely be interpreted as sexual harassment, and not saying anything at all wasn't an option, either, since it could lead Ayano to believe that her appearance really was unsightly...

"...Ayano. You're beautiful and extremely cute...so don't belittle yourself like that."

"Th-thank you very much. I think you are very charming and wonderful yourself, too."

"...Thanks."

After shrugging off her compliment, Masachika lay back down in an attempt to escape the awkward silence and turned his back on Ayano. For once, even she managed to read the room, immediately closing her mouth in order to become one with the air, unlike her "husband," who would read the room and still choose violence.

Sigh... What a day this turned out to be. There better not be some kind of repercussion for all this tomorrow.

Not only did someone confess their love to him for the first time in his life, but he got his own fan-service scene when he got home, too. Objectively, he was extremely lucky, and that was why he was worried he had used up all his good fortune for a lifetime.

Wait... This isn't the first time someone told me they liked me.

He realized that, long ago, Mah also told him that she liked him, and although embarrassed, Masachika had expressed how he felt about her, too. The feelings were mutual. That much he could still remember. Nevertheless, he felt that it had merely been two kids acting like they knew what love was.

But Masha wasn't playing... She was serious...

It would be easy to say they were just pretending and call it a day, but at the very least, Maria's feelings for Masachika remained unchanged, and that was why he couldn't give them such a cheap label and move on.

Ha-ha! It's really cliché for characters to promise to get married when they're kids in rom-coms, but I've never heard of a rom-com where the heroine already has a steady boyfriend.

The hollow laugh echoed in his head until it suddenly hit him.

Hmm? Wait... Don't tell me that Masha's boyfriend is...

At the beach, Maria had told him that her boyfriend was that teddy bear, but...

Was she...talking about me...?

The instant he came to that possible conclusion, he began to feel a sort of uncomfortable, tingly sensation in his chest...but it almost immediately passed.

No, technically, it wouldn't be me. It would be Masachika Suou—Sah.

He was simultaneously overcome with a sense of loss while his mood rapidly fell until it hit rock bottom.

Dammit... I'm being negative again.

He realized this was a bad habit of his, but that still wasn't enough to stop his thoughts from spiraling.

Tsk. What do Masha and Alya see in a guy like me?

The hearts of most people would be brimming with joy if they discovered that those attractive, charming siblings had feelings for them...but all Masachika felt was guilt. He felt sorry that this was the kind of person he was, and he was ashamed to bother these two wonderful girls.

I can't do it... I'm not good enough for them. Maybe I should just run away from it all. Maybe I could just lock myself in my home and cut everyone out of my life...just like I did when I ran away from the Suou residence. I wouldn't bother anyone that way and—

The sliding door swiftly slid open before he could finish his thought.

"Ahhh, I feel like a new woman! Boing!"

Masachika immediately sensed an incoming object and rolled away.

"Nice try!" she shouted.

"Bff?!"

Yuki read him like an open book, body-slamming her brother and knocking the wind right out of him. Then with a slight frown, she observed Masachika, who was coughing and gasping for air, before a mischievous grin twisted her lips once more.

"Oh? What's wrong? The summer heat beating you down? Don't feel good?"

She lightly slapped his forehead while digging her chin into his chest.

"Stop hitting me." After he heedlessly knocked her hand way, she abruptly sat up and straddled him instead. "I don't have time to point out all the ridiculous things you do… You're sick," he stated with a completely straight face.

But Yuki simply raised her middle and index fingers in front of her chest, got into position, and—

"Happiness beam! Make my brother feel better! Pewww! Pew! Pew! Pew!" she rattled off, stabbing Masachika in the chest and stomach with her extended fingers.

"Abbffft! Stop it! How old are you?! And what part of this is a beam?!"

"My feelings for you are a beam!"

"What kind of beam is that?!"

She froze, a blank expression on her face, the moment he screamed.

"Do you really want to know?"

"…I would love to know."

"Oh, really? …Very well. Listen carefully."

She played coy, dragging things out by brushing her bangs aside with her right hand and peering down at her brother with a serious gaze. Then, with a grave and unsympathetic tone, she revealed:

"It's an 'I Wuv My Big Brother Sooo Much' beam."

"Oh, an 'I Wuv My Big Brother Sooo Much' beam, huh?"

"Yes…"

"…"

"…"

"…Go on. I want details."

"What are you trying to do? Make me die of embarrassment?"

"As if you had any shame to begin with."

"Hold on!" Yuki suddenly smushed her face into the top of Masachika's shoulder. "…That's a woman's scent."

"Seriously?!"

"Wow… Look at you, you sly dog. I was wondering why you seemed so down in the dumps. Having lady troubles, eh?"

"…"

"Oh? Exercising your right to remain silent? Which means I'm right, huh? I'm right, aren't I?"

"..."

Masachika closed his eyes and kept quiet while she glared down at him with her chin raised haughtily.

"Hmph..." She pouted.

"I'm going to have to kiss you if you're going to be that way!"

Yuki opened her mouth as wide as she could and began to lean forward.

"Quit it!"

Within a fraction of a second, Masachika had his hand on her forehead, pushing her away. If someone passing by witnessed this, they probably would have thought she had turned into a zombie and was about to eat her brother. It didn't help that she was still stubbornly pushing as hard as she could to bite his neck.

"What's up with you trying to bite me all the time lately?" he asked with a fed-up tone.

"You're seriously going to ask me that?"

Her response to his casual question was surprisingly stern, far different from when she'd been pretending to be sincere earlier. Yuki's blank expression was almost terrifying, even, as she quietly gazed into his eyes without even blinking, making Masachika recoil a bit.

"...What?"

Perhaps there was a specific reason she was acting this way? But there was no telling why. Masachika gave it some thought, but before he could reach any meaningful conclusion, Yuki, still wearing her blank expression, quietly replied:

"I'm waiting for you to say, 'You took a bite, and now you better clench your jaw and not let go.'"

"Guh."

"I've been waiting for you to say the line for sooo long," she revealed, digging into her brother's old wound while she peered hard into his lifeless eyes. Although he shot her a reproachful glare, she emphasized the spite in her voice and smugly mimicked him once more:

"You took a bite, so now you better clench your jaw and not let go."

"You little…!"

"Hee-hee-hee-hee! Oh my gosh! My brother is sooo lame!!"

After tumbling off him and onto the floor, she began to wildly kick her feet while literally rolling on the floor, laughing…until her expression suddenly clouded over. She swiftly sat up with a serious look on her face and raised an index finger.

"But now that I think about it, it could have two meanings. It could mean, 'You better finish what you start,' but it could also mean, 'You better not let go. Because the moment you let your guard down, I'm going to strike.' When you think about it, this is actually very cool—"

"Quit it! Stop analyzing what I said."

Although his face was tense as he glared at his sister, he eventually let out a single sigh and rolled over. Of course, Yuki immediately poked her head over his shoulder.

"Oh, come on. You're no fun, bro. You're supposed to be like, 'Aw, get over here, ya little runt,' then roll on the floor and laugh with me."

"We're not kids anymore."

"High school students are still kids," she whined, tickling Masachika's sides, which gradually started to get on his nerves… Then it hit him.

Wait… Does she just want to spend time together? Maybe she needs a hug?

The realization reminded him of the love he felt for Yuki at the park and what Maria had said to him at the beach.

I guess physical intimacy really is important…

After he reflected on what Maria told him, he rolled onto his back, grabbed Yuki, who was sitting by his side, and pulled her in without saying a word.

"O-oh?"

Although somewhat hesitant, she allowed herself to fall on top of

Masachika. He wrapped his left arm around her petite back and rubbed her head with his right.

"O-ohhh? Huh? Hmm?"

Yuki's eyes widened at the sudden sweet embrace for a moment before she cracked into a smug smirk as if she had picked up on something from her brother continuing to rub her head in silence.

"Heh. What's gotten into you? You're embarrassing me." She bashfully snickered, rubbing her forehead into her brother's chest like a cat showing affection. Feeling her love and affection began to warm Masachika's heart, slowly melting his sense of self-disgust and any urge to run away from it all.

Yeah... This is actually kind of nice.

He could finally understand what Maria meant when she mentioned how important human touch was. Feeling loved was a wonderful feeling.

Even I'm surprised how simple of a guy I am.

Feeling Yuki's love directly through touch made Masachika wonder why he took Maria's confession so negatively. Her embrace was warm, and she was extremely considerate with her words, and yet...

"Masachika."

"Hmm?"

Yuki suddenly spoke up, drawing Masachika's eyes toward his chest, where her face remained buried.

"You don't have to feel guilty for what you think you did to me. I'm happy...and never once have I blamed you for any of that."

"...!"

"I know even telling you this isn't going to stop you from thinking whatever you want to think and worrying yourself over it...but in my eyes, you're still the same brother I've always loved. And that's why...you don't have to care about the Suou family. You're allowed to find happiness for yourself."

Masachika knew that those words, beyond a shadow of a doubt, came straight from Yuki's heart. His sister's very mature words, which were overflowing with love, touched his heart just like they had that special day.

Yeah… At the very least, both Yuki and Masha have told me that they like the person I am now…

As he carefully reflected on his sister's advice, Yuki slowly lifted her head off his chest and smirked again.

"Is it just me, or did I really sound like the heroine just now?"

"Ha-ha… Shut up."

Masachika began wildly ruffling her hair with a grin.

"Aggghhh," groaned Yuki in a monotone voice while burying her face back into his chest.

Thank you, Yuki.

He thanked his loving, extremely kind sister in his heart.

Heh. I can't believe I'm being consoled by my little sister. I'm pathetic.

Although he added a touch of self-deprecation in the end, the dark self-resentment he once had was no longer there. No longer was he going to be tormented by his own self-hatred. No longer was he going to look back. Of course, he still couldn't love himself, and he still considered himself a loser…but even then, there were people who cared about him and loved him. He simply hated himself because it was the easy way out. It was selfish. Because what he should have been doing was putting those who loved him first. Perhaps that would eventually lead to him being able to face Alisa and accept that she had feelings for him as well.

That conclusion evoked a gentle air that filled the room. Silence continued to follow for a while after that…until the wind chime on the porch jingled softly. Yuki suddenly lifted her head with a furrowed brow.

"…Hmm? Main heroine? …Ah!"

Her face was suddenly overcome with alarm as she swiftly sat up and looked down at her brother's quizzical expression.

"Is this what I think it is?! Did you just start the little-sister route?!" she shrieked, her voice trembling.

"…What?"

"Yo, yo, yooo. Seriously, bro? Are you really going to pick the controversial little-sister route on purpose?! A route that's even controversial among the nerdiest of the nerds?!"

"That route doesn't even exist."

"Heh! Very well. If that's what you want, then I will do everything in my power to make your dream come true!"

"Yuki?"

"Ah! We need a child to take over for the Suou family, though! What are we going to do?!"

"Yuki!"

"What? You think we should just have Ayano bear your child? Wh-what a devilish imagination you have!"

"That's a violation of human rights."

"Lady Yuki, that is a wonderful proposal, if I do say so myself!"

""Ayano?""

Ayano, who had been air in the background the entire time, suddenly dropped a bomb, drawing the siblings' attention in her direction. She was sitting properly on her knees, and although she had her usual blank expression, her eyes were sparkling while she tightly squeezed her fists.

"In other words, I get to use every last bit of myself to serve you two, right?! My everything will be yours!"

"All right, Ayano. Let's dial it back a little. You realize what you're saying sounds insane, right?" asked Yuki.

"Seeing you two happy together is what makes me happy, and if I can be a part of that, then do whatever you want with me!" she passionately exclaimed with a hand on her chest like a devout follower.

"The poor girl's clueless," said Yuki in a monotone voice, then shifted her gaze to her brother and, with a half smirk, gave him a thumbs-up.

"You did it, bro. You started with the little-sister route and ended up in the forced-harem route!"

"Like hell I'm gonna let that happen! All that does is make an already abnormal route even weirder!"

"What's the problem? You get a harem. That's every man's dream."

"If it's 2D, sure. But a real harem is way too much work."

"It's cowardly, ball-less virgins like you who ruin everything."

"Did you say something, you shameless, self-proclaimed virgin slut?"

But she simply ignored Masachika's jab and shook her head like she wanted to roll her eyes… Suddenly, she slapped her forehead in astonishment, as if she just had a great idea.

"Hold up… What if we siblings fought for Ayano and made this an Ayano-harem route instead? Wouldn't that solve all our issues?"

"Sounds more like I'm a third wheel here who's meddling in your *yuri* relationship. The author's obviously going to kill me off. In fact, the back of my neck is already starting to tingle."

The moment he mentioned being a third wheel in their girl-on-girl relationship, he felt a powerful aura burning with rage coming from somewhere, and he began to rub the back of his neck. But in spite of that, he shifted his gaze back to Ayano and changed the subject.

"Anyway, Ayano, you need to relax. I don't want you throwing your life away for others, even if you were joking."

"…? When did I tell a joke?"

"Ha-ha! What innocent little eyes you have."

Masachika knew. He was well aware of the fact that Ayano didn't tell jokes, but seeing her curious and sincere gaze sent him into a daze as he stared off into space. Ayano, on the other hand, placed a hand on her chest as if she was offended that anyone would even suggest it was a joke.

"I am your maid, and nothing brings me more joy than serving you two."

"Ya sure ya don't just get off on being used? You're the M in BDSM," barked Yuki with a reproachful look. After blinking two or three times in silence, Ayano shifted to face Yuki.

"By the way, Lady Yuki, the other day I learned what BDSM popularly refers to…"

"Oh! You finally figured it out, huh? Yeah, the M doesn't really stand for 'maid.'"

"So you really were joking with me... Well, there is something I need to clarify, then."

"...What's that?"

Ayano stared straight back into Yuki's quizzical expression and firmly replied:

"I am not a masochist."

"...Oh?"

"Uh-huh."

Even Masachika squinted at her skeptically. Nevertheless, despite their obvious doubt, Ayano continued earnestly:

"I do not get any sexual satisfaction out of being mentally and physically abused."

"...Didn't you ask me to step on your head before summer break?"

"I was simply acting on instinct as a maid."

"Oh. Well, I guess it's okay if it's instinct."

Yuki shot Masachika a disappointed look after Ayano steamrolled through his argument, then asked:

"Are you claiming that you are not motivated by self-interest?"

"Yes."

"How curious. Then give me one logical reason why a maid would serve her master."

The maid adjusted her posture as if she were about to give an eloquent lecture on the holy teachings in her sacred book.

"We maids are continuously working hard to improve ourselves for our masters."

"...Go on."

"However, my two masters are extremely kind individuals, so of course this is not a complaint, but I almost forget how inexperienced and incompetent I can be at times."

"...Uh-huh."

"Pride is the enemy of improvement. Letting one's guard down is the beginning of the end. And that is why I must always strive to be better."

"..."

"Therefore, I would like to request daily guidance from you two so that I will never forget just how inexperienced I really am."

Yuki and Masachika considered what she was requesting for a brief moment. Most people would love it if their boss praised them for the smallest things and never got angry, even over a mistake. On the other hand, there were people who would complain about a lack of motivation with nobody there to set them straight. Ayano was more like a cute little sister than a maid to Yuki and Masachika, and that was why they were always extremely grateful for everything she did, and they would definitely not scold her for making a mistake. However, perhaps Ayano felt as if she weren't being taken seriously as a maid. Perhaps spoiling her and not acting like a proper master ended up actually making her anxious...

Oh... So Ayano wants us to scold her...

It sounds like we accidentally hurt her pride as a maid... We should probably reconsider how we're treating her.

Their expressions were somewhat solemn after they each came to a similar conclusion. Ayano, as a proud maid, boldly added:

"I want you two to show me just how worthless I am compared to you! Show me that I'm an object who only deserves to be used! Scold me and punish me!"

""Oh, come on!!""

In the end, Ayano really was a filthy masochist.

What were you planning on doing with my armpit?

"And that should do it for math…"

After closing the exercise book of summer homework, Masachika did a big stretch in the living room of the Kuze residence. Sitting in the seat across from him was Alisa, who was quietly running her red pen across her exercise book. They were once again in the middle of doing their homework together, but eventually, Alisa also closed her exercise book and pushed it off to the side.

"You all done?"

"Yes, I did every last problem."

"Whoa. Seriously? Good job."

She had apparently finished all her homework—unlike Masachika. She must have been diligently working on it at home in her spare time, too. Masachika, on the other hand, did not even touch his homework while he was home alone, so he still had to do his English and physics homework. Having said that, he was still progressing at a far quicker pace this year compared to last.

"Okay, then…"

"…"

Coincidentally they both glanced at the clock in the living room at the same time and realized it was still only a little past three thirty PM. In other words, they still had a decent amount of time before Alisa left, since she usually went home at around six PM.

So… What now…?

Masachika began to pour some barley tea into their teacups to buy time while he racked his brain for ideas. They had technically achieved their goal, since they only met up to do homework together, but simply blurting out, "Good job! See ya around!" seemed a bit too curt, and it sounded like what someone who couldn't read the room would do.

Yeah... Read the room, Masachika. She's glancing at me suggestively!

Alisa was fidgeting with her hair and glancing at him with expectant eyes, as if she wanted to say, "Oh, look at that. It looks like we still have some time before I go. Whatever should we do?" Masachika fortunately (or perhaps unfortunately) had come to a good stopping point with his homework right around the same time as Alisa, so he couldn't pretend he didn't notice her waiting, either. All he could do was slowly bring his teacup to his lips to buy more time.

I mean, what else can I do?

It wasn't like he had the courage to say, "Wanna go on a date?" Maybe he could have said it like a joke if this was before they went to the beach together, but now that he knew how Alisa felt and he was aware of his own shortcomings, there was no way he could ever allow himself to say something like that, even as a joke.

But...

Masachika was determined to face her and not run away anymore. Anything else would mean betraying Maria and the courageous request she made.

...All right! I'm doing it!

While placing the teacup back on the table, Masachika lifted his head with determination. He stared at Alisa until she looked at him as well. Facing each other like this was nothing out of the ordinary, and yet he felt like there was something different about her usual gaze—now that he knew she had feelings for him. It was as if there was a fire burning in those sapphire eyes, and it made his breath catch in his throat.

"So... It's still early...," started Masachika while desperately trying to calm his racing heart. In his mind, the angel Maria and the devil Yuki were dancing with pom-poms and cheering him on, which surprisingly gave him the courage he needed to continue.

"So...how about...we discuss the election?"

A deep silence fell upon the living room as the twinkle in Alisa's eyes seemed to fade. The imaginary Maria and Yuki lowered their pom-poms and glared at him coldly.

"You're such a coward, Kuze."

"You're trash."

Stop. Don't look at me like that.

Masachika mentally curled up in a ball on the ground, clutching his head as the devil kicked his helpless body while the angel stared down at him in disappointment. However, in the midst of his self-loathing session, Alisa looked down and let out a long exhale.

"*Sigh*... I suppose that is important."

"A-ain't dat da truth?"

"Why are you talking like that?"

"Oh, uh... Ha-ha-ha..."

After a dry laugh, Masachika cleared his throat and fixed his expression. He was well aware that what he did was a pretty pathetic thing to do as a man, but this was the only way he could reboot his mind and focus on something else.

"So, uh... One of the biggest events during the second semester has to be the school festival in the beginning of October."

"I believe every member of the student council has to join the school festival committee, right?"

"Exactly. The committee's basically made up of two representatives from each class, the student council, the student disciplinary committee, the school cleanup committee, the health committee, and the previous student council president and vice president... I think that's all of them."

It was customary for the former student council president and vice president to take on the roles of president and vice president of the school festival committee for Seirei Academy's Autumn Heights Festival every year. In addition, the current members of the student council, along with select members from each class, were assigned positions of significant responsibility under their guidance.

"Put simply, these other members of the school festival committee are going to be watching you and trying to decide whether they can depend on you, so be careful. Sometimes people are forced to join the school festival committee because no one else wants to do it, but for the most part, the students selected to be members have a lot of influence in their class. In other words, you don't want them thinking you're worthless, because it could really hurt your chances in the election."

"Oh... Okay..."

"But, well, you're the student council accountant, so I'm sure you'll be fine as long as you focus on your job. If anything, Yuki, being the publicist, is more at risk than anyone else."

The student council members were usually given tasks related to their positions. The secretary would record meetings, the accountant would manage the budget, the publicist would make pamphlets and flyers, and so on. Although managing the budget was a behind-the-scenes role, the publicist had a very visible responsibility, so while it would be easy to emphasize one's good points, it was also far harder to hide one's mistakes. Therefore, making tacky flyers or messy pamphlets would destroy Yuki's reputation. On the other hand, her rival, Alisa, did not really have too much to worry about in that regard.

With that in mind, Masachika shrugged and added:

"I'm sure she'll handle whatever her task is with ease, though. If there are any mistakes with accounting, it's usually when the balance is calculated, and that's always after the festival is over. Plus, I'll be there to help you, too, so there's nothing you really need to worry about."

"Oh..."

"Seriously. Don't sweat it. If you handle it just like you do in the student council, then you'll be fine."

Even though Masachika tried to be as optimistic as he could, Alisa still seemed a bit concerned, frowning as if she were deep in thought.

I guess this would be awful for someone who prefers to work alone like Alya, and if she has to give orders as a team leader, then...

Alisa was a perfectionist, but she was also aware that what she considered perfect was far too much to ask of most people. To make matters worse, she knew she wasn't an eloquent speaker who could encourage those around her and motivate them to push forward, which was also why she always chose to work alone without relying on others.

Being a perfectionist isn't a bad thing for an accountant. The issue is that she isn't a fan of working as a team, and she is going to have to learn how to lead if she ever wants to become the student council president...

However, this wasn't an issue that could be solved in a day, and a few good words with a pat on the back weren't going to cure her dislike for teamwork. Things were never that easy in life.

If anything, this might end up being a really good experience for her. I'll just have to hope that she uses this opportunity to slowly grow accustomed to teamwork.

After reaching this conclusion, Masachika cleared his throat.

"Ahem! Anyway, why don't we use this opportunity to come up with a method for communication?"

"Hmm? What are you talking about?"

When Alisa looked up with a curious gaze, he quietly stared hard back at her.

"Wh-what?" she asked nervously.

Even though her eyes held a hint of bewilderment, Masachika continued to stare without saying a word.

"Um... Is there something on my face? Come on—say something," Alisa begged uncomfortably as she checked her body and face.

"Read me. Tell me what I want to say," demanded Masachika.

"Huh?"

She frowned and stared right back at him. An entire ten seconds went by before she averted her gaze with a hint of a blush in her cheeks.

"<Wait. I'm still not ready...>"

"Hold up. What do you think I want to say?" Masachika interjected immediately after hearing her somewhat suggestive Russian whispers. But after a brief sigh, he decided to just tell her. "I wanted you to get that kitchen towel for me."

"What? ...How was I supposed to know that? That's ridiculous."

"Is it? Oh, no. You don't really have to get me the towel. That's not the issue. I was actually pointing at it with my eyes, and I was mouthing 'Grab it.'"

"But..."

"Hmm... All right, let's try this one more time," suggested Masachika to please her. Once again, he began to stare hard at Alisa, who firmly stared back...but after a few seconds went by, she averted her gaze a second time.

"<My armpit? But that's...>"

"Seriously! What do you think I'm trying to say?"

Is she some sort of closeted pervert? Don't tell me she's actually some sort of degenerate, thought Masachika while he glared at her strangely bashful expression. But after scratching his head in a frustrated manner, he leaned back in his chair and relaxed into it. Although he'd had a feeling this would happen, he wasn't expecting them to have this much trouble communicating with their eyes. Yuki would have been able to instantly pick up on what he was trying to say through eye contact, his gestures, and his mannerisms.

It takes time together and experience to learn how to communicate like this...so I guess it's still a little hard for Alya to figure me out.

Other than Yuki, the only people who could at least somewhat communicate with Masachika without saying a word were people he'd known for a long time, like Takeshi and Hikaru. Maybe Touya in the student council as well, but they had good chemistry. Plus, Touya was a very attentive and considerate person, which helped. Chisaki wasn't the kind of person who could pull something like this off, and both Maria and Ayano were too laid-back and were on different wavelengths than Masachika in general. Alisa, however, simply lacked experience.

"Hmm..."

This was going to put them at a slight disadvantage during the election, since being able to communicate quickly in a pinch could make or break their campaign. In fact, it was being almost perfectly in tune with each other that helped Yuki and Masachika overcome countless obstacles together, and that was why he was quite worried about not being able to communicate with Alisa.

"If you think you're so good, you give it a try."

"Huh?"

When he lowered his gaze, he noticed Alisa was staring fixedly at him, so he adjusted his posture and faced her.

"<This happened when we were at the beach…>"

"Wait. Hold up."

"Why? I thought you were so good that you only needed to observe my body language to know what I'm trying to say, so it should be easy for you to guess simply by hearing my tone when I speak in Russian, right?"

"That's not even close to being the same thing."

"<On the last day, when we were having breakfast…>"

"What? No. Stop talking in—"

"<…you accidentally started drinking from my cup.>"

Gaaaaaah?!?!

"<You didn't seem to realize it, though.>"

I had absolutely no idea!!

Masachika barely managed to keep himself from gasping when he heard the unexpected confession. He immediately tried to think back to that morning, but he couldn't remember that moment for the life of him. Everyone's glass had looked exactly the same, so it was possible he'd grabbed the wrong one, but…

"<You drank every last drop before I could even say anything, so I never got the chance to tell you…>"

Seeing Alisa somewhat embarrassed made it obvious that she wasn't lying, either.

That Time I Already Had an Indirect Kiss by Accidentally Drinking from the Same Cup.

Masachika began to stare off into space with a blank expression while Alisa's lips bashfully yet devilishly curled.

"<It was kind of like that Japanese tradition where you exchange cups of sake together and make a vow. Do you think this still counts?>"

Nope.

"<You'd better take responsibility for what you've done.>"

A chill just ran down my spine.

Alisa kept saying whatever was on her mind, believing that Masachika didn't understand, so he raised his hands as if to surrender.

"Hold on for a second. I really have no idea what you're trying to do. Like, the whole point of secretly communicating like this is to convey ideas without talking."

"Oh, of course."

She pretentiously shrugged, then started to fan herself.

If you're going to get this embarrassed, you shouldn't even do it in the first place.

But Alisa, who seemed to be thinking about something, didn't even notice his scornful glare.

"Then…how about I test you the same way you tested me?"

Alisa swiftly shifted her gaze to the window, faintly moved her lips, and slowly clasped her hands together. She then slightly angled her hands as if she were begging for something, which led Masachika to only one conclusion: "I want to go out on a date." That was what she was trying to say.

Nghhh!!

He clenched his teeth because the agony was too much to bear. If he hadn't pinched his leg as hard as he could under the table, he wouldn't have been able to keep a straight face.

…! There's no way I can say that!

Saying the right answer would most likely make things awkward, but giving the wrong answer would definitely make her believe he was some overconfident, clueless idiot. The future was bleak, no matter what he ended up going with.

"Come on. Did you figure it out? What do I want to say?"

"Errr…"

Alisa provocatively smirked and crossed her arms as if to say, "You have absolutely no clue, do you?" She was underestimating him. Acting like there was no way he would ever figure it out, and her expression made it clear that she believed she had the upper hand. Masachika suddenly got the urge to see her expression painted with shock and embarrassment, but he immediately talked himself out of it, since the risk would be far too great. Therefore, he had no choice but to choose a bland, harmless answer, even though he knew it was wrong.

"Uh… I'm guessing, 'Nice weather we're having today'?"

"Pfft. Hmph." Alisa snorted, and a condescending sneer twisted her lips.

Tsk!!

Even Masachika couldn't help but grimace, but she paid no heed to his annoyance.

"Not even close. See? *You* don't even know how to read people," she sassed, her words brimming with a sense of superiority.

"…What was the right answer?"

"I was trying to say, 'Summer break's almost over.'"

"Uh-huh…," he replied while closely observing Alisa's expression, then casually added, "I almost thought you were inviting me on a date. I guess it was just my imagination, though."

"Wh-what?! A-absolutely not. That was *definitely* your imagination…"

Alisa jumped as if someone had dropped an ice cube down the back of her shirt, then she quickly looked away. Masachika observed her reaction and kept a straight face—she couldn't have made it any more obvious.

"Oh. Yeah, I guess you would never say anything like that, even as a joke," he replied in a matter-of-fact manner.

"…That goes without saying."

"Thought so."

He spoke in an unamused monotone. After swiftly glancing in his direction, Alisa pouted.

"<What's your problem? Would it really be that strange if I invited you on a date?>"

Errr...

With that sulky whisper, Masachika felt a twinge of guilt, and he promptly tried to smooth things over.

"After all, nothing like that has ever happened to me before, you know? And I know girls never ask guys out on dates, except in comic books." He rambled a bit, hinting that he meant being invited by a girl on a date was weird, not that being invited by Alisa was. Immediately, confidence returned to her gaze, and she smirked arrogantly.

"Oh my. How unfortunate. I've been invited on more dates than I can count."

"Uh-huh. And have you ever accepted any of those date invitations?"

Alisa's fidgeting fingers froze. She glanced to the side and mumbled:

"...I've been on a few dates before."

"Uh-huh."

"..."

She glanced at her seemingly unimpressed classmate, began to twirl the ends of her hair again, and muttered:

"<With you.>"

...Oof.

In other words, she had never gone on a date with anyone other than Masachika. Although this was something he expected, there was no way to avoid taking damage when she put it into words. So he just gritted his teeth. A few more seconds went by, and then Alisa's expression abruptly filled with shock, and she looked at him once more.

"I—I never went on a date with any random guys who tried to pick me up, though!"

"Oh, uh... I never thought you did."

She was constantly ignoring good-looking, smart guys from well-off families at school, so there was no way she would ever go on a date with some random jerk prowling the streets.

"I choose who I go on dates with, and I don't go with just anyone!"

"Okay..."

Masachika took 20 damage.

"I—I only go on dates with…people I li—people I trust!"

"O-oh, okay."

Masachika took 40 damage.

"A-anyway, I get it now…so you don't have to explain yourself."

He desperately tried to defend, but Alisa didn't stop!

"There's no way I'd ever go on a date with someone I didn't like!"

"…"

Masachika took 90 damage but managed to survive with 1 HP left.

"Oh! But that doesn't mean I li— Ahem. I don't dislike you, okay? That's all…"

Alisa used "Bashful"! Masachika "Fainted"!

"<*Giggle*. I got yelled at.>"

"<What were you thinking, trying to sneak into another school's music room?>"

"<Umm… I just wanted to hear Sah play the piano.>"

"<Hmm… Then why not invite him to the recital?>"

"<Hold on. Are you sure?>"

"<Of course… We made a promise, after all…>"

"<Thanks! I can't wait!>"

"—okay?"

"Ah!"

Masachika lifted his head the instant he regained consciousness and noticed Alisa was leaning over the table with a skeptical gaze.

"…Oh, sorry. I lost consciousness there for a second."

"…Hmph. Right."

Out of nowhere, Alisa's gaze narrowed, and a chilling air began to gather around her.

"...?"

What is she angry about? wondered Masachika as he raised an eyebrow. All of a sudden, something hit his shin.

"Owww?!"

An unexpected shock went through him. Alisa had kicked his shin as she sat back down in her seat.

"Do you feel more awake now?"

"Wh-what? I didn't doze off...!" explained Masachika, curling into a ball in pain, but Alisa's gaze was still cold. Then again, most people would probably be upset if the person they were talking to fell asleep mid-conversation.

This is all your fault, though!

But even if he argued that, he would only be digging his own grave, so Masachika had no choice but to clear his throat and get them back on topic.

"Anyway...if we need to secretly communicate with each other in a pinch..."

They ended up practicing different types of eye contact after that despite Alisa's transparent disappointment, and for better or for worse, time passed without the mood ever resembling a rom-com.

"That should do it. Oh, by the way, I made sure to use different patterns from what I used with Yuki for our code language. But she might be able to decipher what we're saying if we overdo it, so we probably shouldn't use it around her."

"Okay."

"Also... Hmm... We should probably come up with something to let the other know we're bluffing, too."

"Why?"

"You know, like when you need to bluff during a negotiation. Like telling a club that we already got permission from the faculty adviser... or when we want to get out of a conversation with someone who's difficult to deal with, you might want to be like, 'The teacher asked me to meet him in the faculty room, so I have to go.' Now, if I said that, and you said, 'What are you talking about?' then they'd know I was lying, and it'd ruin everything. That's why I think we need to have a signal to let each other know when we're bluffing."

"Right..."

Masachika briefly paused to think of a signal, despite Alisa's obvious discomfort, and soon raised his left hand.

"I've got it. How about we touch our hair with our left hand? You have a habit of fidgeting with your hair, right? Well, how about doing it with your left hand...?"

"What about you?"

"I...guess I could scratch my head? At any rate, whenever we're touching our hair with our left hand, that means we're bluffing. Sound good?"

"Fine... I'll probably forget, though."

"...It's not a big deal. Just keep it in the back of your mind." Masachika shrugged. He then adjusted his posture and composed himself because the next issue made him rather nervous. "Now, what if we can't make eye contact? One way we could communicate if we're right next to each other is to write on each other's palm..."

"...? What?"

"We could do it like we're typing on a keyboard, but instead of a keyboard, we're using each other's palm. Like...we could hold hands under a table or behind each other's back and write words on each other's palm," he hesitantly explained.

"...?!"

Alisa instantly frowned, which was no real surprise.

"You're suggesting holding hands...and rubbing each other's palms?"

"Well, it's more like typing than rubbing. We could use flick-input just like when we text on our phones. We can skip the first square, which is just symbols, but the very left—the area closest to your wrist—can be the square for *ABC*, then to the right of that can be *DEF*..."

After explaining the 3 × 3 grid system with one blank space for omitted symbols, Masachika held up his left hand with his right.

"On second thought, since the first square in the grid is blank, we can use that as our backspace, so let's do one tap there equals one backspace."

He tapped the leftmost square of the invisible grid on his palm a few times with his right index finger while explaining. Alisa listened with an unenthusiastic frown until the very end, then revealed her skepticism and said:

"Well, I understand the system...but isn't this a little too complicated? It might be fine for the person 'typing,' but it's not going to be easy for whoever is doing the 'reading.'"

"Yeah, that's going to take some time to get used to, but once you get used to it, you'll be able to communicate just as easily as you can by speaking."

"Sure, but...I don't want you caressing my palm," she replied. She reacted to his superhuman, spy-like plan with a sour expression.

"...Well, there's nothing we can do about that."

Masachika was kind of hurt by how disgusted she sounded. *I thought she liked me?* was the first thought that crossed his mind, but he soon convinced himself that this was a different issue entirely.

"Hey, uh... Alya?"

"What?"

"Are you...a germaphobe?"

Looking back, there had been several signs of Alisa being a germaphobe. Even in PE class, she seemed to always avoid letting anyone touch her, especially her bare skin. "N-no! I'm not a germaphobe! Unbelievable!"

And that was why her extremely adamant denial seemed to have come out of nowhere.

"Really? That's strange. I vaguely remember the president of the cleanup committee reaching out to shake your hand and you doing this sort of half-a-second shake before quickly pulling your hand away."

"That's because... Uh... I don't even know her."

"Sounds like something a germaphobe would say."

"I said I'm not a germaphobe! I... I just—! Imagine you had

something really important to you! You wouldn't want anyone touching it, either, right?"

"Huh?"

Masachika's gaze wandered for a few moments while he thought about the sudden question.

"...I guess a lot of guys wouldn't want people touching their watch or their car, and maybe some girls wouldn't want people touching their bags or jewelry. Since those are like fingerprint magnets."

"Right! Exactly!"

Alisa firmly nodded in agreement with his vague examples, then leaned back and placed a hand on her chest.

"And the most important thing to me is my body! That's why I don't like people touching me!"

"...Okay?"

Masachika felt like he might be able to understand.

"How's that different from being a germaphobe?"

"It's completely different! It's not like I have to go wash my hands after shaking hands with someone!"

"You seem very defensive for someone who's not a germaphobe..."

"Of course I'm defensive! You're making me sound like some sort of neurotic neat freak!"

And you're not? he immediately thought, but he bit his tongue and considered her claim.

Hmm... Well, I guess it wouldn't make her a germaphobe if it's just because of her ego. It's not like she's afraid of germs.

Masachika was persuaded after imagining how stuck-up noblewomen in fantasies say things like, "The only one allowed to touch me is my future husband!"

She's just a real-life virtuous princess...

He half-heartedly nodded to himself.

"Hmm... Well, I guess there's not much we can do about it if you hate being touched..."

It wasn't like Masachika was going to insist on something that made her uncomfortable, so he decided to back off.

"Wait! I never said I wouldn't do it..."

After a moment of panic, Alisa's voice slowly trailed off. Fidgeting with her hair and avoiding eye contact, she then hesitantly asked:

"Do you really want to...touch me that badly?"

"Huh?"

"My hand..."

"Oh, uh..."

Although the discussion had gone off track, when posed with the question of whether he wanted to touch her...

"Yes."

"...No matter what?"

"...No matter what."

"Oh..."

While still looking away, Alisa stopped fidgeting with her hair and held out her hand to Masachika.

"Fine. Here."

Just like that?! What was all that buildup to this for, then? Give me my time back.

Masachika couldn't help but be annoyed as she held out her right hand with a cold expression on her face. But contrary to his furious thoughts, he calmly replied:

"Can I have your left hand instead of your right?"

"Oh...! Sure!"

After a moment, she shyly bit her lips, looked away once more, and held out her left hand. Masachika, smirking, reached out to hold her hand...but hesitated.

Alisa's slender, snow-white hand could only be described as beautiful. Even though this wasn't their first time holding hands, it felt more difficult this time, perhaps due to everything that led up to it.

"...What's wrong?"

"Oh, uh... Nothing. Ahem."

But all it took was one quizzical glance to pressure him into carefully taking her soft, somewhat chilly hand. And although slightly flustered, he took his thumb and gently pressed it against her palm.

"So… Like this…"

I should have cut my nails a little shorter, he thought while carefully using his thumb to type.

"Ngh…"

The faint sound made Masachika lift his head in a flash, seeing Alisa with a slightly knitted brow as she moodily stared at their hands.

"…What?"

"Nothing…"

He lowered his eyes back to their hands and continued to move his thumb.

"For example, I'll tap three times here for *C*. Then if I tap on your palm with my middle finger like this, that's a 'space.'"

After giving her a feel of how the flick-input keyboard was going to work, he looked back up to find Alisa still in a bit of a bad mood. What bothered him the most was the fact that she was biting her bottom lip as if something about this was unbearable.

"…You get all that?"

"…Crystal clear."

"Oh… Okay. Then let me see if I can type out a whole sentence."

Masachika then began slowly tapping and tracing his fingers across her palm.

I'll go with something easy… N.I.C.E.

"Mmm…"

W.E.A.T.H.E.R.

"Hff…!"

T.O.D.A.Y.

"Ahn…"

Gah!! Stop making weird noises like that!!

He had been pretending not to notice any of her strangely sexual moaning, but he couldn't take it any longer. Every time he moved his finger, her hand would tremble, and it made him feel like he was doing something dirty, even though he wasn't doing anything shameful.

"He's fingering her! He's making her moan!"

Shut up.

Masachika kept his cool while shutting up the boisterous devil-Yuki, in his head.

"Did you figure out what I was trying to—?"

He suddenly fell silent. Who could blame him, though? After all, a faint crimson had colored Alisa's pale cheeks, and tears were welling in her eyes as she glared at him.

"<Pervert...>"

What'd I do?!

To reiterate, Masachika was not doing anything lewd that he should be ashamed of, and yet this was how she reacted. *Perhaps she misunderstood what I wrote?* wondered Masachika, but that idea was immediately shot down.

"Did you write, 'Nice weather today'?"

"Y-yeah, good job. You got it right on your first try."

"..."

Alisa averted her displeased gaze despite his praise.

"So, uh... Did that tickle or...?"

"...A little."

"O-oh. Well, I guess we shouldn't use this method, then. We can't really communicate secretly if your expression gives you away..."

She glanced at him once more, then softly muttered:

"<It didn't really tickle. It was more like—>"

"Don't worry about it! For the first few times, even Yuki—"

Sensing that she was about to say something in Russian that he shouldn't hear, Masachika suddenly cut her off, but the instant he mentioned Yuki, he noticed a reaction from her. It was at that moment, he knew he messed up.

"I'll do it."

"What...? You shouldn't force yourself to do it if you don't want to."

"It took Yuki several tries before she got used to it, correct? I can get used to it, too."

The flames of competition burned in her azure eyes as she confidently turned back to Masachika. The moment he saw that look in her eyes, he knew there was nothing he could say to stop her.

"All right, then… Shall we continue?"

They spent the next hour practicing until Alisa was able to read as quickly as she could listen to normal conversation.

"Incredible… I can't believe you picked it up that quickly…"

"H-hmph. It was nothing," she claimed, smirking boldly, but her cheeks were completely red and her bangs were glued to her forehead with sweat. Her breathing was somewhat rough as well.

How lewd.

His brain couldn't help but make that comment in reaction to her sexy appearance. In fact, Masachika felt like he was being given a test on self-control as he was forced to watch her pant suggestively with flushed skin.

Well, that should do it for now… Good job, me! You passed the test!

He let go of Alisa's hand after patting himself on the back for his self-control.

"Anyway—"

Right as he let go, she fiercely grabbed his wrist. His eyes were naturally drawn toward her, and he noticed the flames in her eyes and the menacing grin curling her lips.

"Now it's my turn to practice writing, right?"

"Uh…"

"Right?"

"…Right."

For the next hour, Masachika was used as her guinea pig until she was satisfied with her "handwriting" skills as well.

CHAPTER 4 Who wants to see a guy blush?

One morning, when there was only a week left of summer break, Masachika received a simple voicemail from Takeshi: "Help."

The unusual message prompted him to call his friend immediately, but nobody picked up. It appeared that while his buddy was in some sort of trouble, it would be difficult to explain over the phone. Regardless, Takeshi's tone was clearly exhausted, so Masachika quickly changed into his school uniform and headed to Music Room B, where Takeshi and Hikaru were hanging out.

"...Ugh," he groaned when he peered into the room through the window in the hallway. Hikaru had installed himself in a corner, where he was mumbling something to himself with dilated pupils, and Masachika could practically see a rain cloud hanging over his head. Although Masachika expected it to be bad from the voicemail, he wasn't expecting to run into Shadow Hikaru today, especially with this level of darkness tormenting his soul.

I'd do anything to go straight home right now...but I can't turn my back on him.

There was no escape after coming this far, so Masachika let out a brief sigh, pumped himself up, and opened the door to the classroom.

"Oh, Masachika... About time ya showed up..."

Takeshi, who seemed to have been trying to talk to Hikaru, instantly approached his classmate with a pleading look in his eyes.

"Hey... What's up? What's the situation?"

In fact, why were they the only ones here? Takeshi and Hikaru were supposed to be practicing for their school festival performance with three other members. The student council was in charge of keeping up with the reservation status of rehearsal spaces in general, so Masachika was well aware of their situation.

"Wait until ya hear this..."

Takeshi began to explain the situation.

"I'm sorry."

Those were the first words that came out of the girl's mouth. She was a fierce-looking girl with almond-shaped eyes and shoulder-length black hair tied in pigtails. Her name was Nao Shiratori, and she was the lead singer in Takeshi's band, Luminous. She was unyielding, proud, and hardly ever bowed to anyone, which was somewhat of a problem for the other members of the band.

Perhaps that was why she ended up apologizing with downcast eyes in a voice strained with emotion. Apparently, she was going to have to transfer to a new school due to family issues, and she wasn't able to go to the school festival anymore. After talking to the other band members, she revealed that the family issue was that her father's company was on the verge of bankruptcy. This was presumably the cause of other issues within their household as well, although Nao never said so outright.

"This is probably my last day at this school, too. Anyway...I'm sorry. I know this is sudden, but I have to quit the band."

The abrupt news had the other four members lost for words. A few moments went by until a certain young girl slowly approached Nao.

"Why...? Why didn't you tell us sooner?"

The pained question came from a petite girl who resembled a small animal, with short hair that curled slightly at the ends. She trembled in utter shock because she, Riho Minase, was not only the keyboardist in the band but also Nao's childhood friend. Nao couldn't even look her in the eye, averting her gaze while curtly replying:

"Because it wouldn't have changed anything… Am I wrong?"

"Maybe it wouldn't have changed anything, but I would have preferred it if you gave me a heads-up…"

Riho explained that although she couldn't have done anything about Nao's father's company, she could have at least been there to support Nao and share her pain. If anything, Riho seemed more shocked that her childhood friend didn't even come to her to talk. Nevertheless, Nao simply continued to avoid eye contact with her friend.

"It's sometimes harder to say things to people you're close to, and you're her best friend, Riho," chimed in Hikaru, trying to calm his teary-eyed friend before it was too late. Thankfully, it seemed to work a bit, and Riho even apologized to Nao.

"I'm sorry, Nao. I didn't mean to snap at you like that…"

"No… It's fine…"

An indescribably awkward silence filled the air between the pair until Takeshi cheerfully spoke up to lighten the mood.

"H-hey, this doesn't mean ya can't come to the school festival and perform, right? I mean, there are no rules stating that ya have to go to this school to sing onstage…right? …Right?"

"You're actually right… The thought never even crossed my mind, but I think you just found a loophole."

"Right?! Even if ya transfer to a new school, you could just make it seem like you're joining on the fly and sing with us!"

"Yeah… Yeah! Nao, don't give up! Let's do this!" exclaimed Riho happily, agreeing with Takeshi's suggestion as if she were trying to make up for her behavior earlier.

"Now that you mention it…that might actually work…"

Nao must have been upset that she wouldn't be able to perform with the band, since she had been working hard toward this goal for so long. Her eyes, which were usually brimming with confidence, had a touch of uncertainty in them as she stared at her friends one by one. That was when a plump guy, who had been quiet the entire time, suddenly patted Nao on the shoulder and declared:

"Don't worry, Nao. I'll handle things with your dad's company, too."

"...?"

His name was Ryuuichi Kasugano, and he was not only the band's bassist but Nao's boyfriend as well. Nao looked skeptical of his over-confident declaration. In fact, the other band members immediately shifted their quizzical gazes in his direction, but Ryuuichi smiled proudly and pointed his thumb at himself.

"My grandfather is the president of Eimei Bank, after all."

"Seriously?!" shouted Takeshi, and his eyes nearly rolled to the back of his head. It was an understandable reaction, since there wasn't a single person in Japan who didn't know that bank. Even Hikaru and Riho were wide-eyed in astonishment.

"So come on. Everything's gonna be okay, Nao. I'll ask Granddad to figure out a way to save your dad's company."

"Ryuuichi..."

Her boyfriend's promise put tears in Nao's eyes, and she bit her lip. However, she swiftly lowered her gaze and replied, her throat tight:

"...It's okay, though. It's already too late. Besides...you and your grandfather don't get along, right?"

"Huh? Oh... Not really. But it's fine. He may be stubborn, but he's not going to ignore his grandson's once-in-a-lifetime request!"

"Don't try to act cool when it's your grandfather who has to do all the work," chimed in Takeshi.

"Come on—I may be smart and good-looking, have a great personality, and be a beast on bass, but you can't really expect a pudgy little guy like me to change the world on my own," replied Ryuuichi, giving a good slap to his belly at the end.

"Where does that confidence come from?!" joked Takeshi once more, sending everyone other than Nao into a fit of laughter. The gloomy, serious mood was instantly swallowed by a bright, friendly atmosphere. Ryuuichi's eyes filled with relief when he looked at his girlfriend, who was still down, and he gently added:

"It's not going to be quick, and it's going to be hard...but don't just quit the band on us so easily, okay? I'm going to see what I can do and talk to Granddad, okay?"

The others nodded and looked at Nao with compassion, gathering around her. However...

"I said it's fine. I don't want your help," she insisted firmly, rejecting Ryuuichi's offer once more with downcast eyes. Although Ryuuichi grimaced, frustrated at his girlfriend's stubbornness, he tried to laugh it off and lightheartedly replied:

"Seriously. Don't worry about it. I don't mind groveling to a family member if it means helping you. Besides, I'm already used to bowing to my teachers when—"

"I said I don't want your help!"

Her unexpectedly adamant refusal cut Ryuuichi off before he could tell another self-deprecating joke to lighten the mood. She immediately lifted her chin and shot her boyfriend a piercing glare that wiped the grin off his face.

"How many times do I have to tell you no?! I don't want you to do that!"

"C-come on, Nao. Let's calm down a little."

Takeshi tried to smooth things over between the couple but to no avail.

"I—I didn't mean to upset you... I—I just wanted to be a good boyfriend and help—"

"Then let's break up! It's not like long-distance relationships work anyway! It looks like that's settled, then!"

"Nao?! Seriously?!"

"Wh-what?!"

"Nao?!"

Nao's decision made everyone but Ryuuichi shout in astonishment. Meanwhile, Ryuuichi's eyes widened, then he slowly lowered his head and softly muttered:

"Oh... I guess you never liked me that much, huh?"

"Wh-what? I never—"

Nao sounded almost offended, but her refusal to meet their eyes did not go unnoticed, and that was more than enough to convince Ryuuichi that his assumption was correct.

"No, I always knew. You never seemed like you were having fun when you were with me, and I honestly wondered why you agreed to go out with me in the first place… But even then, I figured you felt something for me—probably sympathy at the very least—since you still decided to hang out with me all this time…"

Not even Takeshi or Hikaru knew what to say after hearing that, and it was actually Riho who first spoke up.

"Nao, he's wrong, right? Because I specifically remember you telling me that there was someone in our band who you liked when you first joined."

"…!"

After Riho took a few steps over to Nao, she looked right into her friend's wide eyes. They were the eyes of someone in trouble, and they eventually drifted toward Hikaru. She had to come clean.

"Yes, I used to like Hikaru! But he doesn't trust women…so I thought I might as well give Ryuuichi a chance and go out with him! Okay?! So it doesn't matter anymore!"

Nao instantly grabbed her bag and fled out the door of the music room, leaving everyone standing there in shock.

"But…I like…," muttered Riho unconsciously. Even though her voice was soft, it sounded strangely loud in the silence.

"Oh, uh… I…"

A flash of panic widened her eyes when she realized everyone was staring at her, then Riho, too, raced out of the music room, leaving three disturbed boys behind.

"R-Ryuuichi, uh…"

Despite being flustered himself, Takeshi tried to search for the right words to console his close friend, but it was simply too much for the boy. Ryuuichi smiled weakly through tears and slowly shook his head.

"I'm sorry… I want to be alone right now."

And then Ryuuichi left the music room with dejection in each step he took. All Hikaru and Takeshi could do was watch helplessly as he disappeared around the corner.

◇

"Sounds like hell." Masachika groaned automatically after hearing Takeshi explain what happened. It was chaos, and it was the worst kind of mess for someone like Hikaru: It was a disaster caused by love, passion, and jealousy.

No wonder he's acting like this...

Masachika sympathized with his friend's descent into darkness. Hikaru had a traumatic experience involving a girl falling in love with him—multiple experiences, in fact. But what hurt him the most was when he would open up to someone who he thought was a friend, only to find out that they actually had romantic feelings for him. He had lost both female and male friends in the past because of this.

This incident was extremely familiar. It was probably going to be hard for Ryuuichi to still act the same around Hikaru after learning that his ex-girlfriend had actually had feelings for Hikaru their entire relationship, and that was why it was only natural that Hikaru would be this depressed. However...

"Bunch of disgusting bitches. That's what they are. Guys only think with what's in their pants? Yeah, right. That's what girls do. All I do is act a little nice to them, and then they tell me they like me without even thinking about how much they might hurt others. The only person they think about is themselves, and then when things don't go their way, they ruin all the relationships around them. They think it's okay to do what they're doing in the so-called name of love? Piss off with that. I wish they'd all just die."

"Hikaru, that's enough," demanded Masachika, interrupting Hikaru's foul curse before he went any further off the deep end. Hikaru slowly lifted his head, revealing his lifeless eyes.

"...Masachika? What are you doing here?"

"Takeshi told me to come. I heard what happened. That's, uh...

That's rough, man," he commiserated and took a seat by Hikaru's side, then wrapped his arm around Hikaru's shoulder. Takeshi promptly took a seat on the other side and wrapped his arm around Hikaru's other shoulder.

"These girls just won't leave you alone, huh? Don't worry about it, though. I'll gladly take some ladies off your hands for ya if ya want."

"Takeshi, seriously? You make it sound like you actually have a chance with the opposite sex."

"Huh?"

"Huh?"

Masachika and Takeshi stared hard at each other over Hikaru's shoulders as a silence soon reigned over the room. Only when Hikaru let out a faint chuckle was the silence finally broken.

"Pfft! You guys… Thanks. I mean it."

"No problem… I'm glad you're feeling a little better."

"Wait. I do have a chance with the opposite sex, right?"

"Read the room, Takeshi."

"There's your answer."

"What's my answer?!"

Masachika and Hikaru shot Takeshi scornful looks, creating a slightly more relaxed mood, but the moment didn't last for long, as there was a knock at the door.

"Sorry for bothering you guys. I'm in the piano club, and I believe we reserved this room to practice, so…do you think we could have the room now?"

A charming boy with cupid-like features stepped inside the room. Calling him a "pretty boy" would most likely be the best way to put it, given his tall, slender figure. He had graceful features with a hint of melancholy in his eyes, and his noble-like behavior seemed somewhat theatrical, which only made him more picturesque.

The boy, Yuushou Kiryuuin, was the son of the chairman of Kiryuuin Corporate Group, which was extremely successful. In addition, he was considered one of the top three best-looking guys in school, and as if he couldn't get any more perfect, he had performed

extremely well in piano recitals domestically and abroad, which earned him the title Prince of Piano. Nevertheless, some people, such as Takeshi, didn't think so highly of him, which was made clear by Takeshi's audible gagging the moment he saw the boy's charming, beautiful face.

"Oh, Yuushou. Sorry about that. Give us a second to clean up," announced Masachika while pretending like he didn't hear his friend gag. After Masachika looked back to his friends and signaled with his eyes that it was time to leave, Takeshi and Hikaru hurriedly began to clean up. Of course, Masachika wanted to help, but since he wasn't a member of their club, he wasn't sure how he could. Therefore, to avoid getting in his friends' way, he decided to strike up a conversation with Yuushou to buy them some time.

"Sorry about this. We ran into a little trouble earlier."

"Oh, it's fine. I sometimes get so into playing piano that I lose track of time as well."

"...Thanks for being so understanding."

While Yuushou seemed to be very understanding of their situation, the female club members behind him didn't seem to share that feeling. It was as if their piercing glares were saying, "Stop wasting Yuushou's time."

"Anyway, Masachika, it's pretty unusual to see you in the music room. Did you join the music club or something?"

"Hmm? Oh. No. Takeshi just asked me to come over to help him with something. I'm still super busy with the student council."

"I bet. Music not your forte?"

While it seemed to be casual small talk, Yuushou's gaze made it appear as if he were fishing for answers, although Masachika had no idea why.

"I don't exactly hate music, if that's what you're asking. When I was little, I played violin...and a little piano."

"Pfft! Who does he think he is, even mentioning piano in front of Yuushou?" muttered one of the girls behind Yuushou with a sneer, followed by numerous other foul comments made by the other girls.

Obviously, Masachika could hear their rude remarks, but he figured nothing good would come of saying anything, so he simply ignored them, not even glancing in their direction. Yuushou, on the other hand, couldn't tolerate their mocking.

"That's enough, ladies. Don't be rude."

"Sorryyy."

"But can you blame us for laughing? He just said he could play piano in front of *you*—someone who puts even pros to shame."

"Ha-ha-ha! Me? Putting pros to shame? I play as a hobby. I have no interest in competing against professionals."

"You're this good, and you only play as a hobby? Yuushou, you're so cool!" squealed one of the girls. The others nodded, showering him with their passionate gazes.

"Okay, it's all yours," reported Takeshi in an annoyed tone as if he wanted to click his tongue in disgust.

"Really? Great. Is everybody ready?"

""""All ready!""""

Yuushou, along with his posse who had already forgotten that Masachika even existed, stepped into the room as if to replace Takeshi and Hikaru. After Masachika wryly smirked at Takeshi's annoyed glare following Yuushou, he walked out of the room and into the hallway with his two friends at his side.

"Hey… Don't you think you hate Yuushou a little too much?" asked Masachika to Takeshi once they were far enough away.

"I wouldn't say I hate him. It's…"

Takeshi mumbled but paused, since he didn't genuinely hate the guy. In fact, he wasn't the kind of person who could seriously hate another human being. His eyes wandered awkwardly for a few moments until he eventually pouted in a childish manner.

"I mean, the guy's a punk. 'I only play piano as a hobby. Derp.' Nice humblebrag, bro."

"I'm not sure that's exactly how he said it."

But pointing out Takeshi's malicious impression only heated him up even more.

"And what's with that harem of his?! Like, is he seriously the only guy in that club?! Piano club? More like harem club, if ya ask me!"

"Yeah, uh… I guess…"

"I even asked him once who he was going out with! And do ya know what this punk said to me?!"

"…I'm guessing he said he didn't have a girlfriend?"

"Exactly!"

"Seriously?!" replied Masachika with a half smile, somewhat taken aback that he'd actually gotten it right. Takeshi, however, promptly held his hands in the air and began moving his fingers as if he were playing two invisible harps.

"Seriously! But that wasn't the problem! It was how he said it! It was…strangely suggestive, like he was insinuating something!"

"Ohhh. Like, 'I'm technically not dating anyone. Wink, wink'?"

"Yeah, like that!" shouted Takeshi, pointing at Masachika with his index finger.

"No doubt he's having his way with every one of those girls in the piano club."

"Where's your proof?! And is this really what you're mad about?! You're just jealous!"

"What's wrong with that?!"

"Wow, Takeshi. So that's the kind of person you are…"

"Ah! Hikaru, no! I was only joking…"

A dark aura immediately began to surround Hikaru while Takeshi desperately tried to backtrack.

"…You guys want to go get something to eat?" Masachika sighed, rolling his eyes at them.

"So… What are we gonna do about the band?"

They had been at the restaurant for twenty minutes, and Hikaru had finally started to calm down a little when Takeshi opened his big mouth like he couldn't stand having a moment of peace.

"Seriously?"

Masachika immediately sensed danger and glanced at Hikaru. Thankfully, Hikaru didn't seem too bothered, so after breathing a sigh of relief, Masachika replied:

"Not much you can do besides find a new member to replace her, right? At the very least, you need someone to sing."

"Yeah… *Sigh.* I'm kind of worried we're not going to be ready for the school festival."

"Wait. You still plan on performing at the festival?"

The school festival took place during the beginning of October, which meant they had only a little over a month to prepare. Not only did they need a new vocalist, but they needed to make sure that Ryuuichi and Riho were coming back as well, and only after that could they start practicing. Put simply, any chance of pulling this off in time was slim. It didn't help that almost nobody in their right mind would agree to be the lead singer for a band that was performing in a month. After all, vocalists were basically the face of any band.

"I think it's going to be rough…"

"Yeah… But I promised Kanau I'd put on the most badass performance in the world for him at the school festival."

"Oh, your little brother? He's in fourth grade now, right?"

"Yeah! And he's so adorable! He looks up to me so much, too!"

The corners of Takeshi's eyes wrinkled the moment he started talking about his little brother, but it wasn't long before despair once again clouded his expression, and he clutched his head.

"And that's why, as his big brother, I can't break my promise to him, no matter what…"

Masachika flinched when he heard that. He then thought about it for a few moments before carefully replying:

"I actually might know someone who could sing in your band…"

"Wait. Are you for real?"

"...Is it somebody we know?"

"Yeah. We need to ask her first, though..."

"Oh! Alya! Over here."

Masachika stood a bit from his seat while waving his hand at Alisa, who had just walked into the restaurant he was in. A smile briefly flitted across her face, but then she promptly put on her usual composed expression and approached the table, drawing the attention of everyone around her.

"Sorry for suddenly asking you to meet me like this."

"It's fine. I wasn't doing anything important...," she replied while still coming toward the table.

"Hey."

"Uh... Hello?"

Her face went blank the instant she saw the two guys sitting at the table with Masachika.

"...So you want me to sing in this band?"

"Y-yeah, what do you think?"

Masachika had been explaining the situation for the past ten minutes, but the entire time, Alisa simply sipped on her melon soda and frowned. Both Masachika and Hikaru, who was sitting across from him, appeared tense in the presence of her undeniably foul mood.

H-hey, is it just me, or is she in a really bad mood?

You can say that again...

Masachika and Hikaru communicated through eye contact as they waited for Alisa to reply. Takeshi, on the other hand, was grinning and drooling all over himself while staring at Alisa, partially because she was wearing something other than her school uniform for a change. He was absolutely clueless.

"<You invited me out of the blue…so I was wondering what it could be, but…>"

That was when Alisa began to grumble to herself in Russian… which at least helped Masachika guess what she was so upset about.

Huh? Oh… I guess I should have explained things better.

All he did was tell her to meet him at this restaurant if she wasn't doing anything, since explaining things on the phone would have taken far too long… However, it appeared that Alisa thought she was being invited to hang out and have fun. It didn't help that Takeshi and Hikaru were also there, so it was understandable that she was upset.

"<Would it kill you to invite me somewhere just to hang out sometimes…?>"

"So, uh… Alya? Think you could do it?" asked Masachika once more, since Alisa had started to chew aggressively on her straw. However, she just shot him a piercing glare before looking away once more.

"Why me? I've never sung for a band before. There must be plenty of other people who are more qualified, right?"

"Why you? Because you're the best singer I know."

Alisa's eyebrow suddenly twitched as if she were finally expressing some interest.

"…Well, I guess that's understandable. My family often compliments my singing… But that's it?"

"What do you mean, 'that's it'? You're a talented singer. What more could we ask for? Think about it. The only opportunity most people get to bring someone to tears is at their wedding when they read the speech they wrote for their parents. But great singers can move hundreds of thousands of people to tears with their beautiful voice alone, and that's pretty incredible if you ask me."

"Don't you think you're exaggerating a little too much?"

"Not at all. Honestly, I think being able to sing well is the most incredible and rarest talent the heavens can give someone."

"O-oh?"

Alisa's slightly crabby mood from a few moments ago was nowhere to be found. She fidgeted with the ends of her hair and smiled happily. The astonishment on Hikaru's and Takeshi's faces as they exchanged glances was a testament to how foreign such a sight was to them.

What the...? All ya have to do is compliment her a little...?

She's really easily flattered, huh?

But Masachika didn't even glance in their direction while they silently communicated their surprise.

"Plus, this could benefit you as well, Alya. You are going to have even more fans if you sing onstage at the school festival. Plus, this will help you with your teamwork skills."

His calculating scheme made Alisa frown, and she glanced at Hikaru and Takeshi. She then poked Masachika's left hand under the table, getting him to hold out his palm for her to type on.

Are you sure you should be saying this in front of them?

Seeing that Alisa had already practically mastered flick-input on his palm warmed his heart, but he purposely replied aloud:

"You don't have to worry about Takeshi and Hikaru. They're on our side, and they're not doing this as a favor. This is a deal that benefits both parties."

Alisa briefly broke eye contact to think for around ten seconds. Then she faced Takeshi and Hikaru once more.

"Very well. I'd be happy to help if that's okay with you two."

"S-seriously?! I can't tell ya how happy we are to have ya on board!"

"Come on, Takeshi. You two haven't even heard her sing yet."

"Oh, uh... But she's good at everything, so I figured... Ha-ha-ha..."

Masachika and Hikaru rolled their eyes at Takeshi, who couldn't even make eye contact with Alisa as he nervously scratched his head.

"At any rate, I'd be fine with her joining, but we need to hear her sing first. Of course, she needs to see us perform as well."

"Yeah, you got to see if you're a good match for each other. How about doing a session together before making up your mind? You're fine with that, too, right, Alya?"

"Of course."

"Then, uh… Like… Should we head over to a karaoke box after this or…?"

"Nah, we're still in our school uniforms, and it's not like you guys can show off your skills at karaoke."

"Besides, all our instruments are at school, so I guess if we're going to do a session, it should be at school, right?"

"O-oh, right. Hmm… I guess we could rent a studio somewhere, too, if we have to. Hold up. I forgot. When were we practicing next?"

Masachika helped them come up with a plan…while still holding hands with Alisa, who once again began to type something onto his left palm.

Hmm? What's she writing…?

Even if he were in the middle of a conversation with someone else, Masachika could easily read what someone was writing on his palm with this method, so he directed half his attention to his conversation with the boys while focusing the other half to his left hand.

T.H.I.S. W.A.Y. "Look this way"?

Masachika looked at Alisa, but all he got back was a quizzical stare.

"…What?"

"Nothing…"

I just did what you told me, he thought in bewilderment. He wondered if he had misread what she wrote, so he began to think back to—

"Masachika?"

"Bro, you've been staring at her for a while. Get lost in her beauty?" teased Takeshi, making Masachika suddenly face forward, flustered.

"Oh my. I had no idea you felt that way." Alisa giggled by his ear as she flicked her hair back with a provocative grin. Just seeing how much she was enjoying this made Masachika grit his teeth.

You little...!

Though he was frustrated about being set up, he maintained his composure and replied:

"Oh, no. I thought I heard Alya say something. That's all."

"Okay."

Although Alisa seemed to have given up easily, the mischief in her eyes remained as she immediately began to write something else on his palm.

You're so cute when you panic.

"I know it's a little late for me to be saying this, but wouldn't we need her to officially join the music club first?"

"Hmm? Oh... Good question. That would probably make things easier..."

"But we only have a little over a month until the school festival. Having her join for a month and then immediately quit would be..."

"Yeah, good point."

Look this way again. This time I'm serious.

"Hmm... We'd have to discuss this with the captain, I guess. I really doubt there's a rule where you can't perform if you're not in the music club, but having a member of the student council join could lead to some issues."

"Y-yeah, good point. I'll call the captain and see what's up."

What's wrong? Are you sulking?

"Hold on. Maybe you should wait until she officially joins our band."

"Yeah, that would be better. Your next practice session is two days before the opening ceremony, right? You can make your official decision there, and if Alya ends up joining the music club, then she can join as a second-semester recruit..."

You're acting like a little kid. How adorable.

She's already using the flick-input technique I taught her for evil!!

Masachika screamed internally while still managing to converse with Takeshi and Hikaru. He was making sure to concentrate on Alisa's fingers while keeping a straight face in the hope that she might actually have something she needed to tell him in secret...but she was only messing around with no end in sight. It was as if she were compelled to keep teasing Masachika, since he wasn't giving her a reaction, and if that was the case, then there was no reason to keep paying attention to her. In the end, that was the conclusion Masachika reached, so he put his attention solely on the conversation with Takeshi and Hikaru. However...

Ngh... This just makes it...

While he may have stopped trying to read what she was saying, he still couldn't ignore the fact that she was caressing his palm with her fingers. If anything, that fact stood out even more now as the tips of her fingers tickled his skin. Every time she tapped on his palm, his fingers twitched closed, making him almost hold her hand.

O-oh, gosh... This is starting to tickle like crazy!

A chill slowly ran down his spine, alerting him that danger was near, but he felt it would be rude to brush her hand away, and it would make him feel like a loser as well. He couldn't come up with a good reason to get up out of his seat mid-conversation, either.

But... Wait. Hold on. This is seriously bad. I'm starting to feel like I'm doing something naughty with all this rustling under the table...!

He could feel his body gradually getting warmer, so he did everything in his power to end the conversation as soon as possible, but it wasn't going as well as he had hoped, thanks to Takeshi, who kept bringing up whatever new topic came to his mind. Nevertheless, Masachika managed to use every bit of rational thought he could to maintain his composure.

"Yeah, then first you should probably send her the lyrics and background music for the songs she's going to sing."

"Yeah, good idea. By the way, Masachika..."

"Hmm?"

"Is it just me, or are you really red?" asked Hikaru.

"...?!"

Masachika froze.

"Yeah, your face is kind of red, bro. You okay?"

Takeshi looked him over. Their consideration was innocent, and their eyes were pure…which made Masachika just want to crawl into a hole, guilty about worrying his friends when it was his own fault for playing with fire and not expecting to get burned. Furthermore, his heart swelled with humiliation, embarrassment, and self-disgust for succumbing to Alisa's teasing by blushing.

Ahhh! I just want to disappear! I don't want to be alive anymore! Somebody, kill me! Please!

He didn't even have the energy to explain himself as he hunched over.

"Oh my. What's wrong? I hope you don't have a fever," Alisa whispered into his ear. The audacity prompted Masachika to sharply glare at her out of the corner of his eye, but she didn't seem to care in the least. If anything, she seemed to be extremely proud of herself; her lips curled with satisfaction and her fingers danced on his palm.

That should do it for today.

And with that, Alisa let go of his hand, grabbed her melon soda, and began to indulge herself in the fruit of her success—happy as could be.

Hiding Feelings in Russian, AKA the Verbal Exhibitions

"Oh. No go, huh?"

"Yeah… I don't blame them, though."

Masachika was talking on the phone with Takeshi in his room the day after Alisa agreed to do vocals for the band, and they were currently talking about the band's bassist, Ryuuichi, and keyboardist, Riho.

"Anyway, both said they wanted to take a break from the band for a while… I don't know how long 'a while' is, but I really doubt we're gonna be ready for the school festival."

Takeshi's uncharacteristically jaded voice made it transparent that he was exhausted from dealing with them.

"I feel for you. I guess it'd be hard to perform with all the jealousy and bitter feelings going around anyway."

"Yeah, you're probably right… Anyway, I still can't believe that Riho had feelings for Hikaru, too…"

"…Hmm?" A puzzled expression crossed Masachika's face. "…Did she say that?"

"What? Remember what she said before she stormed out of the room? She was like, 'But…I like—' She had to have been talking about Hikaru, right? That's part of why he was so depressed."

"…Oh."

That was what it sounded like she was trying to say, given the context, but something still felt off about it to Masachika… In fact, something had felt off even before all that. Although he wasn't close with those three, they were friends of his friends, so he had hung out with them more than a few times and knew them relatively well, and that was why Takeshi's account of what happened seemed strange to Masachika. Takeshi and Hikaru were perhaps far too shaken up over what happened to have noticed, because if anything, this probably went even beyond a simple feeling that something was wrong.

"*Sigh*... Anyway, what are we gonna do without a bassist and keyboardist now? We finally get Princess Alya's support, and now this...," mumbled Takeshi despondently, breaking Masachika's train of thought while simultaneously making him realize that Takeshi didn't have the luxury of quitting. But even after coming to this realization, he had to ask:

"Are you still planning on performing at the school festival? Even though you lost over half your band?"

"Hmm? Yeah... I promised Kanau I would. Besides..."

"Besides?"

"If we cancel, then Hikaru's never going to be able to put all this behind him," suggested Takeshi, conveying nothing but love and consideration for his friend. "Plus, there's no way I'm going to let the once-in-a-lifetime opportunity to perform with Princess Alya slip by!" he added as if to conceal how much he cared about his friend.

"...Ha-ha. Yeah, good point."

But it was obvious that Alisa wasn't really the reason why he felt compelled to make this work. Because in the end, he was the kind of person who prioritized his friends over his lust for women. That was just who Takeshi Maruyama was.

"All right, let me take care of your bass and keyboard problem."

"Wait. Do you *really* know someone who can play? Someone who plays keyboard, maybe. But someone who can play the bass? I doubt there are many people outside our club who can play..."

"Yeah, I might know some people. And if that doesn't work, I'll play."

"For real? Can you even play bass?"

"I've never tried, but I can play violin, and stringed instruments can't be all that different from one another, right?"

"They're completely different! And since when can ya play violin?!"

"Oh, I didn't tell you? I'm not brag-worthy good or anything, but I can still play something like Czardas at double speed."

"What kind of devil did you sell your soul to?!"

They chatted over the phone for a while after that, until Takeshi had finally returned to his usual self. Right after hanging up, Masachika opened his instant messenger app and texted the person who might be able to help them.

◇

"...All right. I understand the situation you're in."

The next day, Masachika met with the person he'd texted at a café where they were sitting facing each other. It was his former clubmate during his time in the student council in middle school, Sayaka Taniyama, who had been quietly listening to Masachika explain the situation while they waited on their order.

"So...? What do you want me to do about it?" she asked softly.

There was no indication in her distant gaze or cold voice that she was going to meet him halfway. Sayaka was usually laid-back and levelheaded when dealing with most people, but she was especially strict with Masachika due to their past rivalry during the election. It didn't help that she was acting like an uncompromising boss who was interrogating her subordinate. The penetrating light in her eyes made it clear that she couldn't be fooled, either, and that was why Masachika decided to be straight with her instead of bending the truth or joking about it.

"Okay, I'll get to the point. Would you play bass for Takeshi's band?"

"Why me? And bass? I—"

"You know how to play bass."

He interrupted her as he stared hard into her eyes, and she stared back into his as if she were trying to uncover his true intentions. But

when Masachika shifted his gaze to her hands on the table, she sighed and leaned heavily back in her seat.

"Even if I could play bass, what's in it for me?" she asked in a matter-of-fact tone. A flash of light reflected off her glasses, which hung over her faint smirk.

"Don't tell me you're asking me to help make Alisa even more popular out of the goodness of my heart, because—"

"Sorry to keep you waiting. One Nakucia Healing Sandwich and MP Potion for the lady."

"W-wow! This looks incredible!"

"Sigh..."

Masachika seemed unenthused as he observed how easily Sayaka switched from playing hardball to squealing over the food the waiter brought. Incidentally, this wasn't any ordinary café. It was doing an anime collab and was designed to look like a pub in a fantasy setting where mercenaries and adventurers would gather. The café was even serving cuisine from anime and had several drinks based on characters from the show as well. It was extremely elaborate.

"And one Kelger Dragon Burger and Dwarf Firewater for the gentleman."

"Thanks."

The food Masachika had ordered was placed in front of him next. Although this went without saying, the dragon burger was not dragon meat but a mix of ground pork and beef, and the firewater didn't have any alcohol in it. These were simply designed to look like the cuisine in the anime.

They did a great job with the food, though... I bet Yuki would have a blast here.

Masachika had actually made reservations at this café to come with Yuki, but his sister suddenly had urgent business to take care of, so he ended up inviting Sayaka instead. Therefore, he took out his phone, figuring he could send her a picture of the food at the very least. Coincidentally, Sayaka also took out her phone for a picture, so they spent the next few minutes taking pictures in silence. Of course, they didn't forget to switch seats to take photos of the other's food, too.

Once they had finished the photo shoot and checked out the free coasters that came with their drinks, Sayaka's expression slowly regained its seriousness from earlier.

"So? Do you really expect me to help Alisa out of the goodness of my heart?"

"Don't force it. Do you really think I can take your tough-guy persona seriously after all that?" replied Masachika blandly while he reached for his fork. "Anyway, there's a time limit on how long we can stay, so let's eat first, okay?"

Although Sayaka frowned a bit, she reached for her sandwich and began to eat. Only after they had finished their meals at the twenty-minute mark did Masachika get back on topic.

"Okay, so let's talk about the band now because I think this can be really fun for you, too. The band's short a few members, but everyone's still doing everything they can to perform at the school festival. Sounds kind of like *K-OFF*, if you ask me."

Sayaka's eyebrow twitched at the thought. *K-OFF* (official title: *K-Off, Winter Won't Come to the Music Club*) was an anime about a school music club on the brink of being disbanded due to a lack of members after one of the members transferred to a new school, and in an attempt to avoid losing their club, they made it their goal to put on an incredible performance at the school festival. The *Winter Won't Come* part of the title had two meanings to it. One referred to the sense of impending danger, since the club would be disbanded by winter if they didn't do something. However, it was also an expression of determination that was meant to convey that they wouldn't accept winter's coming and that they were going to fight until the bitter end. The anime was extremely popular three years prior and probably convinced numerous nerds to join their school music clubs.

From what Masachika could ascertain, Sayaka was most likely one of those nerds. He had two pieces of evidence to back up this claim:

Sayaka's overenthusiastic reaction to Yuki's T-shirt when they ran into each other at the park and the faint calluses on Sayaka's fingers.

"...Well, I suppose I can see your point. Kanamin also joined the band as a replacement after the original bassist left, after all." She slowly nodded while pushing up the bridge of her glasses, concealing her eyes behind a reflection of light. "I suppose you really do have a point. The lead singer, Luna, was also a silver-haired maiden, and hearing that your friend wants to show off to his little brother does remind me of Hikari's love for her little sister, which was her reason for performing. Plus, 'Hikari' does kind of sound like 'Hikaru' when you think about it—"

"Well, I'm glad you see things my way."

Masachika rolled his eyes at his motormouthed schoolmate, who kept pushing up her glasses. She rambled on about *K-OFF* for three minutes nonstop after that, until she finally snapped back to reality, softly cleared her throat, and composed herself.

"At any rate...that doesn't mean I can simply help Alisa without—"

"Stop forcing it already. I can't take you seriously anymore today."

I'm honestly surprised she managed to keep up the facade this long, he thought, inwardly sighing as he reached below his chair.

"Anyway, I'm not asking you to do this for free."

The look in her eyes changed the instant she saw what he lifted into the air.

"What...?! I-is that...?!"

Sayaka stood up so quickly and with such force that she almost knocked her chair to the floor, and she leaned over the table. When she realized that she was most certainly not seeing things, she mumbled in a trembling, hoarse voice:

"Is that an original collector's card personally autographed by one of the voice actors? Those were only given to people who wrote into the anime's official radio show and had their letter read on air, and that looks like it's from the final episode..."

"You really know your stuff. They used a different design on the collector's cards every time they did the event. This one in particular is a group photo of every character in the last episode, which was specifically drawn for this card. There are only five in the world, by the way, and I've never seen even one of them put up on any online auction."

Sayaka gulped, making Masachika grin as he placed the collector's card, which was sealed inside an acrylic case, on the table.

"But I'd be more than willing to part ways with it if you accept my proposal."

The obvious bribe had Sayaka suddenly narrowing her usual chilling gaze. She dropped back down in her seat and sighed cynically.

"Do you really think you can buy me? I'm insulted."

"Then let go of it and say that again."

As Masachika grabbed the collector's card on the table and jerked it away, along came Sayaka's hand, still firmly gripping it.

The band had just gotten a new bass player.

Masachika decided to meet up with the potential keyboardist the next day.

"And…? You want me to, like, play keyboard for that band or whatever?" asked the girl with lustrous blond hair in a ponytail who was sitting across from him.

"What's it gonna be?" asked Masachika with a smirk, staring back into Nonoa Miyamae's heavy-lidded eyes.

"Excuse me?"

Her reaction curled his lips even more, and he nonchalantly proposed:

"If you're interested, then I can work something out with the band. I'm sure they'd be happy to have you on keyboard."

It was a proposal, not a request. A request would mean that Nonoa would have to get something in return, but Masachika couldn't come up with a single thing that would please her, and there was nothing more frightening than being in debt to her, either. Therefore, he wasn't going to ask her to do this as a favor. He was going to simply offer her the opportunity while using Sayaka as bait. He was essentially giving Nonoa the chance to play in the same band as her best friend.

"...Ohhh, now I get it. No wonder you chose different days to talk to Saya and me."

Once Nonoa utilized her innate perceptiveness to promptly see right through Masachika's scheme, she lazily leaned back in her seat.

"And, like, what are you gonna do if I say no?"

"Then I'll just play keyboard in the band. You might be more appealing visually, but it'd work out," admitted Masachika with a shrug and a composed expression.

"Uh-huh."

Nonoa shot him a suggestive look, but she soon closed her eyes as if she had lost any interest in the conversation and waved her hand.

"Yeah, whatever. I'll do it. I'm not exactly thrilled about it, but I'll do it."

"Really? Thanks."

And just like that, the band once again had five members.

"And that's what happened. You have your five band members now."

"Hold up."

"One girl... Two girls... They're all girls..."

"Hey, do you think Shadow Hikaru could hold on for a second?"

That was how Takeshi and Hikaru first responded to Masachika's announcement during their group phone call.

"I get ya have connections, being in the student council and all... but I can't believe you convinced those two to help, too..."

"When I told you I might know some people, you should have at least been able to guess that Nonoa was one of them. I mean, everybody knows she's good at piano."

Seirei Academy Middle School put on a choir competition every year, and it was customary for the best piano player to play piano at the competition. There were countless students from wealthy families at Seirei Academy, and a decent number of them had been learning piano from a young age, so whoever was chosen to accompany the choir students was undoubtedly a talented pianist. And for three years in a row, that talented musician had been Nonoa, whose skills were considered second only to the Prince of Piano, Yuushou Kiryuuin. Even Takeshi was well aware of this. However…

"Dude, how was I supposed to guess that you were gonna ask one of the most popular girls in school?"

Although Nonoa was well known as a talented pianist, everyone knew she expressed absolutely no interest in any music clubs. (In fact, she expressed no interest in any clubs at all.) And that was why Takeshi was so shocked that Nonoa would agree to do this so easily.

"More important, is she going to be okay? Piano and keyboard look similar, but they're actually pretty different."

"Wait. Seriously? Are they really that different? …Regardless, Nonoa said she could do it, so I'm guessing it'll be okay."

"Very reassuring, Masachika. Thanks… Anyway, I had no idea that girl Sayaka could even play bass. She doesn't really look like the kind of person who'd play."

"Yeah, I know what you mean."

"…? How'd ya even know she played?"

"…It's a long story," Masachika replied ambiguously before immediately changing the subject. "Anyway, are you pleased with your new bandmates or not, Takeshi?"

"Huh? Oh, I'm fine with them…but I feel a little intimidated, I guess. You know, with how amazing they all are. I'm worried they're going to overshadow me, and I'm just gonna fade into the background…"

"You don't have to worry about that. None of them are tall enough to overshadow you."

"Come on! You know what I mean! I don't wanna feel completely dominated onstage. Now, offstage—that's another story."

"You don't have to worry about that. You have zero chance with any of them."

"Bro?! Maybe I have no chance with Sayaka, but Nonoa might want a piece of this."

"Even if by some miracle that did happen, don't. Seriously. Anyone *but* Nonoa," warned Masachika in a dead serious tone before shifting his focus toward Hikaru. "Anyway, Hikaru, you've got nothing to worry about because there is absolutely no way any of those three would ever fall in love with you."

"...Really?"

"Really. Even if someone does develop some kind of feelings for someone else in the band, I will deal with it as your manager."

"...?! Manager?" squeaked Takeshi.

"...Yeah? That was my plan from the very start. I was the one who scouted the new members, so of course I plan on making sure everything goes smoothly until the very end," replied Masachika, surprised by his friend's reaction.

"Oh... I guess that makes sense."

"Besides, you guys are going to have trouble even talking to your new bandmates without me there to help you."

"Yeah, I guess you do know them better..."

After persuading Takeshi, Masachika focused on Hikaru once more.

"Anyway, that's the deal, so I need you to trust me. Let's do this."

"..."

A few long moments of silence went by until Hikaru let out a sigh.

"...Fine. These are people you carefully selected yourself, and it wouldn't be right for me to be selfish. Besides, it's my fault the original three members left the band..."

"Don't even think about that."

"Yeah, it's not your fault, Hikaru. You don't need to feel bad about anything."

"...Thanks, guys."

Hikaru chuckled softly at their prompt support and gave his

approval for the band. However, it would be two days later before all five members of the band got together in Music Room A to meet.

“““““………”””””

And unfortunately, it was extremely awkward. Or maybe it was simply awkward for the boys… Nonoa, who arrived early, had been on her phone the entire time, Sayaka had been adjusting and tuning her bass in silence, and Takeshi was glowing angelically with joy before the sparkling, glamorous girls. Hikaru was already in a somewhat gloomy mood, and Alisa was simply a poor communicator who kept to herself. Nobody said a word. Two entire minutes had gone by, and nobody was even trying to get to know the others, despite that being the point of gathering that day.

Sigh… This is even worse than I thought. Looks like I’m going to have to take over.

But right as Masachika was about to suggest that everyone introduce themselves, Sayaka, who had been quietly messing with her bass the entire time, suddenly spoke up.

“Okay. It appears everyone is here, so how about we get started? We don’t have much time, after all.”

“A’ight.”

“Huh? Oh, uh…”

Nonoa promptly began to set up her keyboard, and Takeshi and Hikaru started to prepare in a fluster as well.

“Hold up, Sayaka. Shouldn’t you guys at least introduce yourselves before you start?” Masachika chimed in before they started their session, since they still hadn’t even conversed yet.

“It isn’t as if we don’t know one another. We’ve already introduced ourselves before, so there’s no reason to do that again now. Besides…”

Sayaka slowly traced a finger down her bass’s neck, then smugly snorted out a laugh.

“Music speaks louder than words. This will help us get to know one another far better than any chitchat.”

“Heh. Now we’re talking. Hold on. I don’t remember you being this cool," Masachika jokingly interjected with a straight face, but Sayaka was far too full of herself to even notice.

Now that I think about it, that bass...

It looked very familiar. In fact, it really resembled a bass guitar used in a certain anime that was popular around three years ago.

...She really is a nerd.

Masachika looked away from the girl rubbing her bass with a twinkle in her eyes and turned his focus over to Nonoa.

"I didn't know you had your own keyboard, Nonoa," he casually mentioned while she was setting up. This caused her to lift her head and reply:

"Hmm? I just bought it."

"What...?! Don't tell me you bought a keyboard just for this?!"

"Yeah?"

"Uh... I really appreciate it, but I feel bad. The music club could have just rented one, you know?"

"I wanted to play on my own instrument. Besides, it's, like, not even close to how much a piano would cost, so it's no biggie," she replied in a matter-of-fact voice, shrugging.

"Uh-huh...," said Masachika with a half-hearted nod. That was when Takeshi, with a guitar strapped around his shoulder, approached him and whispered:

"Bro, that keyboard alone goes for around a hundred thousand yen, and all the equipment she has with it probably cost around a hundred and thirty thousand."

"Seriously?!"

The fact that this was "no biggie" to her was proof that professional models like her valued money quite differently.

While Masachika stood quietly in shock, he suddenly heard Alisa begin to hum and sing to herself, so he decided to listen under the impression that she was getting warmed up. Then...

"*<Pay attention to me. ♪ Pay attention to me. ♪ Look at meee. ♪>*"

"...?! Bff?!"

"H-hey, uh… What's wrong?"

"Nothing…"

He tried to pretend like nothing was wrong, despite being in shock for the second time in as many minutes.

I-is this what I think it is?! I haven't heard this song in forever!

Incidentally, the official title was "A Feeling Gone Unheard" (words and music by: Alisa Kujou). At any rate, Masachika shot her a piercing gaze as if to say, "What is going on in that head of yours?" while she sang to herself in blissful ignorance. But after a brief sigh, he decided to walk over and talk to her.

"How are you feeling? Unheard?"

"Hmph. As opposed to you, who won't stop chitchatting?"

"Sounds like you're going to be fine."

After shooting Masachika a somewhat chilling glare, Alisa shifted her eyes down to the phone in her hand.

"I made sure to practice the music they sent me until I could sing without looking at the lyrics…but this is still our first time, so there's no telling how it's going to go."

"Yeah, makes sense."

"Hmph… You're the manager, right? How about some advice?"

"What? No way. I can't give any advice. I've never even been in a band before."

"Well, you're no help," she snapped, frowning as Masachika shrugged.

"The only bit of advice I can give you is to not hold back. You need to speak your mind. Also, don't worry about trying to adapt to how everyone else is doing, and just sing your heart out."

"What kind of advice is that? That's it?"

"It may sound easy, but I doubt many people can actually pull it off, to tell you the truth."

"All right, guys! Is everyone ready?" Takeshi shouted suddenly.

"Go show them what you're made of," encouraged Masachika, gesturing toward the microphone.

"Okay."

Once everyone was in position, Alisa stepped in front of the microphone, thus beginning their first jam session together.

"Whoa…!"

The performance was slightly awkward at first, but everything changed once Alisa started to sing. Although her beautiful voice was relaxed and transparent, it was still steady and powerful. It was as if it were slowly drawing the other four performers closer until they were truly one. By the time the chorus was about to start, everyone was fired up, and once the chorus began, the room was bursting with excitement. That enthusiasm lasted until the very last chord on guitar finished ringing out.

"Nice!!"

After a moment of silence, Masachika erupted with applause from the bottom of his heart. While there were still a few parts that didn't sound quite perfect, the band proved that they were more than capable of putting on an incredible performance together, and it wasn't only Masachika who felt this way, either.

"That was unbelievable! Alisa, you're an incredible singer! And Sayaka and Nonoa?! You were amazing, too!" squealed Takeshi in excitement.

"Right? I honestly wasn't expecting to have this much fun during our first jam session together."

Unlike the two boys in the group, however, the female band members maintained their composure.

"Hmm… That was a whole other vibe from playing alone, huh?"

"I was really rushing to catch up in the beginning, but I managed to pull it off thanks to Alisa."

"…I suppose that wasn't bad for our first try."

Takeshi and Hikaru smirked somewhat wryly at how calm they were, but Masachika knew Alisa was only trying to act cool to hide her embarrassment.

"At any rate, how about we practice that a few more times? After that, we can go through the whole setlist," suggested Sayaka.

"O-oh, right. Good idea."

They practiced for forty minutes straight after that.

"Something sounds a little off during the third measure of the chorus, so let's practice that a few more times."

"Good thinking."

"Okay."

"Word."

"Sure."

Before anybody even realized it, Sayaka had naturally taken command of their jam session.

That's Sayaka for you. She's very observant and always watches others carefully.

Sayaka was a born leader as far as Masachika was concerned, and he felt there weren't that many people who had the talent to direct groups like she could. She was the complete opposite of Alisa, who always felt like she could do everything better alone. Nevertheless, Sayaka was convinced that everything ran better and more efficiently when it revolved around her giving the orders, and she had actual results to back that up. These results became achievements, and before long, everyone around her started to feel as if everything would go smoothly if they did just as Sayaka ordered, and those who disturbed the group's harmony were shunned.

Sayaka didn't try to appeal to someone's emotions or rely on her charisma but instead yielded results and gave practical benefits, which impressed those around her. Being able to rule over others was her natural-born talent.

Sigh… On one hand, she's a good ally to have, but on the other hand, she could be trouble for us. Are you picking up on this, Alya? Even if you do become the student council president, Sayaka might steal your role right from under your nose.

This was also what Masachika meant when he told Alisa earlier not to hold back and to speak up. She didn't seem to get the hint, though.

But, well, I guess I shouldn't be too hard on her, since I can't expect her to figure all this out on her first time. There's still plenty of time for her to make that realization.

The five band members practiced enthusiastically for a while after that. Masachika pondered alone.

◇

"All right, then. We're almost out of time, so let's clean up and start the meeting, shall we?" suggested Masachika as he clapped his hands, since they had the music room reserved for only fifteen more minutes. "I thought we were just getting together to say hello today, but you guys went straight into practicing. Anyway, these are going to be your bandmates for the school festival. Is everyone cool with that?"

"No problem here! I couldn't have asked for better bandmates!"

"Same here. I am looking forward to working with you three."

"Let's put on a good show."

"Word."

"I have no issues with that."

This was the exact moment that these five members officially became a band. After they came up with a date for their next practice session once the semester started, they agreed that each member was to try to think of a band name in the meantime.

Once the meeting was over, they all started packing to head home when…

"Oh! Alya, hold up. We still need to talk about the opening ceremony, since we only have two more days to prepare," suggested Masachika. He scratched his head with his left hand before glancing at the other four.

"Ohhh. All right. I'll just be on my way, then. Later."

"See you two later."

"See you all next semester."

"Later."

"Yeah, see you guys."

"Bye."

Once the other four bandmates were out the door, Alisa immediately sent a quizzical stare in Masachika's direction.

"So? What about the opening ceremony did you want to talk about? I thought we were going to prepare for it tomorrow during student council."

"Of course, I was just using that as an excuse to get to talk to you. Didn't you notice me give you the sign?"

"Huh?"

"You know, touching my hair with my left hand."

"Oh…"

That was when Alisa seemed to remember that they were supposed to touch their hair with their left hand whenever they were bluffing. Her shoulders slumped, and she swiftly averted her gaze.

"…Sorry. I completely forgot about that."

"Well, it's not a big deal. Anyway, want to head over to the courtyard for now?"

They decided to change locations to avoid being rushed out by the next group who had reserved the music room. Normally, the hallway neighboring the courtyard would be packed with students, but it was entirely empty that day because it was still summer break. After taking a seat next to Alisa on a bench under a tree, Masachika immediately asked:

"So… How did you feel about your jam session?"

"It was honestly a lot more fun than I expected it to be. I had no idea making music with others could be so enjoyable," she replied without even a second of hesitation.

"Really? I'm glad you had fun," replied Masachika earnestly after hearing her genuine impression. If Alisa had found working with others fun, then that was already a step in the right direction.

"<It would have been more fun if you played with us, too, though.>"

There she goes, exposing herself in Russian like a verbal exhibitionist.

Just when he'd been getting a little sentimental, Alisa had verbally stabbed him in the heart with her sweet Russian whispers, nearly killing him on the spot. But even then, he had no choice but to clear his throat and get down to the heart of the matter.

"Anyway, you need to come up with a band name before the next practice session, right?"

"...? Right."

"Usually, the leader of the band gets to decide the name."

"Huh?" grunted Alisa as if she were taken by surprise.

"...That would be Takeshi, right?" she asked, tilting her head in curiosity.

"He originally was the leader, but I'm guessing that's going to change, now that over half the band members are new."

Masachika assumed a sterner attitude than usual as he turned to face Alisa.

"And if that happens, who do you think the new leader is going to be?"

Her eyes briefly widened before she hesitantly replied:

"Sayaka, most likely..."

"Exactly. Sayaka unquestionably acted like a leader today during practice." Masachika wasn't going to sugarcoat it for her, which seemed to help him finally get his point across. Alisa bit her lip nervously. However, Masachika didn't stop there. "Put simply, you just acknowledged that you didn't show them you had what it takes to be a leader. You lost to Sayaka. I'm sure Takeshi and Hikaru feel the same way, so if things don't change, she's going to end up the band leader."

"...Yeah," she agreed, although reluctantly, as if she couldn't even argue with him.

"But don't worry about it!" he said in a carefree tone, shrugging.

"...?"

"I know I made a big deal out of it, but you guys actually won't be deciding on a new leader during your next practice session."

"What do you mean?"

As she quizzically stared at him, Masachika nonchalantly replied:

"I already asked the other four if they could wait until the day of the performance before deciding on a band leader. More specifically, I asked them to wait until your final rehearsal."

"What?"

Alisa's brow furrowed in confusion, as if she had no idea what was going on, and Masachika put on a serious expression, gazed right into her eyes, and revealed:

"Alya, you have to prove to those four that you're fit to be the leader. You have one month, and if you can't do that, then there's no way you're going to be able to become the student council president."

"...!"

"Not many people at this school can claim to have top-level leadership skills like Sayaka. Learn what you can from her until you surpass her in your own way."

After lowering her gaze for a few seconds, Alisa looked up at the sky in silence for a while until...

"I'll do it," she said with determination in her voice.

"...Great." Masachika felt a sense of satisfaction and adoration while he gazed at her determined profile. He then shifted his eyes toward the sky as well and vowed in his usual tone, "As always, I'll be there by your side, supporting you every step of the way."

"I'm counting on you."

Their hands naturally drew closer until they gently became one, as if they were conveying their trust in each other through their warmth. Their oath sworn to the summer sky was planted inside their hearts...and bloomed in the new semester.

CHAPTER 6 I'm innocent! I swear!

"Whoa...," muttered Masachika dispassionately as if he was witnessing something that had nothing to do with him.

It was September 1st, the first day of the second semester, and both the opening ceremony and homeroom had already ended, so Masachika was looking out the classroom window, down at the schoolyard, where a huge line was extending outside the gymnasium entrance. A group of students were even sprinting over to join the line as if there were somebody famous waiting for them inside. Obviously, there weren't any celebrities, though. They were selling new school uniforms inside the gymnasium today—the summer uniforms, which Touya Kenzaki, the student council president, had been fighting to improve.

Of course, that didn't mean everyone had to wear one. The new summer uniforms were only being sold to those who wanted one. At the very least, for the next three years, students could choose whichever summer uniform they wanted to wear, whether it be the old uniform or the new one. The student council had predicted that there would be a ton of students who wanted one, so they arranged a staff meeting, voted on it, and ended up putting together a temporary shop in the gymnasium just for that day. The absurdly long line alone made it obvious they had made the right decision. If they had decided to sell the uniforms at the school store, then the line for the uniforms would have blocked people trying to go home, which would have made for one chaotic hallway.

"Everyone must be sick of these long-sleeved blazers," muttered

Alisa. Her facial expression made it seem like she had mixed feelings while she watched her classmates dash down the hallway.

There were students who were against the idea of changing the school uniform, so they decided on a rule that allowed the student to choose. As it turned out, however, most students seemed to have opted for the new summer uniform. Perhaps some threw in the towel when they realized how hot it still was when the new semester started, or maybe some people simply didn't want to stick out like a sore thumb after seeing how many of their peers went with the new uniform, so they followed the crowd. Either way, Touya's proposal to improve the summer uniform seemed to be accepted by most.

"I bet everyone's gonna end up going with the new uniform. Today's crazy hot, too."

Takeshi fanned himself with his hand.

"I'm so grateful that we don't have to wear these blazers to school tomorrow, especially since school rules said we had to wear them even on our way to school," exclaimed Hikaru, nodding in agreement with his friend.

"I don't mean to rain on your parade, but the new collared shirt is apparently a little hot."

"What? Why?"

Takeshi and Hikaru stared at Masachika as if he were speaking in tongues.

"They're apparently using some sort of slightly thicker material that's not see-through, since they wanted to make sure students still looked proper in public, no matter what happens." Masachika shrugged.

"W-wait. Hold up… Are you telling me—…?"

After Takeshi paused, appearing stunned, he glanced at Alisa, then lowered his voice so that she couldn't hear him and asked:

"Does that mean we're not gonna be able to see their bras through their shirts…?"

Despite his friend having the most ridiculously serious look on his face, Masachika gravely nodded back.

"That's exactly what this means."

"No… Nooo!"

Grief-stricken, Takeshi leaned weakly against the window as his eyes darted around, surveying the outside world.

"What have we done…? Hopes and dreams are but a thing of the past now…"

"You say as you live in Japan during a time of peace."

"It's a new semester, and not even one beautiful girl transferred to our school and told me she was my fiancée…"

"Yeah, like that'd ever happen in real life. By the way, that trope is already outdated. Popular tropes for transfer students nowadays are former heroes or former soldiers who dream about living normal lives."

"Maybe if they're the protagonist! But I'm going to be a side character!"

"…Oh."

"Why did you just hesitate there for a second?"

"No reason…"

Masachika swiftly averted his gaze while Hikaru and Alisa both frowned uncomfortably. The awkward silence continued for the next few seconds until Hikaru decided to speak up with a cheerful note in his voice and added:

"Anyway, I'm impressed. I always assumed that it'd be impossible to get rid of an outdated tradition like this, since I didn't think there was any way to convince the First Light Committee."

The First Light Committee was the official title of the committee made up of former student council presidents and vice presidents who had graduated from Seirei Academy High School. The academy may have been a private school for the elite, but the tuition was relatively inexpensive. If anything, the tuition was rather cheap when considering all the facilities and systems that had been put into place. The reason for this was because the school was receiving tremendously generous donations from its alumni. The First Light Committee's donations were extraordinary, which proportionally gave them a lot of say in regard to school policy.

Needless to say, a not-small portion of their donation was used to make the new summer uniforms, so this plan would have never come to fruition without their approval.

"From what I heard, it was actually the relatively younger members of the group who were against the idea." Masachika shrugged again, causing Takeshi to curiously raise an eyebrow.

"Wait. For real? You'd think some stubborn old man would have been the one who was against the idea."

"The geezers on the First Light Committee are all leading figures in the business world and in politics, so maybe they just don't let little things like school uniforms bother them."

"...Yeah, I guess I can't really imagine Niikura complaining about school uniforms, since he used to go here."

"Right?"

"...? Niikura?"

Alisa appeared confused.

"Prime Minister Niikura," clarified Masachika, surprised that she wasn't aware.

"...?! What?!"

"Oh, ya didn't know?" asked Takeshi, since she seemed to be genuinely taken aback.

"It makes sense, though. It's not like the First Light Committee goes on TV to talk or anything, so there's no way you would know unless someone told you."

Nevertheless, this was a relatively well-known fact among the students at Seirei Academy, and it wasn't something even worth gossiping about, so it made sense that Alisa, who didn't have a lot of close friends, wouldn't know. At least, that was what Masachika figured when he tried to make her feel better about being out of the loop.

Incidentally, the only reason it wasn't worth gossiping about was because it wasn't anything unusual. After all, four members within the committee had been the prime minister at some point in their life, and the number was most likely even higher than that if they included former members of the committee who had already passed away.

Although most schools would probably use the fact that a former student of theirs became the prime minister as a selling point, it was so common at Seirei Academy that nobody really batted an eye.

"By the way, the minister of finance, Onuma, and the governor of Tokyo, Nanase, also graduated from our school—just to name a few. You've also got Sayaka's dad, who's the CEO of Taniyama Heavy Industries; the CEO of Gilkes; the head of Eimei Bank; the CEO of Clarique—the list is endless."

Masachika started to list off members of the committee on his fingers until it started to bore him, and he stopped.

"Also, I believe Yuki Suou's grandfather used to be an ambassador to the United States," Hikaru casually added.

"...Oh, right."

Masachika realized that his enthusiasm had plummeted to the point that he was worried the others would pick up on it. While Takeshi didn't seem to notice, both Alisa and Hikaru glanced at him quizzically, making Masachika want to click his tongue.

"Yo."

That was when the person they had been waiting for suddenly arrived, which allowed Masachika to nonchalantly shift his focus to her.

"Oh, hey..."

The new visitor stepping into the room was none other than Nonoa, her hair tied in a ponytail. However, the instant everyone saw how she was dressed, they froze because she had already changed into the new summer uniform that they'd just started selling at the gymnasium. Did she somehow manage to buy it in advance? But as far as Masachika knew, there was no way anyone could have gotten their hands on the new uniform in advance, and he would know, since he was in the student council.

"...How are you already dressed in the new school uniform?" asked Masachika on behalf of all the inquiring minds, making Nonoa curiously tilt her head with her usual heavy-lidded eyes.

"Eh, you know. One thing led to another."

"...Uh-huh."

He couldn't press her for answers anymore after hearing that. Although it was highly likely that she just didn't feel like explaining, Masachika felt that asking for details wouldn't lead to anything good, so he dropped it. If Nonoa said that one thing led to another, then that was what happened.

"Not on your phone for once, huh?" commented Masachika, changing the subject. Nonoa sluggishly sat in a nearby seat.

"Yeah," she grunted with a shrug.

"My mom got mad at me for being on my phone all the time, so I'm trying to cut back or whatever."

"Oh..."

Masachika was genuinely surprised that Nonoa was respecting her mother's wishes, and he didn't seem to be the only one.

"Wow... You do what your parents tell you to do," mentioned Takeshi a bit hesitantly.

"Uh...? Yeah? Of course I do. That doesn't mean I'm gonna start listening to my teachers or anything, though. Ha-ha."

It was hard to gauge whether she was serious or joking, and her bored expression wasn't helping. Takeshi and Hikaru fake-laughed as well, since they didn't know how else to react.

Mmm... What have I gotten myself into? This isn't going to be easy.

Takeshi was uncomfortable around girls his age despite how he usually acted, and Hikaru simply wasn't a fan of them. And to make matters worse, Alisa was terrible at making new friends. Meanwhile, Nonoa did things at her own pace, and Sayaka didn't really trouble herself over how others felt. In other words, though he was the one who had brought these people together, Masachika had a hard time imagining a future where they really hit it off and had great chemistry as a band.

And that's why I need to act as a sort of mediator to bring them together.

But the instant he renewed his resolve, Sayaka came walking through the door and almost immediately began to run the show.

"All right, how about we start off by choosing a band name? Does anyone have any ideas?"

She stood at the lectern like a teacher, since the six of them were the only people in the room. A few moments went by after she made eye contact with each of them individually. Hikaru suddenly raised a hand.

"I do."

"Okay, let's hear it."

"Uh... How about Colorful? Our band's pretty diverse when you think about it. Plus, it's simple, which I like."

"That's not a bad idea at all," admitted Sayaka as she wrote *Colorful* on the chalkboard. After she asked if there were any other ideas, Takeshi enthusiastically raised his hand.

"Yes, Takeshi?"

He smirked as if he had the greatest idea in the whole world.

"Shan't," he slowly exclaimed, his breath oozing with confidence; however, the other five were clearly unimpressed.

Sayaka's brow furrowed slightly, and she pushed up her glasses by the bridge.

"You mean like as an abbreviation for 'shall not'?"

It was a reasonable question, so Takeshi promptly raised an index finger to explain further.

"The easiest way to come up with team names is to take the first letter of everyone's name. In our case, we have *T*, *H*, *A*, *S*, and *N*, so after thinking about it for a while, I came up with Shan't! What do ya think?!"

"Lame."

Nonoa used "Relentless Strike"! Takeshi "Fainted"!

"...Anybody have any better ideas?"

Even the disciplinary committee member was relentless, rubbing salt into his wounds. After clearing her throat, Sayaka set her eyes on the girl who had absolutely crushed Takeshi.

"What about you, Nonoa?"

"Me? For real?"

When Masachika glanced at Nonoa, who was twirling her hair as her eyes wandered, the first thought that came to his mind was, *There's no point in even asking her, since it's probably going to be something flashy or trashy. It's just going to be something ridiculously long about being "lit" or having "rizz" or something stupid.*

"Oh," Nonoa suddenly muttered before Masachika's speculating gaze. "How about God of Grilled Chicken Meatballs?"

"Are you okay?"

"What? It's a legit good name."

"It sounds like the name of a pub," interjected Masachika with a straight face.

"How did you come up with that name anyway?" asked Sayaka, frowning.

"Hmm? It just came to me," replied Nonoa.

"..."

Even though Sayaka placed a hand on her forehead in exasperation, she still wrote *God of Grilled Chicken Meatballs* on the chalkboard.

"What about you, Saya?" asked Nonoa while Sayaka was still facing the board.

"My idea for a band name? Well..."

After Sayaka slightly turned around with a raised eyebrow, she faced the blackboard once more, allowing the chalk to effortlessly glide across its enamel. *Dark—*

"Sayaka, wait."

"What?"

"Just come over here for a second."

The instant Masachika saw what she had begun to write, he tried to lead her to the hallway, but she only stared back at him, knitting her brow in utter confusion.

"...Can it wait until I finish writing my idea?"

"Saya? Like, I think you should probably hear Kuze out first."

"Nonoa..."

Sayaka placed the chalk down at the request of her childhood friend, then stepped out with Masachika into the hallway, where he immediately shut the door, cornered Sayaka against the wall, and placed a hand on the wall by her head.

"What were you planning on writing on that chalkboard?"

"What? ...*Sigh*."

She sighed as if to say, "That's what you wanted to talk about?"

"Dark Alliance," she revealed in a matter-of-fact tone as she adjusted her glasses.

"Wooowee. Now that's a doozy. That was a close one. Even I almost took damage."

"What are you rambling on about?"

"No, what are *you* rambling on about? What other amazing names did you come up with?"

"Well, I was considering Nightmare or something similar."

"Ooof. Aren't you a little too old to be having your emo phase now?"

Although it wasn't an emo phase, Sayaka hadn't been a nerd for long. She had only gotten into anime and manga in June during her second year of middle school—in other words, right after she lost to Yuki and Masachika in the middle school student council presidential election. Until then, she was an overachiever just like her parents wanted her to be, and she never once questioned why she was living solely to satisfy her parents. She was the model student who went to a prestigious school to meet her parents' expectations. In fact, the first time she had ever failed to meet their expectations was when she lost the election.

She wondered how she would be punished for her failure when she nervously went home that day...but what waited for her was her parents' love and affection. It was anticlimactic while simultaneously making her notice that she'd been the one who wanted to become the model student to live up to her parents' supposed expectations. The entire experience was also what pushed her into thinking that maybe she should enjoy her life a little more. That was how Sayaka became a healthy nerd. Two years had gone by, and now she was finally going through her edgelord phase!

"I'm telling you this for your own good. Do not write either of those names on the board. They're going to smell the nerd on you."

"...! That would be bad..."

His warning seemed to work perfectly on this closeted nerd. So after thinking for a few moments, she walked back inside the classroom and casually erased the word *Dark* on the board as if nothing had happened.

"What about you, Alisa? Do you have any ideas?"

"Huh? Me?"

But despite Sayaka suddenly moving on, neither Takeshi nor Hikaru even uttered a word. Perhaps they were slowly catching on to her.

I'm genuinely surprised she has managed to keep her nerdy hobbies a secret this long.

While Masachika's heart was filled with a mixture of admiration and annoyance, Alisa somewhat hesitantly spoke up and suggested:

"How about Fortitude...?"

"Fortitude? That's like one of those words I hear a lot but have never actually looked up in the dictionary," joked Takeshi, except for the fact that it wasn't a joke.

"It means to have courage in the face of pain or misfortune."

"O-oh yeah... I knew that..."

"Yes, courageous... 'Unconquerable' would be another way of trying to get my message across."

"Unconquerable..."

Hikaru rolled the word off his tongue. Alisa continued:

"Just like how humility is viewed highly in Japan, having a never-give-up attitude and overcoming whatever life throws at you is considered a virtue in Russia. I understand this might be a unique value held by Russians who grew up in adverse environments, though."

"Overcoming whatever life throws at you..."

Both Hikaru and Takeru seemed to pick up on what Alisa was trying to say.

"I like it. I like it a lot," said Hikaru with a grin as he nodded at Alisa.

"Me too! It has a nice ring to it!"

Their acceptance instantly suggested that they were going to use Alisa's idea, prompting Sayaka and Nonoa to exchange glances as if they were communicating through eye contact alone.

"Great. I think we should go with Alisa's proposal, then. Does anyone have an issue with that?"

Their silence said it all.

Takeshi somewhat hesitantly spoke up. "Uh… This isn't an issue or anything. I was just wondering what 'unconquerable' was in Russian."

"Hmm? Oh. Несгибаемые."

"Neese-gee bayayaya…? Okay, then… Let's just go with Fortitude."

Thus, the group decided on Fortitude as the band's name.

"Now, we need to discuss the songs we're going to play at the school festival. Each group has roughly fifteen minutes of stage time, which means around three songs if you include our self-introductions. However, the tabs I received the other day were for three covers and one original, so…what do you want to do?"

Takeshi made eye contact with Hikaru after hearing Sayaka's query, then weakly mumbled:

"Oh, right. My bad. I know I was the one who sent ya the tabs, but that original was actually a song we made with the original band… so it wouldn't really feel right if we played it without them."

"Oh. That's fine. Shall we go with the three covers, then?"

"Yeah, I guess that would be our best bet when you consider how little time we have to practice before the show."

But there was a faint note of disappointment in Hikaru's tone, as if he really wanted to play an original deep down inside.

"If you want to play an original, you should. You guys still have a whole month to practice."

"A month isn't a lot of time. Besides, while Takeshi and I might be able to write the lyrics, writing the music, too, on such short notice would be impossible..."

Even though Masachika tried to be encouraging, he still couldn't convince Hikaru to give it a try. Takeshi looked like he wanted to say something as well but ultimately maintained his silence. They were most likely hesitant, since they didn't want to put any pressure on the so-called guest members, much less bother them. However...

"If you want to do an original, then I think we should. I've already agreed to help, so that's what I'm going to do. Let's put on a show that none of us are going to regret," an unexpected voice suddenly chimed in. Takeshi and Hikaru were wide-eyed in astonishment at Alisa's support. Even Masachika was somewhat taken aback by how unexpectedly motivated and aggressive his partner was being.

"None of us." *She put the team first...*

She wasn't solely pursuing her ideals but instead giving a common goal for everyone to pursue. It almost brought tears to Masachika's eyes.

"I appreciate the thought, but as I mentioned, we don't have time..."

"Then how about you use one of Saya's original songs?" interjected Nonoa, making everyone turn to look at Sayaka. "You wrote a few originals, Saya, right?"

"I did write a few, but they're all for guitar."

"Wait. Sayaka, you can play guitar, too?"

"I'm average at best, but yes," she smoothly replied, so Nonoa shifted her heavy-lidded, unmotivated gaze at Hikaru.

"So there you go. You have an original. Besides, you guys picked out those covers with the original band, too, right? Like, one of the songs is a bad match for Alisa's voice, so maybe we should make a new setlist altogether?"

"Yeah... I guess you're right."

"Yeah, I agree."

"Then let's start from the very beginning. It won't, like, matter if we practice covers or originals if we're starting all over, right?"

Takeshi and Hikaru exchanged glances and nodded after seeing how confident the female members were being.

"All right... Yeah...let's do it! Let's do this!"

"Now we're talking! Sayaka, do ya have any recordings of your originals? I wanna hear them."

"Well...I have a video of myself that I took on my phone for practice."

"For real?! Let me hear it!"

The burning motivation and excitement pushed Takeshi and Hikaru over to Sayaka's side, where they all listened to her originals.

Uh... Is it just me, or do these all sound like anime songs?

Even the song titles sound—

That's enough. We get it.

The boys in the room froze, speaking to one another only with their eyes.

"What do you think? I take pride in my work, and I feel like the quality's there."

Meanwhile, Sayaka seemed strangely confident.

"Oh my god."

It was an ambiguous phrase that young girls like Nonoa could use to avoid saying how they actually felt.

"I thought all the songs were wonderful and really conveyed how you see the world," replied Alisa genuinely, only making the other five like her even more than they already did.

"I especially enjoyed the second song."

"Oh, really? I'm surprised you like that one the best."

"The second song was really bad—uh, ass. Really badass, and I agree with Alisa."

"Yeah, it was rather relaxing. I enjoyed it a lot!"

"Oh my god."

After everyone agreed to go with the song Alisa selected, which also happened to be the least *unique*, they decided on two more songs, completing their setlist for the school festival.

"All right, let's go with Sayaka's song 'Anthem' for our original. Is everyone else okay with that?" asked Alisa.

"Oh, it's actually called 'Phantom.'"

"What...? Oh, uh... Okay."

Once again, it was a mystery how most people didn't pick up on how much of an anime nerd Sayaka really was.

No, no, no...

The following day, Masachika was tottering down the hallway and feeling overwhelmed by a sense of imminent danger.

I have to...hurry...

His legs were trembling, and his vision was blurry, but even then, he desperately pushed forward, for if he stopped moving for even a second, it would all be over. Because at that moment, he would surely...

I'm going to fall asleep standing up at this rate!!

Although it may have sounded like a joke, it was the truth. Ever since becoming a member of the student council, Masachika had actually scaled back his carefree lifestyle and changed his day-to-day behavior so that he wouldn't humiliate his partner, Alisa, in any way. For instance, he had been gradually increasing the amount of time he slept at night and worked hard to pay off his sleep debt so that he wouldn't have to take naps at school any longer.

But once summer break started, he got into the habit of going to bed late, getting up late, and taking naps on the side, instantly destroying his progress on the good habit he had been building. The new semester had only just begun, and he was already battling against the almost unbearable urge to sleep. That said, he still managed to stay awake during all his morning classes… Perhaps that was an exaggeration, since he hardly had any recollection of what happened during the second half of fourth period, but Alisa didn't reprimand him, so it wasn't as bad as it could have been. Nevertheless, Masachika did sense that she was catching on to him, so he decided to make a run for the student council room.

I should be able to take a nap there…without anyone finding out…

Eventually, he managed to make it to the student council room without falling asleep, although 30 percent of his brain wasn't functioning any longer.

Oh, right… I should set my alarm…

Once inside, he pulled out his smartphone and headed to the couch, then picked a good time to wake up from his saved settings, kicked off his slippers, and collapsed onto the couch. Only after placing his phone on the table in front of the couch did he finally allow his body to go completely limp.

After finishing lunch, Maria grabbed the paper bag with her new summer uniform inside and headed over to the student council room. The ridiculously long line the day before convinced her to wait until the next day, so she came to school in her old uniform…but it was unreasonably hot for September. To make matters worse, she sat in one of the window-adjacent seats, which were always the hottest. Her peers were all wearing cool, short-sleeved shirts, while she was wearing a collared shirt, a jumper, and even a blazer, as if she were spitting right in the face of climate change. She was already far beyond what she could take.

Therefore, she bought the new uniform at the school shop in between morning classes and decided she would change into it during lunch. There was only one issue: Where would she change? She wasn't comfortable using the school's dressing room all for herself, and using the girls' bathroom was not an option, either, since she was a member of the student council—and for aesthetic reasons as well. Then where? The first place that came to mind was the student council room, since she could lock the door, which would at least prevent anyone from walking in on her.

"Hello?" she said just in case, even though she figured nobody was there. However, the first thing she saw when she walked inside were slippers randomly lying on the floor and two feet poking out from the edge of the couch.

"Oh, gosh. That scared me..."

She jumped, but whoever was lying on the couch didn't even flinch.

"..."

Maria cautiously approached the feet, stole a peek over the armrest...and lovingly grinned from ear to ear.

"He's sooo cute. ♪"

After throwing any wariness she had out the window, she promptly rushed over to the front of the couch and crouched in front of Masachika. Gazing at his innocent, sleeping face, Maria placed both hands on his cheeks while silently squealing to herself.

"*Giggle.* ♡ Look at you, Mr. Sleepyhead."

She mirthfully giggled as if she were a mother watching her young child rest. Ever since she was born, she had been full of more love than most people and had far stronger caretaking instincts than most, always having the urge to spoil and watch over all those she loved. Up until now, she mainly only had her little sister to take care of and spoil, but Alisa was far more mature and independent than her older sister, so being pampered was out of the question. Therefore, Maria was always overflowing with so much love and affection that she didn't know what to do with it.

But that all changed when she happened across the boy she fell in love with, passed out from exhaustion on the couch, and he was just waiting for her to take care of him (from Maria's point of view), which was why she was on the verge of losing control. If he were sleeping in a bed or on the floor, she would have undoubtedly slept by his side or rested his head in her lap while he slept.

"Mmm. ♪ You're so cute, Sah. ♡"

Maria had no interest in damaging the relationship between Masachika and Alisa, and she genuinely meant what she said when she told him she wanted him to prioritize Alisa, but these were two separate issues entirely. The person who had stolen her heart was right in front of her, awaiting her affection and care, so taking care of him was the only right thing to do. Alisa only had herself to blame for not being there to take care of him.

Oh, Alya. What am I going to do with you? Your partner is exhausted, and you're not even here to support him.

But after telling herself that, she realized that maybe this was intentional. Maybe Masachika didn't want Alisa to see him in such a fragile state, so he chose to rest here in secret. The instant Maria realized that this had to be what happened, her heart became swollen with love and an intense desire to protect him.

Oh, Kuze. ♪ Boys will be boys, I suppose. It looks like I'm just going to take care of you and pamper you if Alya's not here to do it!

Maria needed a cause, and now she had one. She was going to do this on behalf of Alisa, and thus, it began. She started by gently poking Masachika's cheeks.

"*Giggle. ♪ Poke, poke.* Goochie-goochie-goo."

Her fingertip tickled his cheek until she noticed his eyebrow faintly twitching and stopped, gleefully shaking her head as if to clear her mind of the pink hearts that were practically visible around her.

Ah! I have to capture his cute, sleeping face on camera!

She immediately sprang into action, stood in the corner of the room, and began to take pictures from a distance to make sure she wouldn't wake him with the camera's shutter sound. She then got closer and closer to him, zooming right up on his face like a cameraman for a reality show where someone sleeping was about to get pranked.

"Ahn. ♡ I love him so much, ♡" whispered Maria, squirming excitedly while poking his cheek again, enjoying every bit of his cheeks, which were surprisingly smooth and soft for a boy in high school.

Hmm… What should I do next?

While deciding how she was going spoil him, she realized that there wasn't much she could do with him on the couch. Since she couldn't sleep by his side or rest his head in her lap, her only options were essentially rubbing his head or singing him a lullaby…

Oh my. I'm already doing both?

That was the moment Maria noticed that she had been unconsciously humming a lullaby while gently rubbing his head, which surprised even her. However, after she saw how peacefully he was sleeping, her beaming smiling only grew wider. Maria got over things quickly, so she didn't let little things bother her. In other words, although she felt that maybe Masachika appeared to be sleeping so much more peacefully now without a certain someone poking his cheeks, she wasn't going to lose any sleep over it!

"*Thou art safe in my arms* ♪," whispered Maria, finishing the lullaby.

"Kuze, do you think I'm too kind to a fault or too self-giving?" she asked with a relaxed voice. Of course, he didn't reply, but she continued speaking all the same. "Because you would be wrong if you did." She softly smirked. "Because I…"

Maria closed her mouth and paused for a moment before whispering ever so quietly:

"Я думаю, у вас с Алей-тян не ладится."

Her eyes narrowed somewhat sorrowfully and yet affectionately as well while she held Masachika's head.

"Вот увидишь, ты терпеть не сможешь быть рядом с Алей-тян," she added in a voice so soft that it was almost inaudible, then pouted and rubbed his ears.

"So you see…I'm actually not a nice person at all. Got it?" claimed Maria in a baby voice before she began to rub his head once more.

She then brushed Masachika's bangs back on a whim, cracking a beaming smile once more.

"*Sigh*. Even your forehead is adorable. ♡"

...Maria truly did get over things quickly. She was emotionally *unique* and already on the verge of melting as she gazed at his forehead, gradually getting the urge to just kiss it.

I want to kiss that cute forehead of his. I want to kiss it so badly... Oh, maybe I could kiss his cheek?

Out of nowhere, Alisa's face popped into her mind.

Oh, Alya. No. This isn't what you think. It wasn't supposed to be a romantic kiss. It was more like a good-night kiss a mother would give her child...

She instinctively began to make excuses to her sister, but such excuses soon lost meaning as she continued to stare at Masachika's sleeping face. After a soft *gulp*, Maria placed her phone on the floor, then slowly brought her face closer to his.

"It's Alya's fault she's not here..."

Right when she got close enough to feel his breath—

Knock-knock.

"...?!"

There was a knock at the door.

"...? What are you doing?"

Having only knocked as a courtesy, Alisa promptly opened the door with a paper bag in hand and immediately witnessed Maria jumping to her feet...which obviously made her sister curious.

"Oh, Alya? I wasn't doing anything at all. I found Kuze sleeping, so I was just checking on him."

"...?"

Alisa frowned at her sister's unusual overreaction, then she shifted her focus to the couch, where she noticed two feet sticking out, which apparently belonged to Masachika.

"Did you come all the way here to change, too?"

"…? Yes…"

The furrow in her brow deepened as she looked at her clearly flustered older sister, carefully observing her expression. As if to avoid those judgmental eyes, Maria immediately averted her gaze, allowing her eyes to aimlessly wander while she faintly smirked.

"Then I guess we should start changing, since that's what I came here to do, too…"

"No way. Masachika's right there," said Alisa, sending her sister a scornful gaze as if to say, "You're not going to fool me," since it was painfully obvious that Maria was trying to hide something. However, Maria's reaction was beyond anything Alisa could have ever predicted.

"Hmm? So what?"

"Excuse me?"

Maria was not trying to play dumb, and she didn't feel like she was in too deep to back out, either. She was genuinely puzzled. At the very least, that was how Alisa interpreted her reaction.

"Kuze's sound asleep, so just lock the door. It'll only take a minute."

"No, no, no! No way!"

"Alya! Shhh!"

"Ah—!"

Alisa covered her own mouth in a fluster after realizing how loud she was, but when she glanced at Masachika, he was still sound asleep, not even a twitch.

"…See? We should be able to change without waking him up."

"But still—"

"What's our alternative? Did you find somewhere else we could change?"

Maria's question shut Alisa down, since they both specifically chose the student council room after careful consideration. It wouldn't be easy to find another location as good as this, especially since such a place might not even exist.

"Don't worry. It'll be okay. We'll quickly change into our new uniforms and be out of here in no time."

As soon as Maria locked the door from the inside and closed the curtains just in case as well, she placed her paper bag on the table and immediately started to change into her new school uniform.

"H-hey—"

"Alya, you better hurry before our lunch break is over. ♪"

Once Alisa glanced at the clock, she realized that they only had a little over ten minutes before lunch was over. Although she frowned, she concluded that she probably wouldn't be able to go somewhere else to change and still make it to class on time.

But still...

What if Masachika woke up while they were changing? The thought alone made Alisa's entire body feel like it was on fire.

Yeah, I'm not doing this...

After she came to that decision, a certain thought crossed Alisa's mind. What if she woke Masachika up after changing here, waited until he noticed that she was wearing the new school uniform, and then told him that she got changed in this very room? Just imagining the look on his face tickled Alisa's mischievous heart.

The chance to see that carefree joker embarrassed because of something he himself did was extremely appealing to her. Having the opportunity from time to time to witness someone usually reliable turn red in the face like a helpless child was the chance of a lifetime. It was hard for Alisa to not want to see those cute, pathetically adorable blushing cheeks, and she was willing to use her powers as a woman to the fullest to do so in order to tease him to her heart's content.

I wonder how he'd react if I told him I got changed in front of him. Would he be startled? Would he be like, "O-oh?" and try to play it cool?

If he tried to pretend he was fine, then she could show him the outfit she changed out of. Maybe she could let him touch it and she'd say, "See? It's still warm." The thought alone was embarrassing enough to make Alisa feel hot all over, but the joy she got from it overshadowed the negative—so much that she couldn't stop grinning. An exciting chill ran down her spine as she imagined herself toying with Masachika and making him squirm.

He was really cute then, too...

Alisa thought back to how adorably pathetic he was at the restaurant a few days earlier when she was writing on his palm. She'd had to stop herself from going overboard, given the situation, but today—

"Alya...?"

"...!"

Alisa's expression tensed in shock; she suddenly realized that her sister had been staring at her weirdly while removing her blazer, so she shot Maria a piercing glare as if her daydreaming were her older sister's fault, and she promptly began to change before her sister could even get another word in. She made sure to take off her uniform quickly but carefully as to not make a sound. She untied her ribbon, removed her collared shirt, and grabbed the new school uniform when—

"Let's go! Flyyy hiiigher!"

The sudden shout startled Alisa, making her jump and drop the new school uniform on the floor.

◇

"...!"

Masachika instantly sat up in a panic the moment he heard the familiar anime song he had set as his alarm and impulsively reached for the source of the noise.

"Ack...! Ugh...," he groaned, for he had far too much momentum when he reached out to grab the phone, and he slid right off the couch.

"Ah! No!"

The sudden shriek immediately got his attention, welcoming his eyes to paradise, for standing before him were two beautiful sisters wearing nothing more than their socks and underwear. Alisa's large, plentiful chest and rear were both perfectly round and firm. Compared to those, her waistline was slim and toned. Maria, on the other hand, had an extremely mature, feminine body, which didn't seem to match her youthful appearance one bit. While Alisa boasted a perfect, tight figure, Maria's voluptuous body was unparalleled, and both of their bodies were in plain sight. Even their underwear—hardly covering anything—appeared to be nothing more than decorations worn to complement their breathtakingly beautiful naked bodies.

"...??"

Masachika stared in silence with his mouth agape, still unable to discern whether this was a dream or reality in his half-awake state. It was like a flood of data being downloaded onto a freshly rebooted computer and causing it to freeze.

"S-stop staring!"

"K-Kuze? If you keep staring like that, I..."

Only when he heard the blushing sisters speak up did Masachika's brain start to function again. Nevertheless, he still couldn't process everything that was happening, so he just smiled tightly and gave them a thumbs-up.

"Don't worry! This is no different from seeing you two in a bathing suit!"

However, his way of trying to make them feel better apparently didn't work. Alisa's eyebrows furrowed as she grabbed her collared shirt, which hung over the chair, and threw it as hard as she could at Masachika without even giving him a second to dodge. The soft impact was followed by darkness, but he could still feel Alisa's warmth. The smell of a girl's skin and sweat tickled his nose, overloading his mind with so many different thoughts until his brain bugged out, resulting in him being unnecessarily honest.

"Ah, this smells really good."

Immediately, something else hit him right in the face, forcing his consciousness to once again shut down.

Guilty. Straight to jail.

"All right, everyone! Shall we begin?!"

Once he got a good look at each member gathered in the room after school that day, the school festival committee president commenced their first meeting. The committee consisted of each student council member, the former student council president and vice president, two representatives from each class, the captains of each school club, and the presidents of the disciplinary committee, the school cleanup committee, and the health committee.

The disciplinary committee would patrol the school during the festival and keep an eye on students during the preparation period, the cleanup committee would handle decorating the entire school, and the health committee would help people who got hurt during the festival and handle emergencies. Each group needed to work together as a team, which was why everyone had gathered there today. Furthermore, each class had their own attraction for the festival, so the core members who would be busiest on the day of the festival were these three committees and the student council. One school festival committee member representing each class oversaw their attraction while their partner helped other members of the school festival committee. Of course, all members of the committee were given breaks throughout the day, so even though there were a decent number of members, the committee was never going to feel overstaffed.

"The school festival will be held over a two-day period this year as well. The first day will only be open to students from our school, but the second day is open to the public. As always, there will be students who cut loose the morning of the second day and get a little too carried away, so please be careful, everyone."

The meeting was progressing smoothly thanks to the experienced former student council president, and everyone was giving him their full attention, suggesting that they truly believed in him.

"Sometimes, students offer luxurious prizes at their attractions on the second day, which isn't really that big of a deal. But in the past, we have also had issues with female students suddenly wearing clothing that's twenty percent more revealing on the second day while running cafés, so we need to make sure to keep everyone in line this year so that doesn't happen again."

"President! Is it okay if guys wear more revealing clothing on the second day?!"

"Hmm… Just don't be disgusting."

"Does that mean it's okay?!"

"Only if you're built like Touya."

"Me?!"

"I mean, check this out. You're shredded."

The group erupted with laughter as the former student council president teased the current one. Masachika and the others smiled as well, since it wasn't often that they saw Touya teased like a little brother. Well, there was one person who wasn't amused, though.

"Stop right there! These muscles aren't for show! I didn't personally train Touya for your entertainment!"

"C-come on, Chisaki. Relax."

"If you really want to see them, then you're going to have to defeat me first!"

"I'd rather not die today."

"I wish someone loved me as much as she loves Touya."

"You too? Now I've got the former vice president of the student council giving me a hard time…"

The meeting progressed amicably until the very end. Everyone briefly introduced themselves, exchanged information, and was given a specific role for the committee. The only exceptions were members of the student council, since their roles were related to their work in the student council, so nothing was fundamentally going to change for Masachika and the others.

"As usual, each of you will be given two tickets: one for your guardian and one for whomever else. Any questions or concerns?"

"I know this isn't anything new, but I can't believe we're still using physical tickets. Is there any way we can go digital?"

"We definitely do not have the time to do that!"

"Ha-ha! Figured… But I feel like paper tickets like this would be easy to counterfeit."

"I really doubt someone wants to invite so many friends that they're willing to counterfeit a ticket. Every year, students who want to invite more people seem to always ask friends for their extra ticket anyway."

"I guess that makes sense."

"Here, Kuze."

While Masachika was half-listening to them talk, Maria, who was sitting next to him, handed him the sample of the admission ticket that was being passed around.

"Oh, thanks."

He stole a quick glance at Maria's face while thanking her in a whisper, but she appeared to be her ordinary self and didn't seem to care about what had happened during lunch at all… What happened between them during summer break didn't seem to be on her mind, either.

She seriously never changes, does she?

Maria had taken her own advice by acting as if nothing had happened between them at the park, which Masachika really appreciated…but seeing how normal she was acting was starting to make him worry somewhat that her confession was nothing more than a dream.

"…? What's wrong?"

"Nothing…"

"Oh! Were you…?"

Her face suddenly lit up with realization, and she cupped the side of her mouth and leaned closer toward Masachika's ear.

"Were you daydreaming about what you saw during lunch today?"

"...?!"

"You're such a perv. ♪"

Her bashful giggling tickled Masachika's ear, sending a chill down his spine.

Wait. Since when did Masha become such a tease? Are those horns growing out of her head?!

The little angel who was always standing on his shoulder had transformed into a little devil, sending Masachika spiraling into a world of confusion.

"From now on, whenever you're tired, you can come to me. I'll take care of you."

Hold up. So is she an angel? ...Or is she a demon trying to tempt me to sin? Ah! Is she a demon in angel's clothing?!

Maria's whispers sweetly numbed his mind until only the stupidest of thoughts could survive. When he was poked in the ribs on his opposite side, he finally returned to reality. When he glanced over, he realized Alisa had been coldly glaring at him out of the corner of her eye.

Maria smirked slightly, then leaned back in her seat away from Masachika.

Sigh... It has been a while since I felt like I was being stabbed with an icicle.

Alisa's sideways gaze was so piercing that he almost mentally checked out. Was she upset because Maria got too close? Or was she still mad about what happened during their lunch break? Most likely both.

Incidentally, when Masachika woke up after the incident, he found himself in the infirmary at the end of fifth period. However, it would be difficult to prove whether it was Alisa's mystery attack or merely the fact that he was sleep-deprived that caused him to be passed out like a log for so long.

Two admission tickets... I'm not going to be able to use one. Actually, I'm not going to use either of them, since I'm not going to bring my guardian with me. I guess I'll give the spare one to Takeshi this year, too, if he wants it.

Masachika focused on his extra tickets to avoid Alisa's gaze while he passed the sample to her next...but that was when he was suddenly struck with a divine revelation.

Hold up. Couldn't I use this...to invite her?

After finally spotting a glimpse of a possible solution to the issue that had been bothering him these past few days, Masachika immediately gave the idea his undivided attention.

"...?"

Alisa curiously tilted her head, wondering what her frowning partner was suddenly deep in thought about, but Masachika was too focused to even notice her stares, and he continued to be lost in thought until the meeting was about to wrap up.

"Oh, right. As always, very important people from the First Light Committee will be coming on the second day in the afternoon, so... Touya, Chisaki, good luck."

"Thanks."

"Oh, right. Thanks."

"I think that just about does it. Does anyone have anything they want to say? ...Okay, then. Make sure to submit your written proposal before the next meeting! Also, we need a theme for the festival as well, so give it some thought in the meantime, too! Good work, everyone! See you all next meeting!"

Everyone thanked the committee president after the first meeting finally came to an end.

That was a lot more relaxed than I thought it would be.

Alisa was honestly expecting there to be a little more tension during the meeting, so she couldn't help but sigh in relief as she watched each representative, captain, and president merrily walk out the door.

"Kuze, Suou, long time no see."

"Oh, K-Kaji... Long time no see, I guess?"

"*Giggle*. Even though we see each other at school from time to time, I suppose it has been a while since we have actually talked like this."

Masachika and Yuki were chatting with a mild-mannered male student wearing glasses. They seemed to know a lot of people there, most likely thanks to being the student council president and vice president in middle school.

"Oh, allow me to introduce you to my new partner. This is Ayano Kimishima."

"Oh, right. Let me introduce you to my new partner, too. Alisa Kujou."

"It is a pleasure to meet you."

"Nice to meet you..."

"Call me Kaji. I'm the president of the disciplinary committee... I knew you two had new partners, but meeting them for the first time feels kind of weird. Oh, of course, I don't mean that in a bad way."

"Ha-ha-ha. Yeah, I bet."

Kaji glanced at Alisa for a brief second before his focus immediately returned to Masachika and Yuki. Although the three continued their conversation, Alisa didn't have the communication skills to jump in, so all she could do was simply watch them in silence. Unsurprisingly, it had been like this ever since the meeting had started. All Alisa could do was watch her partner casually strike up conversation with these strangers as some sort of dark, burning emotion only grew stronger inside her.

I... I hate this.

The vague, frustrating emotion made her frown. While it was an emotion she wasn't used to, Alisa had a hunch about what it could be: possessiveness.

I don't want you getting along with others like this. I want you to care about me more than anyone else. I always put you first, *so I want to be your first priority, too.*

It was an extremely egocentric, selfish emotion, and even she knew it was an unwarranted response. After all, the fact of the matter was that Masachika and Alisa were nothing more than friends. Alisa was being needy, and Masachika was probably acting how people would normally treat friends…

But still…! Would it kill him to give me a bit of special treatment?! We even went on a d-date together, and I k-k-kissed him, too! He even saw me in my underwear!! We're going to have to get married now!!

But even then, Alisa had to face reality whether she wanted to or not. She was nothing more than one of Masachika's many friends. Even though they may have been partners for the election, Alisa was not as special to him as he was to her. If Masachika had a special relationship with anyone, it was with Yuki. At least, that was how most saw it.

"…!"

The instant Alisa came to that conclusion, she bit her lip. She had noticed that everyone who had been talking to Masachika and Yuki thought it was strange that they weren't partners in the election this year, which was perhaps a testament to how everyone felt they were an unbeatable duo and that their relationship was special. After all, even Sayaka had once screamed about how they were the ideal pair with tears in her eyes.

I…

After hearing that Alisa was teaming up with Masachika, countless people had said to her, "*Why him?*" and "*He's not good enough for you.*" But Alisa knew the truth, and everyone here knew as well. It wasn't that Masachika wasn't good enough for Alisa. She wasn't good enough for him.

I—I…

Alisa was overcome with a sense of helplessness and frustration while her competitive side simultaneously reared its head.

I've made up my mind.

She had to change, for her pride wouldn't allow her to simply sit back while Masachika carried her through the election.

I'm going to show them…!

At that moment, Alisa secretly vowed to herself that she was going to prove to everyone that she was fit to be his partner.

◇

"Oh my."

Two days later, after finishing up her business in the teachers' room, Alisa was heading back to the student council room when she ran into a certain female student waiting in front of the door.

"Alisa Kujou, yes? I believe this is our first time speaking."

Alisa thought back to the school festival meeting as she stood before an older student with honey-colored hair tied into two spiral-curled pigtails that jiggled as she spoke.

"Nice to meet you… You're…the captain of the girls' kendo club, right?"

"Oh, my apologies. I forgot to introduce myself. My name is Sumire Kiryuuin. It is a pleasure to make your acquaintance."

"…!"

Alisa had heard the name before, straight from Masachika's mouth a few months back…

"You were one of the people who ran for student council vice president in middle school…weren't you?"

"Oh? You must have heard that from Kuze."

"I did."

"Great. That should save us some time. Yes, I was once a rival of Suou's and Kuze's in the past."

Her fluffy spiral pigtails bounced as she proudly puffed out her chest. Although somewhat overwhelmed by her behavior, Alisa thought back to what Masachika told her.

The Kiryuuin duo, Sumire and Yuushou, were cousins only one year apart. They were a unique pair, with Yuushou being the son of the CEO of Kiryuuin Group and Sumire being the daughter of the vice president, which probably influenced their decision to have Yuushou run for student council president with Sumire as his partner, despite her being older and in a grade above him. Incidentally, these two used to be the most popular candidates among female voters in the entire school.

"I heard you actually dropped out of the student council presidential race when you lost a debate against Sayaka."

"Yes, and that is exactly why I am extremely interested in getting to know the woman who defeated her in a debate."

Sumire smirked faintly as if she were judging Alisa based on her reaction, but Alisa boldly looked her right back in the eye. A few seconds passed before Sumire eventually let out a soft chuckle and looked away.

"However, I suppose that can wait until another time, since we're both extremely busy individuals. There is work to do," she added, holding out a written proposal for the festival. Sumire then knocked on the door to the student council room and walked inside.

"I apologize for the intrusion."

Masachika, who just happened to still be there, looked up with a quizzical expression on his face.

"Oh. Hey, Violet."

"It's Sumire!" she protested sharply without missing a beat. Alisa blinked a few times, wondering where the composed girl from a few seconds ago went.

"*Sigh.* Unbelievable. Is that really the first thing you wish to say to me?"

As Sumire huffed and gave him an earful, Alisa slipped over to his side and whispered to Masachika:

"Hey, uh… Who's Violet?"

"Hmm? Oh, her real name's Violet. It's written with the kanji for *sumire*, but it's pronounced *Violet*."

"…Oh, that's…"

That's quite the name, she thought. Although Alisa had heard that Sumire also grew up abroad and that she had at least one non-Japanese parent, this unique name and spelling still took Alisa by surprise. But even then…

"I don't think you should call her that if it bothers her."

"Oh… About that…"

Masachika awkwardly pressed his lips together, then focused on Sumire, prompting Alisa to do the same.

"Calling me that sounds far too…intimate…as though we're best friends…"

Although Sumire continued to complain, she seemed to be bashfully blushing, which took Alisa by complete surprise, making her jaw drop.

"She actually really likes her name."

"Oh…"

"And I'm sure she'd love it if you started calling her Violet, too, Alya."

"I would definitely not!" denied Sumire swiftly. She brushed her curls back and glared. "Listen, the only ones who are allowed to call me by that name are those I trust! It is not something that simply anyone can call me!"

"My bad, Vio."

"Stop that! Shortening it makes me sound like some sort of pre-evolved creature!"

"So Vio evolves into Violet… Interesting…"

Sumire scowled at Masachika, who was messing with her in his way, but she was hardly threatening at all.

"*Sigh*. You never change, do you?"

After sighing in resignation at her unfazed schoolmate, Sumire placed her written proposal on the table before him.

"This is the girls' kendo club's proposal."

"Thanks. Wait… Is this…?"

Alisa curiously followed Masachika's gaze to see why he sounded so perplexed.

"A play…? Wow."

Alisa raised an eyebrow at the kendo club's unique proposal, but once she actually read it, she fell silent as well. It was apparently a sword-fighting play where female members of the club would dress like men and stylishly cross swords onstage. That much was fine, but there were numerous issues regarding safety that needed to be considered. Then again, that much was fine, too, for the moment. The real issue was…

"Many students in the girls' kendo club are in the disciplinary committee as well, so we chose the perfect attraction, if you ask me."

Sumire proudly puffed out her chest.

"Yeah… It's a good idea."

The proposal went into detail about how members of the disciplinary committee could patrol the school in their stage costume to promote the show.

"…I bet it's going to be quite the sight."

"Yeah… But, well, there are going to be tons of people cosplaying during the festival, so whatever… Anyway, I'll make sure your proposal gets into the right hands, and we can discuss whether this is feasible during the next school festival meeting."

"Very well. I am counting on you."

After elegantly bowing by the door, Sumire glanced at Alisa, then retired from the student council room. Once she was out of sight, Masachika softly sighed.

"*Phew.* Yet another bizarre proposal."

"Another?"

"Yeah, there's actually one that I need to talk to you about," revealed Masachika as he handed Alisa another proposal, which she immediately started to read with furrowed brows.

"…? A quiz competition?"

It was a written proposal submitted by the quiz research club stating that they wanted to set up a stage in the schoolyard to have a quiz competition between Alisa and Yuki.

"According to the captain of the quiz research club, it's going to be a revolutionary event that integrates elements of the election into a good old trivia show. I have no idea what exactly that means, though."

"Why, though? There's no way the school festival committee is going to allow such a vague proposal."

"They claim it would spoil the show if they delved into too many details, and they said they would only tell the student council president and the committee's president and vice president exactly what they were planning in order to avoid either of you getting the chance to research or plan."

"...What did Touya say?"

"He apparently said there weren't any issues with the proposal itself and mentioned that it sounded fun to him." Masachika shrugged and looked up at Alisa. "But it doesn't matter what everyone else thinks. It's not going to happen if you two don't want to do it, Alya. So what do you want to do?"

"It's fine by me," she instantly replied, making his eyes widen.

"...Are you sure? Personally, I'm not too big of a fan having you two compete at such a bizarre event..."

"Oh? Because you're afraid I'll lose?"

"No, it's not that...," he replied somewhat vaguely before pausing to lower his gaze and think to himself for a few moments. "...Something like this happened during another election in the past. Sometimes people or groups who back a certain candidate try to come up with some sort of competition to set up their rival for failure."

For example, the soccer club could play rough during PE and bully someone until they snapped in front of their classmates and looked like the bad guy. Or the flower arrangement club could hold a flower arrangement workshop under the guise of teaching beginners the art of arranging flowers, but then they could take any beginner's poorly done arrangement and put it on display for everyone to see to embarrass them.

"That's terrible..."

"It's worse than terrible. It's downright wicked. At any rate... there's no guarantee this proposal isn't a trap, either," he concluded, waving the quiz research club's proposal in hand. "For all we know, the quiz research club wants Yuki to win, and they already gave her the answer key."

"That sounds a little far-fetched."

"It's not, though. It's just as possible that another candidate running for student council president proposed the entire event to get rid of both you and Yuki. They might have even put together an impossibly hard quiz to get you two to resort to mudslinging."

"..."

Alisa considered his suspicions for a few long moments, and after weighing the risk...she decided to do it.

"But Touya decided there weren't any issues when they filled him in on the details, right?"

"Well, yeah, but..."

"Then I'll do it. Even if they are plotting something, they aren't going to stop me from winning."

Masachika blinked in disbelief in the presence of her increased confidence. Although he might have been suspicious, Alisa considered this proposal a once-in-a-lifetime chance. Being able to compete against Yuki head-on was a gift from the heavens, regardless of the circumstances, and she was going to get the opportunity to do so in front of countless students at the school festival.

If I can defeat her without relying on Masachika for help...then everyone will have to recognize that I'm good enough for him.

But regardless of how others felt, a win would still make her more confident, and that was all she needed. That was all she needed to—

I'll be able to proudly stand by Masachika's side.

A competitive flame kindled in her heart with that vow to herself. Meanwhile, Masachika narrowed his worried gaze at her before once again turning his focus to the proposal in hand.

"What are you plotting?"

"Well, that's a rude way to start a conversation, bro."

Those were the first words out of Masachika's mouth when he got home and saw his sister relaxing on the couch as if she lived there.

"If anyone's plotting something, it's you, my dear brother," she said with a wry smirk, watching him closely.

"..."

They locked eyes in silence for a few moments, but even though they knew each other inside out, reading the other's poker face still proved difficult. Nevertheless, it wasn't long before Yuki exhaled, seeming amused, then began rummaging through her bag until eventually pulling something out.

"All right, all right. I'll sweeten the pot," she grumbled, and smacked a USB stick onto the table.

"...What's this?"

"This? Heh. I call it the X File."

"I don't know what that means, but you should probably get rid of it. Now."

"Get rid of it...? Are you sure? Because there is some valuable data on the one and only Alya stored in here."

Yuki had one eye closed as her parted lips curled into a devilish grin.

"Probably just pictures of her in a bathing suit," Masachika interjected calmly.

"How'd you know?"

"Seriously?! Let me guess. You're about to say something like 'I told her I wouldn't give the pictures to anyone, but I never said I wouldn't give the image data to anyone,' right?!"

"Tsk! You're good. Too good... You win. This USB is yours."

"I don't want it."

"What? Are you saying this isn't enough? Hmph. You greedy little boy... Fine. I'll throw in Masha's as well."

"What? No. Who do you think you are? Some kind of merchant trying to throw in a few more items to get the protagonist to bite? 'Ah, still not enough? How 'bout I sweeten the deal a bit for ya, eh?'"

"The dialogue at the end felt unnecessary, but I get what you mean," she replied, flashing yet another mischievous smirk. "So? What are you going to do? I'd be willing to part with both USBs if you tell me the truth."

"Joking aside, you shouldn't be walking around with USBs like that."

"Don't worry. They're password-protected just in case. The password hint is my birthday."

"Hint?"

"Come on. Just be honest with yourself. All you have to do is give me a little information, and you'll get access to countless pictures of their scantily clad, tight, voluptuous, jiggly bodies. *Boing-boing!*"

"I could do without the sound effects."

"Vrooom! Brrbrrbrrbrr!"

"Stop pretending you're motorboating their boobs."

"Bo-yoi-yoi-yoing—!"

"I don't have a—!" interrupted Masachika, noticing that she was staring right at his crotch with a straight face. But after a sigh, he slid the two USB sticks across the table back toward his sister.

"More important, why would you even try to use Masha's bathing-suit pics as bait when she already has a boyfriend?"

"...A boyfriend, you say?" replied Yuki slyly.

"...What?"

"I don't know... I just can't help but wonder if Masha really has a boyfriend. That's all."

While it still made his heart skip a beat, he had actually expected her to say that, so Masachika simply raised an eyebrow and feigned ignorance.

"What makes you say that?"

"I don't know. Maybe because I have a wide circle of friends? I've talked to Masha's friends a great deal...and nobody has ever even seen what her boyfriend looks like. Nobody has ever met him, let alone seen a picture."

"Oh?"

"Plus, the only reason why everyone thinks he's Russian is because of the foreign-sounding name. It's just all so strange…and that's why I have some doubts that he even exists."

"Makes sense. She might just be saying she has a boyfriend to keep other guys away. Still, it's none of our business. I mean, even if she didn't have a boyfriend, that's still no reason to just hand over pictures of her in a bathing suit to others. Of course, that goes for Alya, too!"

"Tsk. Looks like I just can't fool you."

Masachika let out an exaggerated sigh while Yuki stuffed the USBs back into her pocket reluctantly.

"…Whatever. Even if you are scheming something, I'll figure it out eventually and use it against you."

"Right back at you. Anyway…I guess this means you aren't involved in this game at all, right?"

"I had nothing to do with it. Whether you believe me or not is up to you, though."

"Hmph… Well, just to let you know, I don't plan on resorting to petty tricks, either. Alya might be a good test-taker, but she's not going to beat me in a quiz competition. I'm going to beat her fair and square."

"I just hope you're telling the truth…because Alya obviously plans on beating you fair and square as well."

Masachika thought back to how his partner was even more fired up than usual for this quiz, and he faintly shrugged.

"…? What's wrong, bro?"

"Uh…"

After pausing, Masachika realized that he wasn't going to be able to fool his sister, and he opened up to her.

"Like, I don't know what's going on with her, but she seems really frustrated lately. I don't know what's stressing her, but I wish she'd relax more and just be herself."

Although it was Masachika who pushed her to improve her leadership skills, he couldn't help but worry that she was straining herself or feeling worked up over it. He also couldn't help but feel that she was being a little distant, too, for some reason…

I don't know why, but it kind of feels like she's keeping her distance from me...

"She takes everything so seriously, after all," he mumbled to himself, scratching his head, not convinced that was the reason. Meanwhile, Yuki, who had been watching him closely, began to stroke her chin.

"My dear brother... Perhaps this is merely the arrogance of those who have it all."

"Hmm? What are you talking about?"

Masachika was genuinely baffled by her comment, so he frowned. Yuki, on the other hand, gently smiled. She stared off into the distance and sweetly said:

"My dear, dear brother... When Masha washes up in the bath, she has to lift her boobs."

"Huh?"

His jaw dropped in disbelief at the deranged, unexpected comment, but Yuki simply continued her monologue with a somewhat sorrowful expression in spite of his bewilderment.

"From what I was told, her boobs are apparently so massive that they are on top of her chest. The bottoms of her boobs are squished against her ribs, so she gets underboob sweat," she explained miserably before slamming her hands against the table with furiously narrowed eyes. Lowering her gaze as if she were struggling to cope with something, she shouted with all her might:

"Gaaaaaah!! Dammit all to hell!! Underboob sweat?! What do you mean they're 'on top of' her chest?! Is that some kind of riddle?! How am I supposed to respond to that?! 'Sure, you can place mine on top of whatever you want if you make them bigger'? You can place flan on a plate, and it still doesn't cast a shadow! If only they were the size of rice cakes, then I'd at least have a shadow!" Yuki lifted her head back up with a smirk as if she felt just fine. "And just like this, the haves unintentionally hurt the have-nots until they feel like they've been driven into a tight corner..."

"Was that story even necessary? And is it just me, or have you become more of a degenerate lately?"

"Puberty and hormones, my brother. And puberty 'bout to make this hor—"

"Okay, okay. I get it. By the way, yours are more like gelatin than flan custard."

"You mean the little containers of jelly that people give out as midsummer gifts that are almost completely flat yet absurdly expensive?"

"Lady Yuki, I love jelly, too."

"Shut your mouth, flan-tits, or they're gonna get squeezed."

"...?! Be my guest."

"Yahoo!"

Yuki wasted no time before diving into Ayano's breasts, enjoying every moment with both hands as she buried her face.

Oh. Ayano was here, too.

That was the first thought that came to Masachika's mind as he witnessed their *yuri* encounter. Although he'd noticed Ayano's shoes at the front door, he hadn't even noticed her existence until now, causing him to secretly shudder at the idea that this maid's stealth capabilities were improving.

Yuki, with her face still buried in Ayano's chest, glanced at her brother and concluded:

"So maybe...it was you who unconsciously ended up driving Alya into a corner, and that's why she's stressed?"

"Huh...?" said Masachika with a grunt before pausing to think.

I'm the cause of Alya's stress...? Was the band too much to ask of her? Wait, no. That's not what this is about.

There was something else that Masachika was doing that was stressing Alisa out, but he couldn't figure out what that something was. No matter how much he thought about it, he couldn't figure out what made him a have and Alisa a have-not.

I mean, I have a lot of wasted potential...and social skills? But so does Yuki… If anything, Yuki's probably making better use of her social skills at school than me.

It would make sense if Alisa was feeling pressured because of her rival, Yuki, but it simply didn't make sense to him that he, her partner, would be the cause. Even after Yuki and Ayano went home, he continued to rack his brain, but he couldn't come up with a single answer.

"Hmm?"

Masachika was about to take a bath when he absentmindedly stuffed a hand into the pocket of his shorts, discovered something in there, and took it out.

"That little…"

He frowned the moment he realized what was most likely on this USB stick: Alisa's swimsuit pictures.

"I told her to take it home with her…"

He started to ponder when Yuki could have slipped it into his pocket…until it occurred to him that she had way too many opportunities, so he gave up. After a single sigh, he took the USB stick back to his room, then placed it on his desk.

"*Sigh*… What are you doing turning the computer on?" griped Masachika with a straight face as if he were disappointed in himself while he took a seat at the desk. But even then, he didn't stop.

"Come on—you've got to be kidding me. What are you doing plugging that USB in, Mr. Right Hand?"

His left hand grabbed his right hand before it could slide the USB stick all the way into the port, but the difference in strength was undeniable as the USB stick gradually slid inside.

Wait! You need to calm down! This USB contains pictures of Alya that she said she didn't want anyone else to see! You would have to be a total scumbag to actually go through with this!

The voice of reason shouted in his mind, granting his left hand the strength to fight back.

"Ngh… Guh…!"

Masachika clenched his jaw while he pulled his right hand back as hard as he could...when all of a sudden, the voice of desire stepped in.

Come on. I was nearby when these pictures were taken, so what's the big deal if I have a peek? It's nothing I haven't seen before.

The voice of desire considerably weakened his left hand's grip.

But even then...! She said she didn't want anyone seeing them, so I should respect her wishes!

She was probably talking about Touya seeing them. She never specifically said she didn't want me to see them, right? Besides, I saw her in her underwear just the other day, so this is no big deal.

Stop making excuses.

No, you stop making excuses.

The intense struggle between reason and desire continued until they ultimately found a point of compromise.

Let's plug the USB in first, then think about what to do after that.

According to Yuki, the USB was password-protected, so it wasn't like he would be able to see swimsuit pictures the instant he inserted the USB. Therefore, he decided to plug it in first and think later. Besides, his hands were getting tired anyway.

He pushed the USB stick into the port. Then...

"What the...?!"

The instant the computer recognized the USB memory stick, it promptly opened a folder with countless pictures lined up side by side without even asking him for a password. It all happened so quickly that he didn't have a chance to look away—

"...Huh?" he quizzically grunted, for each displayed file was nothing more than a white rectangle.

"What the...? Is the data corrupted?"

Masachika scrolled through the files with genuine curiosity as if his struggle from a moment ago was merely a distant dream. But when he reached the bottom of the folder, he discovered a single text file titled To My Garbage Brother, Who Succumbed to Temptation ♡.

"..."

He quietly opened the file...

> These are all overexposed pictures of Alya that ended up just looking white.

"You little…!!"

After slamming his laptop shut, he rushed to his bed in a huff, then dived headfirst into his pillow.

"Ahhhhhh!!"

The sense of humiliation was too much to bear, and even that was overshadowed by his extreme sense of guilt. The negative emotions quickly intertwined, causing him to violently writhe on the bed. It took an entire forty minutes after that for him to finally recover…but the bathwater was already cold by then.

Seriously. Who wants to see a guy blushing and stuff?!

"♪ ♪ ♪"

The band started to seriously practice once they discussed issues and came up with a setlist, and ever since then, the five band members had been borrowing the music room day after day to practice.

Alya never ceases to impress me. She has already pretty much perfected her parts.

Masachika once again found himself admiring Alisa for her hard work while he watched the band perform. They had only just decided on a setlist three days ago, and she was already nailing her parts. Prior to that, she had never even heard these songs, to boot. It was hard to fathom how much she must have listened to them and practiced, since she was hardly ever off pitch. In fact, her voice was filled with so much feeling that the songs were almost transforming into her own arrangements. Masachika couldn't help but feel somewhat overawed by her beautiful, transparent, and yet sometimes intimidating voice. Meanwhile…

"Oh, sorry! I messed up!"

There was also a member who couldn't keep up with Alisa's perfection. Takeshi kept messing up during the same part, bringing their practice to a sudden halt.

"My bad, guys… Can we try that part again?"

"How about we start from *Until now* ♪?"

Practice resumed after Sayaka's suggestion. However…

"Ah! Dammit! My bad!"

...Takeshi messed up again. Of course, a lack of practice was part of the problem, but it was hard to be upset with him, because this was his first time playing this song, too. Besides, that wasn't the only issue.

This was a performance put on by members who still didn't know one another that well. To make matters worse, both Alisa and Nonoa were considered two of the most attractive girls at school, and Sayaka was kind of difficult to approach in general. Those facts alone would make anyone feel self-conscious. Plus...

Sigh... Alya's really frustrated...

As the face of the group, Alisa was silently putting a lot of pressure on him. It wasn't hard to understand how she felt, either, since she had essentially nailed all her parts despite being a beginner. Meanwhile, Takeshi, who had experience playing in a band and asked her for help, kept making mistakes, so you wouldn't even have to be a perfectionist like Alisa to feel frustrated.

But this is just going to make Takeshi feel more timid the longer it goes on... Maybe the silver lining is the fact that nobody is yelling at him. I guess it's time I do something about this.

But right as Masachika was about to chime in as the manager...

"Takeshi, how about we play through the song all the way this time without worrying about small mistakes? This is the first time we're practicing this song together, so today we should focus on simply pinpointing where the mistakes are. We have plenty of time to fix them later."

Alisa's unexpected advice made Masachika's eyes widen in astonishment. Even Takeshi blinked in silence for a few moments, as if he couldn't process what he was hearing.

"Th-thanks. I'm seriously sorry about all this, though. I should have practiced a little more," replied Takeshi, flustered.

"Then make sure you can play it flawlessly next time we practice, okay?"

"Errr... I'll see what I can do..."

"I'm kidding."

Alisa smirked, catching Takeshi off guard. After his jaw dropped in a flash of confusion, he slapped his cheeks and fired himself up.

"Let's do this! From the top, please!"

"...Okay, is everyone ready?"

Once Sayaka shot Hikaru a quick glance, he began to click his sticks, starting off the song once more. While there were still a few minor mistakes, Takeshi...and even Hikaru...seemed to have loosened up quite a bit. No matter how many times Takeshi messed up, he didn't let it bother him, thus allowing them to play through the whole song. When the song came to a close with Alisa holding the last note as Takeshi's final chord rang out, Masachika immediately started to clap, giving the silence not even a second to breathe.

"Nice. That was so good that I actually found myself instinctively dancing to the beat."

Masachika's genuine praise curled Alisa's lips.

"Yes... We still have several issues we need to fix, but that was really nice," added Alisa, immediately planting smiles on both Takeshi's and Hikaru's faces.

"Yeah, that was so much fun! I still made the most mistakes, though! My bad!"

"Ha-ha. Well, I'm in no position to criticize anyone for making mistakes, either. Sayaka and Nonoa sounded really comfortable, though. You guys did far better than us, and we're in the music club."

"Well, this isn't the first time I've played this song, so...

"Yeah, like, the keyboard part in this song isn't that hard, either. Plus, there aren't any solos."

"Guys, can we just take a moment to appreciate Alisa's singing for a moment? That was incredible! I feel bad ya have to be accompanied by my terrible guitar playing!"

"...I can't play any instruments, so I have no idea how hard it must be for you. But I know it isn't easy, so don't be so hard on yourself, okay?"

Alisa's comment instantly unraveled Takeshi's tension until he became a bumbling dope, bashfully scratching his head. He seemed even more pumped up when they resumed practice.

Masachika couldn't help but feel impressed while he watched them perform.

Alya... You did it. You did it all on your own. I didn't even need to say a word.

Never in his wildest dreams did he expect Alisa to not only make Takeshi feel better but to crack a joke to lighten the mood as well. What changed? It was hard to believe this was the same Alisa who despised working with others a short while ago.

Maybe Alya's time in the student council has helped her grow.

Masachika's original plan was to have Alisa get used to working as a team in this band before her work for the school festival shifted into high gear, and if possible, he wanted her to work on her leadership skills, too. Therefore, this was an extremely welcome, heartwarming surprise.

She's going to have no problem as a member of the school festival committee at this rate.

Takeshi, who was overenthusiastically strumming his guitar...

Hikaru, who was telling his buddy to calm down with a wry smirk...

Nonoa, who was somewhat more energetic and excited than usual...

Sayaka, who was secretly having the time of her life...

And Alisa, who was having so much fun singing her heart out with a look of serenity on her face...

Surprisingly, they looked far more like a real band than Masachika had originally expected. There was one thing bothering him, though...

Is it just me...or is Alya being nicer to Takeshi than she has been to me lately?

This feeling.

Uh...? This is weird. She looks a lot more relaxed around him than she does when she's with me, too...

And it most likely wasn't just his imagination. However, when Masachika carefully thought about why she seemed to be in such a bad mood when she was with him…

…Yeah, it's my fault.

After reflecting on his actions, he realized that he was the only one to blame, and he began to grimace.

I should try to be a little nicer to Alya…

Masachika continued to reflect upon his mistakes while he watched them practice.

"A taste test?"

"Yeah, do you think you could give it a try for me?"

A week had gone by, and classes were over for the day, so Masachika decided to check up on his class as a member of the school festival committee. However, once he got there, the class president and a school festival committee member asked him to try a drink they were considering selling at the festival.

There were a decent number of students in Masachika's class who couldn't contribute to this year's attraction, whether it be due to student council obligations or club activities, so after discussing it among themselves, they decided to go with something that didn't require much time or effort.

They named the attraction Café from Another World, and it was actually Masachika who came up with the idea, inspired by the collab café he met Sayaka at the other day. The idea was to have the class dress like they were in a fantasy world while serving all the classic drinks like potions and elixirs. Obviously, they were planning on serving ordinary drinks that only resembled potions or elixirs.

Cooking food was both troublesome and time-consuming, but with drinks, they could simply mix a few already existing drinks to create their own. It was normal for classes to sell authentic black tea or coffee at the school festival at this school. The only difference with this was that they needed to do a few measurements, make a few large batches, and have some paper cups to pour the drinks into. Their costumes were simple as well. All they planned on doing was putting on a pointed hat and a robe over their school uniform to make them look more like wizards. After that, they simply needed to act like they were students at a wizarding school who made magic potions. Students who wanted to put more effort into their costumes were free to do so.

At any rate, Masachika found himself in the classroom on the day they decided to do some trial runs for the potions…

"Everyone else is already filled like a water balloon… We tried to make small batches, but when you're testing different types of combinations, you soon find yourself with way too much to drink."

"Yeah, that makes sense…"

Numerous drinks in paper cups—that looked like they were made for a hazing—were lined up on a table.

Yeah, there's no way that one wasn't made as a prank.

Masachika was tense as he stared at what appeared to be a cup of sludge with tiny red balls floating on top.

You're free to make whatever you want, but you better drink it so it doesn't go to waste, asshole.

"…Hold up. I thought the idea was to only mix drinks, so why do I see something that's clearly not for human consumption floating in that one?"

"O-oh, that? We thought maybe normal drinks would be too cookie-cutter, so we might have used a little seasoning to spice things up."

"…Like what?"

"Uh… Like a little harissa…and some gochujang…"

After the class president trailed off while refusing to make eye contact, the other nearby students swiftly averted their gazes as well, as if they were feeling just as guilty.

"…Well, as long as you stay within budget, you're fine," Masachika assured them, searching for a relatively safe drink. "All right, I'll try this one."

He grabbed a paper cup that was filled with a grayish-brown liquid but was at least free from floating solid matter. It didn't smell particularly weird, either, so he figured the taste probably wouldn't kill him, at the very least.

"Ah…" The class president seemed to unconsciously grunt, making Masachika immediately look up to find every other one of his classmates staring with their mouths agape.

"…What?"

"Nothing…"

"All right, then…"

"Ah…"

"Seriously. What?"

Right as he was about to take a sip, they gasped as if they wanted to say something, making Masachika furrow his brow. Nevertheless, nobody attempted to explain anything to him, so he decided to take another hard look at the liquid and then took a little sip.

Hmm…? Wh-what is this?

The liquid swishing around in his mouth seemed to be mixed with vegetable juice…but it had somewhat of a tea leaf–like quality to it as well, and there was a hint of cacao in the fragrance. But underneath that was a taste of something he couldn't quite put his finger on. And to top it all off, the offensive bubbles from an unidentified carbonated beverage could not be ignored.

It isn't completely disgusting…and it does taste kind of like medicine. So it is potion-like, maybe?

After swallowing, he tilted his head and made an uncomfortable expression. Although it was in no way good, it wasn't bad enough to make him spit it out, so he was having trouble thinking of how he should respond.

Eh, I guess I'll finish drinking it first.

Masachika had already put his mouth on the cup, and he wasn't one to waste, so he chugged the rest in a single gulp. The less-than-stellar flavors made him frown. He poured a cup of oolong tea into his empty cup before chugging that to get the bad taste out of his mouth.

"Well, it wasn't the worst thing I've ever had…but it wasn't good, either."

"O-oh…"

"What did I just drink anyway?"

"That's…a company secret."

"Sure, but I technically work at this 'company.'"

But the class president averted her gaze once more, and the other classmates followed suit.

"What in the world was in that thing…?"

The class president hesitantly glanced at Masachika, who was clearly starting to worry, and timidly asked:

"Hey… Do you feel okay?"

"Why wouldn't I?!"

"Oh, no. It's nothing. There's nothing to worry about if you're feeling okay. There's nothing to worry about…"

"Okay, that's enough! What was in that drink?! You're starting to scare me!"

"It's okay. There wasn't anything in it that could make you sick…?"

"Why did that sound like a question?!"

"But if you do start to feel like something's wrong…you should probably get to the hospital as soon as possible."

"I wish I never asked!"

"If there aren't any side effects within two hours…then you should be fine."

"Side effects?!"

Masachika continued to press them for answers for a while after that, but he never got any more details in the end. In fact, the conversation only progressively got worse and worried him more, so he left the classroom behind and decided to head back to the student council room to work. But after thirty minutes went by, he could tell there *was* something wrong with his body.

Uh... Why am I feeling so horny all of a sudden?!

...This was genuinely the last thing he expected to happen.

Huh? What? What is this? Shouldn't this usually happen to girls? Like a girl who's usually calm and collected is suddenly overcome with these unfamiliar emotions? Everyone would love to see that. Seriously, who would want to see a guy all riled up?! Nobody wins here!

But despite his protests, the situation did not change. Yes... The train was ready to depart, and there were no brakes to stop it!

Dammit! What the hell is this...?! Those punks didn't put an aphrodisiac in this to prank me, right?!

Even though he was doing paperwork for the student council, he couldn't stop cursing his classmates in his mind. Of course, he knew it was his fault for even drinking the unidentifiable liquid, but that didn't change a thing. At any rate, all he could do right now was keep himself solely focused on the documents in his hands... Suddenly a voice called out to him.

"Master Masachika, can I ask you something?"

"...?! Yeah? What?"

He reluctantly looked up from the papers in the direction of the voice to find Ayano looking 30 percent more attractive than usual.

Ack! The guilt...!

Masachika gritted his teeth to bear the pain of his stomach tightly twisting with guilt. He was disgusted with himself for even getting close to feeling lust for his pure, good-natured childhood friend. Therefore, he used every bit of power he had to maintain eye contact with her so that his gaze wouldn't accidentally wander toward her chest or butt. However, despite his efforts, he soon noticed that his eyes were already stealing glances of her faintly pink lips, causing the guilt to twist his stomach even more.

"—So I was wondering if you had any ideas."

"O-oh, we could borrow some from the middle school if necessary."

"But how are we going to get them all the way over here?"

"I'm sure we could ask the janitor to carry them in his truck for us. Obviously, we don't want to bother the guy, and it'd be safer to load the truck with everything at once, so if we're going to ask the janitor for help, we should probably wait until we have everything we need ready to go."

"Oh. ♪ You can do that?" Maria asked suddenly from across the table, making Masachika swiftly bite down on his lip.

"...Yeah, I actually borrowed a lot of the high school's equipment in middle school this way."

"Oh, that's wonderful. ♪ Maybe we could ask the janitor or someone else to help carry stuff for our attraction, too."

"I don't know about that, but I guess it wouldn't hurt to ask."

Even though they were having a serious conversation, Masachika's mind couldn't help but wander.

Guh! Seeing Masha in the new summer uniform...is mind-blowing...!

Even though he tried to keep his eyes on her face, his increasingly overpowering instincts as a man were trying to force his eyes to focus on something less wholesome. Compared to when she was wearing a blazer and jumper, every part of her was more emphasized, making their presence and enormous size known.

"It's really reassuring having someone with experience like you around!"

Maria smiled innocently and clapped her hands, pushing her chest together from each side. A button could pop right off her shirt, and nobody would bat an eye.

Gahhh!

Blood started to leave Masachika's brain, rushing toward his lower body, so he swiftly looked back at the sofa behind him.

"Wh-what about you, Alya? Anything on your mind?"

"...? Like what?"

Alisa looked up from her accounting documents on the table and shot him a quizzical stare.

Oh, gosh. She's simply too good-looking.

The instant he saw her otherworldly beauty, he could feel something burning swell in his chest, so he looked away.

"Like...anything. But it sounds like you've got everything under control, so forget I asked."

"Okay?"

Argh! Dammit! Why is every girl in the student council way above average?! (*Belated realization.)

With the absence of the student council president and vice president, Masachika could see a different beautiful girl whichever way he turned his head. Although this would be a dream for most men, it was nothing more than a nightmare for a guy about to burst at the seams.

The only one I'm safe around is Yuki...!

"...? Masachika? May I ask why you are staring at me?"

When he turned his eyes to the girl on the opposite side of the table for help, she stared right back at him as if she were genuinely puzzled. Then again, who wouldn't be puzzled if their older brother suddenly started staring at them like a desperate wild animal?

Phew... Yeah. Thank goodness. I feel better already.

Thankfully, he felt absolutely nothing when he looked at her... since feeling even faintly attracted to his own sister would have made him want to jump off a cliff. Although she was just as good-looking as both Alisa and Maria, he wasn't remotely interested in her sexually, so all was well with the world as far as he was concerned. If anything, there was something strangely comforting about having his sister there, and it seemed like it was keeping the beast tamed as well.

Perfect. It looks like I'll be okay... I just need to keep my eyes on my work, and if things go south—if things go north, then I'll just look at Yuki.

He had finally come up with a plan to get him out of the hellish chaos born from that mystery drink. Unfortunately, his relief didn't last for long.

"Ayano, I need to go look for a few old files. Do you think you could help me?"

"As you wish."

His safety net had been swiftly taken away.

Noooooo!!

He sat in a daze while Yuki and Ayano withdrew from the room, leaving him alone with the Kujou sisters, which naturally reminded him of a certain *incident.*

...! Oh, crap! Nooo!

The paradise he had seen that day began to play out in his head against his will. A growing sense of urgency made him stand and try to escape before it was too late.

"Er... I'm going to go grab something to drink."

He blurted out the first thing that came to mind, only for it to immediately bite him in the ass.

"I can grab you something to drink. I found a mistake on one of the receipts, so I was going to be heading that way anyway."

"Oh, uh..."

"Are you fine with barley tea?"

"Yeah, sure," replied Masachika before immediately regretting it. "Actually, maybe I should go with you..."

"I'm fine. I'm not a child."

Unfortunately for him, Alisa casually turned down his offer and briskly walked out the door. Masachika's extended hand was left to half-heartedly claw at the air.

"Uh..."

By the time he came to his senses, he realized that he was now alone with Maria. On one hand, this felt like it could be a good thing, but on the other hand, it also felt like being alone with her could lead to some issues.

"Alya seems to be very motivated lately for some reason."

Meanwhile, Maria was clueless in stark contrast with the dangerous feelings in Masachika's heart. She placed a hand on her cheek while innocently tilting her head at the door Alisa had just left through.

"Yeah, I know what you mean. She has been even more fired up than usual... She has been working really hard practicing with the band, too."

Alisa had been constantly turning down his help lately as well… as she demonstrated only a few moments ago. However, there was a part of Masachika that was worried that she might be pushing herself a little too hard.

"Really? Oh, but now that you mention it, she has been practicing her singing at home a lot lately. ♪"

Maria nodded a few times, oblivious to the struggles of the boy nearby, who had wasted his opportunity to escape. He sat back down and tried to relax, but he was still unable to hide his tension.

"Kuze, are you feeling okay? You don't look so good."

Her eyebrows slanted with worry.

"Hmm? I'm fine."

"Why won't you look at me, then?"

Because I can't. If I look at you now, these perverse memories of mine will take over.

But there was no way he could ever tell her the truth, so he kept his eyes on the files in hand and tried to play it cool.

"Sah! Look at me!"

Maria grabbed his cheeks with both hands and forced him to face her. Peering into his eyes was her unfiltered worried gaze along with a hint of anger born from her concern.

"Look me in the eye and tell me nothing's wrong."

"Uh… I…"

He was unable to get the words out as she held him as if they were going to kiss. The sensation of her hands touching his cheeks in addition to her lips being so close to his scrambled his already hardly functioning brain. Perhaps this was why Maria suddenly lowered her brows compassionately.

"Kuze, I understand why you would be confused after learning who I really was and hearing how I feel about you, and I feel bad for troubling you like this, too. But I don't want that to be a reason for you to avoid me."

"…"

"I want you to come to me when you're in trouble. I want you to let me take care of you when you're hurt. I want you to be vulnerable with me, even though I know you refuse to show Alya any sign of weakness. You don't have to worry about giving me the wrong idea, and you don't have to worry about getting my hopes up. We were childhood friends regardless of how I feel about you now...and I'm older than you, so I want you to depend on me more."

"..."

What Maria was saying sounded very important and sweet, but unfortunately...Masachika was having a hard time hearing what she was saying because being in the student council room alone with her, with her hands holding his cheeks, was making his brain overheat.

She'll take care of me...when I'm hurt? Would that really be okay? Does this mean she'd be fine if I threw my arms around her?

His somewhat dazed, heated mind started to push his thoughts into a dangerous direction. Even now, he was on the verge of throwing out all reason and diving straight into her chest.

"I'm back."

As the door opened, Masachika wrenched his head away from Maria's grasp. The momentum brought his gaze toward the door right as Chisaki stepped inside. With her hand still on the doorknob, she knitted her brow, then surveyed the room with a scowl.

"...What the...? It reeks of man in here."

Although her anti-man radar seemed to have been activated for the first time in what felt like forever, Masachika still silently stood out of his seat and slowly approached her with the face of an angel.

"Chisaki."

"Hmm?"

"I need a hard reset. You know what to do."

"Now we're talking."

And just like that, both reason and desire were wiped clean with a hard factory reset.

CHAPTER 9 Aren't these guys *too* strong?

"Everything's finally coming together, huh! I was worried we weren't gonna make it in time for a while there."

"Especially with 'Anth'—'Phantom,' since we had to write the music for every instrument, too."

"Yes, but practicing…'Phantom' as a band has made me realize once again how good of a song it is."

"*Sigh*… I don't care anymore. Just call it 'Anthem' if that's easier for you guys."

"Oh my god. You guys just made the songwriter herself give up."

"I'm sorry, Sayaka. I don't have an issue with the song's name if it seemed like that…"

The five members of the band were really getting along like they had finally opened up to one another. Meanwhile, Masachika watched their exchange from a short distance with his head hanging a little to his side.

Ummm… Do they even need me here?

It was a rather depressing thought. Although he had figured they would eventually get along, he wasn't expecting them to mesh this well together. They obviously didn't need him to intervene or fix anything.

I definitely was not expecting a group of "unique" individuals with such strong personalities to get along this well.

At the very least, they all seemed to be very relaxed around one another. Furthermore, the heart of the group was undoubtedly Alisa now. While Sayaka deserved credit for leading band practice, it was none other than Alisa who united the team. Sayaka had always been skilled at leading others, but she was never someone who would be considerate of other's feelings. She was the kind of person who would, with a straight face, say, "You have the ability to do it. You're not feeling mentally up to it? That's not my problem. Go whine to your friends or cry to your boyfriend, then come back and get to work. If you still can't even manage that, then I'll simply have to replace you." Because to Sayaka, everyone was merely a cog in the wheel, aiming for a greater goal, and that included her. She was a pawn who needed to lead other pawns, since they did not have what it took to lead. She had no illusions about it, no matter how coldhearted this fact may have been.

Sayaka's a top-level commander, but she isn't a leader. It looks like that was what led Alya to unintentionally take on the role of being the caring one who kept everyone happy. But...maybe that was Sayaka's doing as well? What if it was intentional?

Regardless, Alisa was going to earn her title as the band leader without any help from Masachika at this rate. Even though that was something to celebrate...Masachika couldn't help but wonder if there was even a point of him actually being their manager anymore. Alisa's sympathetic support meant he didn't need to step in to make Takeshi or Hikaru feel comfortable, either, so what could he do to help now?

...They should be stopping for a break any minute now, so maybe I should go buy them something nice to drink... What am I? The manager of the baseball club? he thought with a touch of self-deprecation as he quietly left the music room.

"It's like..."

The instant he left the five musicians behind and stepped into the hallway, a strong sense of alienation awakened inside him, and he instinctively began to grumble to himself. However, once he realized what he was doing, it only made it worse, and he smirked bitterly.

What kind of manager complains because everything is going smoothly?

He should have been thrilled that everything was going so well that they didn't even need a manager. Besides, it wasn't like anyone asked him to be the manager. He had decided it on his own, and he had absolutely no right to be upset that he didn't have any work to do. If he were really upset about being left out, then he should have played keyboard himself without ever asking Nonoa for her help.

Ha-ha. Right.

But even he was terribly aware that he couldn't do that because he never planned on playing the piano ever again. In a way, it was an act of rebellion against his mother, but it was also far more than that.

The music I make...doesn't have the power to make others happy.

And it was always that way. Whenever he played piano, people's faces would go blank. Children who had been going wild with cheers whenever their friends performed, and guardians who would enthusiastically clap with a smile for their child's performance, lost any joy they were feeling the instant Masachika started playing piano, and they would stare at him as if he didn't belong.

Looking back, they were all clearly disgusted... Then again, I didn't really act like a kid was supposed to, and I didn't really like piano, either. The only one who genuinely liked to hear me play was Yuki. Actually... I remember someone else smoldering with rivalry while glaring at me when I played.

To sum it up, he didn't have any good memories of the piano, so his playing probably would have been very jarring in the band.

Plus, I have no idea if I can even play piano anymore...

Those thoughts went through Masachika's mind while he bought everyone drinks. He returned to the music room, where he found everyone just getting ready to take a break.

"Good work, guys. I brought you a drink to—"

Raising a can in the air, he made his appearance with a smile as if he didn't have a care in the world, but that smile immediately froze.

"No joke, though. Your singing keeps getting better, Alya. Like, you were always good, but wow."

Takeshi casually uttered Alisa's nickname. Up until now, Masachika was the only guy at school who ever called her by that name, and hearing Takeshi use it instantly lit a bitter fire in his stomach, which began to sear his entrails.

"Hmm? Oh, Kuze. You got us something to drink?"

"Y-yeah…"

After Nonoa's comment snapped him out of shock, he began to walk, albeit awkwardly, toward a nearby desk, where he placed the drinks, but even then, he could hear the band members' conversation whether or not he liked it.

"Nothing in particular… I used to be in choir for a little while when I was younger, though."

"Hold on. Alya, are you Christian?"

"No, it's nothing like that. I think most young people in Russia are becoming more secular, just like in Japan."

Even Hikaru was calling Alisa by her nickname. A restlessness stirred in Masachika's heart, and he was overcome with undeniable jealousy, which made him start to feel dizzy.

"Kuze, Kuzeee. My man, Masachiii, what's wrong?"

"'Masachi'? Nothing, really…"

He smiled uncomfortably back at Nonoa while desperately trying to look nonchalant.

"Everyone's calling one another by their nicknames now, huh?"

"Hmm? Oh yeah. Alisa suggested that."

"Ah…"

It was Alisa's idea. In other words, she requested that everybody call her by her nickname.

"Anyway…I'm going to check out our class's attraction," he stated before leaving the music room once more, since he wasn't confident he'd be able to keep up the facade any longer. He made it all the way to the staircase before…

"Dammit!!" he yelled furiously, then stormed off toward the classroom in a huff. He was pissed. At everything. All of it. He was angry at Alisa for easily letting others call her by her nickname, at his two best friends for using it and acting overly familiar with her, and at himself for being possessive.

"Tsk!"

He stomped down the staircase, his heart in turmoil. But when he reached the staircase landing, a familiar voice suddenly stopped him from behind.

"...? Masachika?"

Alisa seemed puzzled by Masachika leaving so soon after getting back.

"Shouldn't you go after him?" suggested Sayaka bluntly.

"Huh?"

"It's your job to make sure he's okay, so you need to talk to him before things get worse."

"Oh... Okay?"

Sayaka watched the confused girl chase after her partner, then sighed.

"You're so sweet, Saya," Nonoa piped up.

"Excuse me?"

Sayaka frowned before promptly looking away and pushing up her glasses.

"I simply gave her a push in the right direction for the sake of the entire band. We need to be in tip-top shape to practice."

"Uh-huh."

"...What are you looking at me like that for?"

Nonoa's lips curled slyly, and Sayaka faced her once more to give her a dirty look. That was when Hikaru spoke up with a somewhat wry smirk of his own.

"I want to thank you, too. I was almost considering going myself, but I think it's better that Alya talks to him."

"Huh? What's going on?"

Sayaka felt somewhat exhausted by Takeshi's obliviousness, and she was feeling slightly uncomfortable as well, so she walked over to her bag, took out her lens cloth from her glasses case, and began to wipe her glasses.

"Is there a problem?"

"Oh, uh… Ya look really different without your glasses, Sayaka."

"…Yeah, I'm aware that my eyes are intimidating."

"Nah, I don't think so. I think ya look cool. They're nice—your eyes."

"…?"

Despite Takeshi sounding nervous, Sayaka couldn't exactly see without her glasses, and she felt like she probably shouldn't worry about it, either, so she looked away from him before putting her glasses back on and setting down her bass.

"I'll be right back."

"Oh, Saya. Taking a leak? Let me come with you."

Sayaka shot Nonoa a slightly reprimanding glare for unashamedly saying *leak* in front of the others before replying:

"I just want to go outside and get some fresh air."

"A'ight. I'm in."

"…"

After realizing that Nonoa would have most likely come no matter what she said, Sayaka shot her another scornful look. But she quickly gave up and left the music room with Nonoa. However, almost immediately after they walked out the door, Nonoa burst into laughter.

"For real, though. I legit can't believe you'd help those two out like that."

"I told you already. I'm doing it for the team. It's nothing personal."

"Looks like you're being really considerate of Alisa if you ask me. Like, you could legit do a better job of leading the band than her if you wanted to, right?"

"…I simply didn't want to be distracted by anything other than playing bass. That's all. If someone else wants to be the leader, then why wouldn't I let them? Takes a load off my shoulders."

"Does that mean you're gonna let her be the band leader, then?"

"…"

Sayaka didn't answer but instead frowned, feeling as if Nonoa was going to tease her about any answer she gave. After a moment went by, she turned to her friend and went for a gentle counter.

"What about you, Nonoa? You seem to be really enjoying yourself for a change. Is being in a band that fun?"

"Yeah, like…"

Of course, even Sayaka had realized long ago that when her childhood friend showed emotion, it wasn't real. Usually, Nonoa would simply see how everyone else was reacting and play along, giving the people what they wanted. Nevertheless, Sayaka wasn't interested in really pressing the issue because she knew this was the best way she could get along with her childhood friend. That said, Nonoa had seemed to be genuinely having fun lately, which was surprising…yet also something Sayaka was really thrilled about as well.

"…Being in a band is more fun than I thought it'd be."

"Oh. Good."

Sayaka cracked a smile, and a warmth filled her heart as she walked down the hallway. But when she turned the corner up ahead, she saw a familiar face and stopped.

"Whoa. Yuushou. 'Sup?"

"Hmm? Oh! Nonoa, Sayaka, long time no see."

It was the current captain of the piano club and a former member of the middle school student council, Yuushou Kiryuuin. He was also someone who lost to these two in a debate during the student council presidential race. In other words, they robbed him of his chance to become student council president. Nevertheless, Nonoa was as relaxed as always, perhaps not even conscious of what they had done to him. Sayaka, however, couldn't help feeling a little wary.

"It has been a while, Yuushou. Did you need something from us?"

"No, not really. I just happened to run into you two and thought I'd say hi." He shrugged. "But, well…a little bird did tell me that you guys started a band with Alisa Kujou and were planning on playing at the school festival."

"Yes? What about it?"

"I just found that a little surprising. That's it. After all, I never expected you would ever try to help a transfer student like that."

Sayaka's eyes narrowed coldly as she slowly pushed up her glasses. He wasn't even trying to hide how he really felt.

"What do you mean, 'a transfer student like that'? You've never even talked to her, as far as I know."

"But even then, I *know*, and I know that you know exactly what I mean." The corner of his lips snidely curled. "The student council president is someone who can contribute to the First Light Committee in the future. Only people who have enough financial power and public influence to run the country are fit to become the student council president. So let's look at this transfer student. She doesn't have the money, status, or connections required. She has nothing. How much she even understands Japan is up for debate. In other words, she isn't fit to become the student council president… And I know you feel the very same way."

His self-important, almost sinister behavior was far from that of a young gentleman, but Sayaka wasn't particularly fazed.

"I understand what you're saying, but I don't remember agreeing with you," she said with a soft sigh.

"Why? You're the daughter of Taniyama Heavy Industries' CEO, and you were once someone who wanted to join the First Light Committee to be a leader who shapes Japan's future, right? Even you, Nonoa. You ran for student council vice president because you wanted to join the committee to help your family business, right?"

"Me? No. I only did it 'cause, like, Saya wanted to."

Yuushou scoffed, then shrugged dramatically.

"I'm surprised. I thought you two would have a little more sense. No wonder nobody takes the student council president position seriously anymore."

Sayaka's glare sharpened at the unfiltered contempt, but before she could get another word in, Nonoa interjected:

"Pretty cocky today, aren't we, runner-up?"

While Sayaka had no idea what that even meant, the nickname proved to be extremely effective.

A deep crease instantly formed in his brow, and he grimaced, revealing his clenched teeth. But his disgust was almost immediately erased by a smile.

"Really... I honestly don't understand how someone like you is so popular."

"Yeah, for real. I don't get it, either."

Unlike Yuushou, who seemed to be seething with rage, Nonoa was checking her nails as if she couldn't care less. Meanwhile, Sayaka glanced at Nonoa out of the corner of her eye, briefly sighed, and then looked back at Yuushou.

"I'm not interested in being the student council president anymore, but if I have to become the president to join the First Light Committee, then I currently don't have any other choice."

"Interesting. Because I haven't heard any stories about you doing anything for your campaign lately," said Yuushou audaciously.

"Running an election campaign isn't only about trying to curry public favor, right?"

Sayaka knitted her brow at his cryptic remark.

"...What's that supposed to mean?"

"Good question. All I'm saying is it's a little premature to assume that either Yuki Suou or Alisa Kujou is going to be the next student council president. Sometimes, things appear to be running smoothly, and the next moment, someone pulls the rug right out from under you... But, well, this has nothing to do with you two, so I guess you have nothing to worry about."

After shrugging ostentatiously again, Yuushou glared at Sayaka and Nonoa with contempt.

"I'm glad I got the chance to talk with you...because now I know that neither of you are a threat anymore." He stepped around them and began to walk away. "Later, you two. I could care less what you do, but maybe you shouldn't get any strange ideas and think you can win, okay? Just enjoy your little band," he said mockingly as he passed by.

But before he could get away, Sayaka looked over her shoulder at him, pushed up her glasses, and replied:

"It doesn't really matter, but for your information, the phrase is 'I couldn't care less.' Saying you 'could' care less means you *do* care, so maybe you should start worrying about yourself instead of worrying about Alisa."

"Oh my god, Saya. You're so aggressive today. Hilarious."

Yuushou didn't particularly react to her small act of revenge, so Sayaka snorted softly, faced forward, and began to walk in the opposite direction.

"*Sigh*. What was he even trying to say?"

"Totally sounded like he was bragging about plotting something. Yuushou craves the limelight."

"Yeah, I can see that..."

"What do you wanna do? Should we subtly warn Yuki and Alisa?"

Sayaka's brow furrowed as she considered the question for a second, and then she shrugged.

"I doubt we need to. Even if he was plotting something that could hurt Yuki's or Alisa's chances in the election, then oh well. It has nothing to do with us."

"Word. We can just sit back, relax, and enjoy the show."

Even though Nonoa sounded calm, there was a faint hint of disaster hidden behind her mirthful grin. But despite noticing this, Sayaka didn't point it out.

"Unless whatever he's plotting gets in our way. *Then* we'll have a problem." She shrugged again.

"Masachika!"

A frown instantly twisted Masachika's expression when the voice called out to him from behind. She was the last person he wanted to see right now, after all. Regardless, he put on an air of nonchalance and turned around as if there was nothing wrong.

"...Alya? What's wrong?"

"...I..."

His quizzical glance rendered Alisa speechless, and her eyes wandered the air as she descended the stairs. When she reached the landing, she pondered for a few seconds, then hesitantly continued:

"You were acting strange...so I came to check on you."

"...!"

Masachika didn't know what to say, since he never expected Alisa, of all people, to notice that he was acting any differently, but his astonishment went unbeknownst to her as she continued to look away.

"I kind of feel like...we haven't been as close lately. Is it something I did?" she asked timidly, but those words ended up offending Masachika a bit.

"Yeah, and whose fault is that?"

"What...?"

"Ah—"

Masachika regretted those words the instant the accusatory statement left his mouth. He genuinely did feel that they hadn't been as close lately. Claiming she was avoiding him would be a bit of an exaggeration, but he did feel like she was keeping some distance between them. Regardless, she still wasn't the one to blame, and he knew he was simply taking his frustrations out on her.

"Ummm..."

After Masachika roughly scratched his head as if he were trying to get all the bad thoughts out, he awkwardly bowed to Alisa.

"I'm sorry. You didn't deserve that."

"Oh... Sure..."

"*Sigh*... It's... Like, seeing how close you guys have gotten... It's..."

It made me jealous.

But he still couldn't throw away his shame and tell her the whole truth.

"It made me feel really lonely!"

So instead, he blurted out something that was neither the truth nor a lie, but it was still just as embarrassing, so he lowered his gaze and clenched his teeth to power through the shame.

"...Oh? Heh."

There was clear amusement in Alisa's voice, and when he looked up at her, that gloomy, somewhat worried expression from moments ago was nowhere to be found. Her sinister grin was like a cat that had cornered a mouse.

"You were feeling lonely...because I've been getting along so well with Takeshi and Hikaru?"

The "so well" part created a crease in Masachika's brow so deep that even he knew it had to be obvious.

"Oh?"

Alisa's eyes narrowed sadistically like a cat slowly closing in on its prey while she brought her face even closer to his until he could almost feel her breathing. She then whispered:

"Wait... Don't tell me you're jealous?"

"...! Fine, you got me! Yes, I'm jealous! I got jealous! And I got annoyed with myself for getting jealous, so I ran away! Happy now?!"

Masachika gave up trying to hide it any longer and spilled the beans, making Alisa smile more brilliantly than ever before. She quickly stepped back.

"*Giggle.* Yes, I'm very happy now."

She mirthfully slid to Masachika's right side with a bounce in her step, provocatively placed a hand on his trembling shoulder, and gave him a soft peck on the cheek.

"...?!"

Although he froze the instant her lips touched his cheek, he quickly darted his eyes in her direction in disbelief...where he found her looking up at him with the most mischievous of grins.

"Don't worry."

She paused before softly whispering in Russian:

"<Because you're special.>"

Masachika's heart almost burst right out of his chest.

"Wh-what?" he awkwardly replied, only to be met with a smug snort as she slightly raised her chin, nose in the air. Alisa then began to nimbly run up the staircase, but she stopped halfway, looked back, and devilishly placed a finger to her lips.

"Very well. I suppose I could give my jealous, lonely partner a bit of my time."

"Huh?"

"I'll give you the honor of hanging out with me at the school festival when I'm free. So you better show me a good time, okay?"

She then swiftly turned her back to him, dashed up the rest of the staircase, and disappeared down the hallway, leaving Masachika to watch in mute amazement for the next few seconds. Once she was out of sight, he staggered back so he could lean against the wall, then slid all the way down until his butt touched the floor.

"Gaaah… What the hell?" he groaned, and ran his hands through his hair. "…It should be illegal for her to do that," he muttered, his voice trembling.

Even he knew that his cheeks were burning red, and there was no way he could deny that he probably looked like a blithering idiot in his excitement. He couldn't deny how much it made him feel better, either. His racing heart was so loud that it was almost too much to bear. Alisa had accepted him and his revolting jealousy—which even he was disgusted by. Moreover…

"…!! Gyaaaahhh!!"

Touching his cheek reminded Masachika of the sensation, causing him to uncontrollably writhe as he twisted his body violently and ground his forehead into the wall. That was when he could suddenly hear voices coming from the bottom of the staircase, which instantly brought him back to his senses.

"Ngh…"

After standing back up in a fluster, he brushed his pants off, then escaped straight into a nearby restroom, where he spent the next few minutes cooling off. When he finally managed to calm down somewhat, he awkwardly tottered back to the music room.

"Oh, you're back."

Masachika tilted his head, wondering why Takeshi made it sound like they were waiting for him.

"…Did something happen?"

"Not exactly. We were just talking about calling one another by our nicknames or preferred names from now on. You know, make things more casual and act more like friends."

"Oh… Yeah. Why not?" Masachika nodded, making sure to show no signs of his heart rate increasing. Immediately, Takeshi's face lit up with a beaming smile.

"Right?! It makes us really feel like a band!"

Masachika couldn't help but wryly smirk back at his friend's innocence, but Hikaru soon chimed in as well.

"That includes you, Masachika."

"Huh?"

"What do you mean, 'huh'? You're part of Fortitude, too, right?"

Hikaru's comment caught Masachika off guard for a moment until he was finally able to process what was said, and he laughed nervously.

"Yeah… I am."

He then casually glanced at Alisa, who shrugged back so subtly at him that only he would notice. It was that gesture and what she said to him earlier that finally put him at ease.

Yeah… What was I so jealous about?

He instantly felt embarrassed for having such negative feelings toward these incredible friends. As if to shake off the embarrassment, he faced Sayaka and Nonoa next.

"So, uh… Are you two fine if I start acting more friendly with you, too?"

"Sure…"

"Yeah. Whatever."

For Masachika, this moment was almost bittersweet. Never had he imagined that one day he would become this close to former rivals he used to work with in the student council, and before he even realized it, the dark feelings burning inside him were gone.

"Mmm… So, Masachika… Buddy?"

"Uh… Sure?"

"…No, that sounds weird."

"Ha-ha-ha! Yeah, I know what you mean. We spent so much time together in middle school that it feels kind of weird that we're just now trying to get to know each other better."

That was when he started to feel extremely hot again for some reason.

What the...? Is it just me, or is it getting hot in here?

A cold sweat slowly dripped down his back while he shifted his gaze in Alisa's direction...and he noticed her chilling glare. However...

Hold up... This might be my chance to get back at her.

Memories of being at her mercy earlier tickled his mischievous heart. It made him move toward Alisa's side, where he softly whispered so that only she could hear:

"Wait... Don't tell me you're jealous?"

Alisa immediately averted her gaze in utter embarrassment—

"Shut up."

—or at least, that was how Masachika imagined she would act, but her reaction ended up being far nastier than he could have ever imagined.

"Ouch. Harsh."

In the end, his plan backfired and broke nobody's heart but his own.

"Really? I'm glad to hear everything is going smoothly."

Yuushou was standing in a room in a high-rise apartment with a smartphone in hand.

"Yes, I am sure a few people will get injured...but it would be pointless otherwise, right?"

His casually wicked comment was met by backlash from whomever he was speaking to on the phone, but Yuushou didn't care a single bit, and the corner of his lips curled upward.

"Don't tell me you're planning on backing out now. If you quit, then your dear vice president will... I don't need to continue, do I?"

Yuushou's beautiful face twisted maliciously while he cackled as if he were laughing at all the fools beneath him. And yet there was a hint of kindness in his voice as well when he sweetly whispered like a demon luring someone onto a dark path…

"I'm counting on you to follow through with the plan… Mr. President."

The ulterior motives of countless people intertwined as the week went by…until the day of the school festival finally arrived.

Pride and Stubbornness

"Let the sixty-sixth Autumn Heights Festival begin!"

With the president of the school festival committee's announcement, Seirei Academy's much-anticipated event began. Since the first day was for Seirei Academy students only, it wasn't going to be total chaos for the school festival committee…or at least, that was what they naively believed.

"Kuze! The next performers aren't going to be ready in time!"

"Where are they?"

"They haven't even arrived!"

"How long do we need to stall?"

"Uh…"

"Please check and get back to me as soon as you can. I'll handle things here. Host, once these performers get off the stage, I need you to buy us some time. Can you do that? Thanks."

There were three stages set up for performances: the gym, the auditorium, and the schoolyard. For the most part, each stage was run by the school festival committee, the broadcasting club, and the drama club. In addition, the president of the school festival committee specifically put Masachika in charge of making sure everything went smoothly in the auditorium. Of course, they were working in shifts, so there were still two others who would take his place when he was on break.

"Kuze, I talked to the performers, and they need two more minutes."

"Roger that. Host, try to buy us three minutes just in case. Cut the stage lights, leave the audience's seats as is, and shine the spotlight on the host. This stalling is cutting into the next break as well, so I need the next props master to switch out with the current one while the host is buying us time."

As he checked the task schedule and time schedule, Masachika used a transceiver to give instructions to the other auditorium workers, who quickly responded.

Although most of the others were older than him, there wasn't even the slightest hint of disrespect in any of their voices, which was a testament to the trust that he'd built with them during multiple rehearsals. Although they ran into a few bumps along the way, thanks to his direction, the auditorium's stage plans went smoothly, until it was time for their break.

"All right, I'm going to start my break. I'm counting on you."

"Sounds good. Enjoy."

After one of the third-year school festival committee members took over his shift, Masachika quickly washed his hands, then headed straight for the stage in the schoolyard. The stage area in the schoolyard was partitioned off with traffic cones of various colors, and there were around a hundred metal folding chairs set in front of the stage for the audience. Even though there were a few empty seats here and there, Masachika decided to stand behind them, close to the traffic cones. Shortly after that, two sets and a lectern were brought out onstage and set up before two familiar faces eventually stepped onto the stage.

"Thank you all for coming to watch the quiz research club's very own quiz show!"

The final person to join them onstage was the quiz research club's leader, wearing a silk hat and all. Masachika watched from afar as the club leader introduced the show, but it wasn't like he was forced to stand so far away. This was a choice Masachika made himself so he could immediately take action if an emergency arose, since there was no telling what was going to happen on such a secretive trivia show. Ayano seemed to feel similarly...or at least, that was the conclusion

Masachika came to when he suddenly noticed her standing as still as a statue nearby.

"Without further ado, allow me to present today's two contestants!"

After introducing himself as the host, the quiz research club's leader held out his hand toward the two competitors sitting in the center of the stage. A close-up shot of Yuki appeared on the screen above.

"Born into a well-known family that cultivates foreign relations, this young woman has the brains to become a diplomat herself one day! Politics, economics, pop culture, subculture—you name it! She knows it! But will she be able to utilize this extensive knowledge of hers during today's quiz?! Give it up for Yuki Suou!"

The instant Yuki waved at the audience with a smile, the crowd erupted into cheers and whistling, which gradually attracted the attention of other students in the vicinity.

"Next up, we have the top of her class—a girl who has gotten the highest grade on every exam since she transferred to this school! There isn't a single soul here who can deny that she is talented! She has both brains and brawn, and she is just getting started! Will she continue being the undefeated prodigy after this show?! Give it up for Alisa Mikhailovna Kujou!"

"Damn, he's good," commented Masachika as a close-up shot of Alisa was suddenly displayed on the screen. Alisa bowed slightly with a serious expression on her face. Her reaction was, in a way, the opposite of Yuki's, so although she was welcomed with cheering and a warm round of applause, the audience did seem less enthusiastic.

Hmm… I was honestly expecting there to be a distinct, bigger difference in support…but maybe they liked her indifferent reaction. Some people like it when celebrities are cold and blunt, after all. Anyway, I'm glad I was wrong.

Masachika was pondering the audience response while clapping when he noticed the influx of spectators was starting to die down a little. It was already a huge crowd, perhaps because two of the most beautiful student council presidential candidates at school were about to duke it out, but the fact that it was lunchtime seemed to help as well. In fact, most students in the crowd had some sort of snack in hand, as if they wanted something to watch while enjoying their meal.

There's not an empty seat left. Counting the people standing in the audience and those outside the venue peeking in, then you'd have around 130 people watching.

In other words, a little under 20 percent of the entire student body was currently here. While there was no way all of them were going to watch the entire show, there were still more than enough people here for details to quickly spread to every single student in school.

"Now, let the game begin! This competition will contain elements related to the election as well as elements you'd usually see on good old-fashioned quiz shows. So while most rules follow what everyone's used to, there will be some rules like you've never seen before, too. Of course, our two contestants aren't the only ones who can play. Everyone here is allowed to participate. All the questions will be multiple choice, and there will be no free response questions, since free response questions would be wayyy too hard to judge."

The host added a playful note in his voice when explaining their reasoning, then continued:

"You get ten seconds to think after I read the question, then you have to give us an answer! There will be six topics with five questions per topic and a final question at the end, making a total of thirty-one questions. Whoever gets the most points wins. We have a very nice prize for our winner tonight, whether or not they are one of our two contestants, so give it everything you've got. Now, the question is: How do you participate if you're not one of our two contestants? However, before I tell you all that, there is something important we need to discuss first."

The host waited a beat before raising his voice loud enough for everyone in the venue to hear.

"Of course, this should go without saying, but I need everyone to be quiet during the show. You are not allowed to give the contestants any hints or answers, and if we find anyone cheating, they will be immediately kicked out of the venue. If that happens, we will have to start over and ask a new question. Is everyone fine with that? I'm counting on you all to keep quiet."

The audience gradually got quieter until the area was completely silent, making the host smile with evident satisfaction.

"Thank you all so very much! Now, I need everyone to take out their phone and scan the QR code on the screen. This will take you to an answer sheet we made just for the show. We also have a few signs set up at each corner of the venue with the URL and QR code, so please use those if you need to."

Masachika took out his smartphone just like those around him and scanned the massive QR code displayed on the screen.

This is really impressive... I can't believe they did all this just for the show... What the—?

The web page that came up made him raise an eyebrow. Who do you think is a better fit for student council president? Under that question were the names Yuki and Alisa, which you could select as an answer.

The hell is this? Some kind of survey? Is this going to be used during the quiz? Are our votes going to be added like bonus points to their score?

When Masachika surveyed his surroundings, he noticed there were numerous others curiously looking around as well.

"Since I'm sure most of you are still opening the web page, I will use this time to explain the special rules for only our two contestants here. As I mentioned earlier, this quiz will contain elements related to the election. For example, our contestants' partners, Ayano Kimishima and Masachika Kuze, will be able to participate as guests!"

Suddenly hearing his name made Masachika immediately look toward the stage.

"Each candidate pair is allowed to 'phone a friend' one time. One pair being Ms. Suou and Ayano Kimishima, with the other pair being Ms. Kujou and Masachika Kuze. I know it's self-explanatory, but 'phoning a friend' means they are allowed to ask their partner for help. Therefore, if you ever want to phone a friend, you need to raise your hand and say, 'Help.' After that, you are allowed to talk to your partner on the phone for ten seconds tops. Oh, and you need to put your phone on speaker so that everyone can hear."

Yuki promptly raised her hand. After the host acknowledged she had a question, she spoke into her microphone with a well-projected voice and asked:

"I have two questions. First, how does the time limit work when we phone a friend? Furthermore, if we put our phone on speaker, wouldn't the other contestant also be able to hear the advice that was meant for us?"

"Oh, my apologies for being unclear. When you phone a friend, your rival's answer will already be locked in. In other words, the ten seconds for answering the question have already passed. However, if you phone a friend, you get an additional ten seconds to receive help from your partner, then you get another ten seconds to answer the question."

"Interesting. What happens if we both phone a friend about the same question?"

"Only one person may phone a friend per question. In other words, if one contestant declares first that they would like to phone a friend, then the other will not be able to call their partner anymore."

"That makes sense. Thank you very much."

"No, thank you for your wonderful question. By the way, it is against the rules for either of your partners to give you hints during the duration of this quiz with the exception of when you call them, but I'm sure that much was obvious. Please be careful, though."

Hmm... So I only get one chance to help Alya if she gets stumped. Then again, if she doesn't know the answer to something, I really doubt I would...

Masachika thought about the rules while shifting his gaze back down to the second choice on his phone screen.

Of course, I'm going to choose Alya.

After he tapped on Alisa's name, another page popped up with the words please wait while the page was loading.

"Last but not least, I would like to explain how the point system works. Not all questions are worth the same number of points, and the general percentage of people who get the question right will affect the score."

"What?"

When Masachika looked up, the host had just taken his eyes off the contestants and shifted his gaze toward the crowd.

"I'm sure everyone here has watched a trivia-based game show at least once before, right? Ordinary people are asked several questions, and then the show checks the average percent of correct answers that they had. Put simply, the more people who get the answer right, the easier that question is. Fewer people answering a question correctly means the question is harder. We, the quiz research club, have the technology to use our own personal surveys to calculate the percentage of correct answers. Normally, trivia shows have ten easy questions and twenty hard ones, but we will be using the formula one hundred minus the general percentage of correct answers equals the number of points! Put simply, if eighty percent of people answer a problem correctly, then the problem will be worth twenty points. However, if only five percent of people get the correct answer, then the question is worth ninety-five points!"

"That's, uh…? I don't know about that."

In other words, easy questions were worth next to nothing, but difficult questions could create a massive gap in the score between the contestants in the blink of an eye. To make matters worse, it was a multiple-choice test…

You could make a lucky guess on an extremely difficult question and instantly get seventy points. If all the other questions are painfully easy ones that 90 percent of people get right, then there would be almost no way to ever catch up. It's a scary thought…but I'm sure they worked on balancing the game before making it.

This point system seemed to be one of those unique rules the host mentioned earlier.

All right, to sum things up… There are thirty-one questions, and you get ten seconds to answer each question. Each question is worth a different number of points, which is based on how many individuals get the correct answer when they're surveyed. Furthermore, both Alya and Yuki are allowed to phone a friend for help but only once.

Other than the scoring system, there wasn't anything special about the rules for the most part and that included phoning a friend. The audience appeared to think so as well, seemingly getting sick of listening to all the rules. However, the host was not oblivious to this and proceeded by asking the contestants if they had any final questions. After they both shook their heads, the host faced the crowd once more and spread out his arms.

"Sorry to keep you all waiting. Anything goes in this battle between two student council members! Let the game begin!"

The host then moved to his lectern, where he began to use the opened laptop lying there.

"Your first topic is...social studies! First question!" shouted the host while the question was simultaneously displayed on the screen.

"Out of the Seven Summits, which of the following has the lowest altitude?!"

What the...?! Who the hell knows that?!

But despite his bewilderment, the multiple-choice answers were promptly displayed on the screen.

"One, Vinson Massif. Two, Kilimanjaro. Three, Aconcagua. Four, Kosciuszko. Your ten seconds starts now!"

"Oof! Seriously?!"

In the midst of his astonishment, a ten-second countdown appeared in the top-right of the screen, prompting Masachika to immediately rack his brain for ideas.

Uh... Okay, Kilimanjaro is definitely not it, and I've never even heard of Kosciuszko. The hell is that? Wait. Hold on. The Seven Summits are supposed to be the highest mountains, so size-wise, the smallest ones are somewhere like Australia or Antarctica, right? Wait. Antarctica is deceptively huge, isn't it? Which leaves Australia... I'm pretty sure Aconcagua is in the Americas somewhere...but where is Vinson Massif again...?

Not even two seconds went by as those thoughts flew through his brain. But when he directed his gaze back to his phone...he froze.

"...? What's this?"

Because there was something he was not expecting to see. Displayed on his phone's screen under the timer in the top-right corner were the question and multiple-choice answers. This much was no different from what was displayed on the screen above the stage. However, there was something else displayed above the question on his phone that was nowhere to be found on the main screen. There were two square frames with Alisa's name written above one and Yuki's name written above the other.

Uh...? Oh, does this have something to do with that vote from a few moments ago?

Masachika tried tapping on the box and Alisa's name, but nothing happened. The ambiguity even caused him to forget about the quiz itself for a moment. But when the timer reached the four-second mark, the mystery naturally solved itself.

"Hmm?"

The number 4 suddenly appeared in the box under Yuki's name, followed by another 4 written in Alisa's box one second later.

Wait. Don't tell me these are their answers...

A wave of bewildered grunts stirred the crowd, provoking the host to tell everyone to settle down, which immediately silenced the audience.

This must be one of the features of the game... Anyway, I need to answer before time runs out. I guess I'll go with Kosciuszko, wherever that is. Seems suspicious.

Seeing Yuki and Alisa choose the same answer gave Masachika the confidence he needed to tap the fourth multiple-choice answer. Another second went by, bringing the countdown to zero and locking in the answers.

"Time's up! Now, let's get straight to it! The correct answer was… number four! Kosciuszko! Congratulations to both of our contestants for getting it right! Furthermore, sixty-eight percent of you all got the correct answer, which means each contestant will receive thirty-two points!"

…? Don't they usually check the contestants' answers before telling us the right answer? Oh! Right. The contestants don't have a screen in front of them, so I guess there's no way to show their answers to the audience.

The two contestants had ordinary classroom desks in front of them, which were covered with a tablecloth to keep their tablets from getting scratched. It was an extremely simple setup, with the cloth hanging down in front of their desk, which was common with trivia shows, and there was no screen displaying their answers, either.

The questions and answers displayed on the main screen were likely made in advance, so they probably have no way of showing the contestants' answers. That must be why they went with this answer form to show the contestants' answers… But still, something feels off…

Although the next question was announced, most of Masachika's focus was on the quiz research club's puzzling solution to displaying the answers. It felt extremely unnatural and obtuse, which made him think there had to be something else he wasn't seeing. So he decided to follow his gut and began racking his brain.

Common sense would tell me that this just allows everyone to base their answers on the contestants' answers, right? But giving the audience such big hints only takes away from the fun of the game, right? Is this a feature where you're supposed to just choose the same answer as the contestant you like? So the survey in the beginning was— Wait. No. If that were the case, then why show both contestants' answers? Why not only show the answers of whomever you chose in the beginning?

"Time's up! We have an incorrect answer this time! The correct answer was number two! Ms. Kujou got it right! Number three, which Ms. Suou selected, was unfortunately the symbol for steel cans."

Masachika suddenly looked up when he heard the host's announcement. It appeared that Alisa had already taken the lead.

Good job, Alya. You learn that from one of those trivia books?

There was no way Alisa would lose to Yuki when it came to knowledge that could be found in simple textbooks, but Masachika knew this wasn't enough to win a trivia show. Therefore, when he had stopped by the quiz research club to discuss the trivia game, he casually memorized all the names of the trivia books he saw lying around. He then got copies for Alisa to study at a later date, which she ended up using to memorize every single fact in them like a sponge, exceeding even Masachika's expectations.

They most likely pulled a decent number of problems from those trivia books… I'm sure they modified some of them, but it's nothing Alya can't handle!

Simply watching his dependable partner lifted his mood tenfold; he gazed at her with praise and support. Alisa, however, didn't notice his stare, since she had her eyes glued to her tablet and wasn't planning on letting her guard down for even a second.

…She still looks pretty tense, though. I really hope she can remain focused until the very end…

A bit of anxiety clouded Masachika's heart when he realized that he missed how many points the last question was worth. Wondering how much of a lead Alisa was in, he immediately looked down at his phone…and discovered that their score wasn't displayed.

What the…? Their score isn't written anywhere onstage, either. Dammit. Is this going to come back and bite us in the ass?

He panicked somewhat until the host announced their score.

"All right! That does it for our first topic. The current scores are Ms. Suou, 148 points! Ms. Kujou, 192 points! It looks like Ms. Kujou has a slight edge over her opponent!"

"Oh, wow. She has an even bigger lead than I thought."

Masachika honestly didn't believe she would already be in the lead after the first five questions. *Unexpected but greatly appreciated*, he thought, but it was still soon to get comfortable yet because depending on the next topic, there was always a high chance of Yuki taking the lead in the blink of an eye. Alisa was especially ignorant when it came to subculture and pop culture, so all Masachika could do was pray nothing like that ever came up…

"Let's move on to our next topic! Our next topic for the day is…"

Masachika naturally tensed in fear as the host began to announce the next topic.

"…cuisine! Here is your first question!"

After breathing a sigh of relief, Masachika returned his focus to the curiously displayed answers of the contestants, since he was sure that Alisa could handle the quiz itself without him.

This show contains elements related to the election…which means people can use the contestants' answers to cheer on their favorite candidate. That seems like the most natural reason for doing this. So would that mean the survey in the beginning was to let the audience know this was to cheer on their favorite…? But wouldn't this just motivate the audience to give their favorite candidate a hint if they end up selecting the wrong answer…? Then again, that is against the rules, so…

Or was it only against the rules if they got caught? Still, the issue here was that it was unlikely that either of the candidates had realized this mechanism even existed. Plus, the ten-second clock made it hard to have any sort of effective system set up for cheating.

On second thought, if you did manage to tell a candidate about this system, then it would be an easy enough system to abuse. The candidate could just slowly choose each answer until their accomplice in the audience gave them a nod when they picked the right answer. That should work, and it would be subtle enough for someone to pull off without anyone noticing, right?

A little cheating during the election race wasn't a problem as long as you got away with it. You could even be kind of obvious about it if you left no evidence. In fact, it could improve your reputation if you did pull it off without the other person finding out how you did it.

But how am I going to tell Alya all this? That's the issue. Plus, the problems are honestly really hard, so this might actually not help her at all.

Masachika had been making sure to look up each question until now, but most of them didn't seem like they were something you could look up online and find an answer in under ten seconds. In reality, the accomplice would probably have only a maximum of five seconds to find the right answer online.

Hmm... I guess it wouldn't really be feasible.

But even then, he turned his focus to Alisa onstage, since he figured letting her know about this was still better than nothing. Having said that, she was still completely focused on her tablet, never glancing even once in his direction.

...Alya?

A seed of anxiety and panic began to grow inside Masachika when he realized that she clearly wasn't paying attention to what was going on around her.

Hold up. Relax... How is panicking going to solve anything? If Alya is nervous, then I need to be the calm one.

He shook his head, shifted emotional gears, and looked back down at his phone.

I should keep an eye on Yuki first. If she's already cheating, then there has to be some kind of hint of it within her answers.

Once he reached that conclusion, Masachika peered hard at Yuki's answer while glancing a few times at Ayano to see if they really were up to no good, but neither of them seemed to be doing anything suspicious.

They aren't acting any different from how they were acting earlier... Besides, I doubt Ayano has it in her to cheat.

Maybe she could do it if Yuki gave her the orders, but Ayano wasn't the kind of person who would even get the idea to cheat, let alone be able to pull it off. She was far too pure to do something so dirty.

"That does it for our second round. The current score is Ms. Suou with 304 points and Ms. Kujou with 390 points! Ms. Kujou is still in the lead!"

"Oooh!" Masachika exclaimed when he heard the host's announcement. He immediately looked over at his partner with genuine admiration in his eyes, but Alisa was still far too taut with tension to notice.

Meanwhile…

I've answered every question correctly so far. All that studying has paid off. I can do it. I can beat Yuki all by myself.

The extremely short ten-second period for thinking, in addition to the subsequent anxiety and relief felt once the answer was announced, ended up being far more mentally draining than Alisa had imagined. The fact that this was only a third of the entire show made her slightly less confident that she would be able to focus until the very end. Nevertheless, she fought through her fears and focused on the questions before her.

…That is, until the host announced the next topic.

"Our next topic is trends! Here's your first question!"

Alisa was suddenly overwhelmed by a sense of danger that was almost immediately proved to be well-founded.

"Last year, the TV show *Detective Family Holiday* took the world by storm. Your question is: What did the protagonist famously say in episode eight during this scene?!"

…! I have no idea!

Although she had heard of that TV show on the news before, she had absolutely no idea what it was even about. At the very least, she thought she could guess which line was right based on the scene, but all the choices were extremely similar. The only difference was vocabulary used and the order of the words, but all the lines essentially meant the same thing.

Whoever wrote the question expects us to have a general idea of what the protagonist said, so the question is simply testing if we remembered it correctly… I basically just have to go with my gut and guess!

The option to phone a friend did cross her mind, but Alisa immediately ruled that out.

I'll be fine. I can beat Yuki in any ordinary topic. Even if she gets the lead on me this round, I can still pull ahead in the later rounds.

She convinced herself of that while going with her gut to pick an answer, but when the time came for the host to announce the answer…

"The correct answer is…number one! Oh nooo! Ms. Kujou got her first answer wrong! Ms. Suou is catching up, folks!"

She got it wrong. The fact was like a heavy weight in her stomach. It was emotionally devastating whether or not she wanted to acknowledge it, but her iron will wasn't going to allow her emotions to get in the way.

I'll be fine. I have a one-in-four chance of getting the answer right, so even if I guess every time, I should still get at least one or two of them right. In addition, if I do get two of them right, there's almost no way Yuki will outpoint me, even if she does answer every question correctly.

"Question number two! This mascot has been a huge hit on social media lately! But what city and prefecture is he originally a mascot of?"

It's okay. Just two questions. As long as I get two correct…

"Question number three! This hot product is used for what?"

It's okay. I can still…

"Whoa! Would you look at that?! Ms. Suou has finally taken the lead!"

Just one more question. If I get this one correct…

………………

"That does it for round three! Ms. Suou is now in the lead with 496 points, with Ms. Kujou still with 390 points! I bet everyone was as shocked and upset as I was to see Ms. Kujou getting every question wrong this round! This is major! Anyway, that does it for the first half of the game, so let's see how our contestants are feeling! Let's start with you, Ms. Suou. That was one impressive comeback."

"Thank you very much. I was quite surprised by how difficult these questions turned out to be. Are the trivia questions you ask one another in your club always this difficult?"

"No, these questions are actually…"

Even though the host and Yuki were speaking, Alisa hardly heard a word. Her unfocused eyes stared at her tablet, and she gritted her teeth. Being stubborn ended up only putting her far behind in points, and it was going to take more than one right answer to catch up. Despite being prepared for a bad round, Alisa couldn't help but curse her poor intuition after getting every single answer wrong.

"I try hard to keep up with trends in order to stay informed about others' interests…but trends are seemingly unimportant to Alya. If I were her, I would have phoned a friend…"

Hearing Yuki call her out snapped Alisa back to reality. She looked up from her tablet and turned to face Yuki, who was staring in her direction with a very ladylike smile.

"Did you not phone a friend out of pride, even though you knew the topic would be difficult for you? Or perhaps you only plan on phoning a friend if I do so first?"

Pride… It was pride, but it wasn't her rivalry with Yuki that made her too stubborn to ask for help. Alisa was doing this for herself, and her pride wasn't going to let her back down.

"…Why did you agree to do this show?"

Yuki blinked in confusion, as if Alisa's question had caught her off guard, but before she could even get a chance to reply, Alisa continued:

"I agreed to come on this show to demonstrate what I was capable of. I want to prove that I am fit for running for student council president and that I am fit to stand by Masachika's side. And that's why…"

Alisa grabbed her smartphone off the desk in front of her, then flipped it over as if to show that she wasn't planning on using it.

"…I don't plan on getting Masachika involved in this. Whether I win or lose this battle depends solely on me."

Her determination was awe-inspiring, still shining even in the face of despair, and it was this great pride of hers that captivated the audience.

"I will not rely on anyone but myself to defeat you, no matter what."

The perfectly still audience swallowed their breath when they heard just how determined she was. Even the host was speechless for a few seconds. Of course, Masachika was no different as he watched over Alisa from afar.

"Alya..."

He unconsciously muttered his partner's name as she shone so brightly that he wanted to squint.

Heh... She's so cool.

And he meant that from the bottom of his heart. She was putting everything she had into improving so she could become the ideal version of herself. Masachika truly felt that her single-minded pursuit was not only beautiful but admirable as well.

Ha-ha... I guess we don't need to cheat...

He lowered his smartphone with a bit of shame. All he could do now was believe in his partner, trust that she could turn this around for herself, and watch over her.

Anyway...I had no idea she felt that way.

Masachika himself seemed to be the cause of Alisa's unusual tension lately. In other words, although he hadn't really taken what Yuki said seriously at the time, she turned out to be right.

I was only trying to help her with the election, since I have experience, but it looks like I might have ended up only making her feel cornered.

Looking back, he did feel like he might have been helping her too much. Perhaps his overprotectiveness made Alisa believe he didn't trust her. Perhaps it made her feel like she wasn't good enough to do anything on her own.

But you have nothing to worry about... You're always going to be walking ahead of me and going farther than I ever could.

Masachika gazed at his partner onstage with a hint of sorrow in his heart. She was a brilliant star in the night sky, and he was but a single spectator watching her from the ground. It was as if this were some kind of metaphor for the future to come, which drained his heart, leaving him with a strange sense of loneliness.

"Now, let's move on to the final half of the show!"

The audience erupted with passionate cheers the instant the host announced that they were resuming the show. There was probably not a soul left in the crowd who saw this as merely an attraction for the school festival anymore. This was a serious match with two student council presidential candidates' pride on the line, and the passionate cheers from the crowd were proof of that.

"Our next topic…is math! Here's your first question! Which of the following is the correct geometric net for this three-dimensional object? Timer starts now!"

"Whoa?!" exclaimed Masachika at the strangely difficult question. This was obviously not something you could solve within ten seconds, no matter how you looked at it. Maybe you could put two of the nets together in your head if you were quick enough. As a result, both Yuki and Alisa punched in their completely different answers almost simultaneously when there were only two seconds left to go.

"Time's up! The correct answer is number three! …Oh no! This is the first time both contestants got the answer wrong!"

"Yeah… Not much anyone could have done about that," said Masachika with a bitter smirk.

It was essentially a luck-based question, after all.

"Incidentally, only eleven percent of people got the answer right! I guess ten seconds was a little too short, huh?"

"…What?"

Masachika's smile fell.

Wait… What did the host just say?

A chill ran down his spine, and the clearly unusual comment instantly put Masachika's slowly drifting brain into overdrive.

Only 11 percent of people got the correct answer? That doesn't seem right. Probability-wise, you have a one-in-four chance of getting the answer right. But if we assume there were at least a few people who actually knew the answer, then wouldn't at least 20 percent be more realistic? There's no way only 11 percent of people got the answer right… Unless…

Unless the people answering were influenced by Yuki's and Alisa's incorrect answers.

"...!!"

The instant it hit him, Masachika's heart began to race. He couldn't even breathe as something similar to fear shot through his body.

Wait, wait, wait. Then that means...

There was no time to worry about how the quiz was going any longer. Masachika placed a hand on his chin, getting lost in his own thoughts.

The percentage of correct answers from non-contestants wasn't something they calculated beforehand after surveying strangers. They're using the audience's answers to calculate the percentage. In other words, the audience can manipulate the score. But that sounds like it would be pretty pointless if Yuki and Alya kept getting the right answer... Wait! How stupid am I?!

There was an obvious way to manipulate the scores to one's advantage, and it was right under Masachika's nose.

So that's why they have the answers displayed here!

Although an extreme example, what if everyone here copied Alisa's answer? If she got the answer correct, then the general percentage of correct answers would be 100 percent. In other words, she would get zero points. But if Alisa got the answer wrong and Yuki got it right, then the general percentage of correct answers would be a whopping 0 percent, which would instantly give Yuki a hundred whole points in the blink of an eye. And if that were to happen, then there would be no way for Alisa to catch up, no matter how many questions she got right.

Ha...ha-ha... This is a feature of an election. Each answer the audience gives is a vote that directly influences how many points Alya and Yuki get.

There were probably not that many people in the audience who had realized this...yet. But what if people started to catch on? How many people in the audience were fans of Yuki? At the very least, she had far more people who would vote for her over Alisa. Which meant...

I need to get as many people on my side as possible and have them copy Yuki's answers! That should at least prevent her from getting a huge advantage! There's one more thing I need to do—

Masachika sprang into action, pulling out the contact list on his phone while turning on his heel to leave the area.

...Masachika had the right idea, but he made a huge mistake in his calculation... There was already someone who had caught on to this point system long before he did.

"Sorry, Kuze, but I need you to stop right there."

"Huh...?"

Once he started to walk away, a familiar female student suddenly appeared right in front of him. Immediately, another familiar face appeared on his left and yet another right behind him.

"You guys are..."

They were friends of friends, so he had met them a few times before, and there was only one reason why they would prevent him from leaving.

"I am deeply sorry, Master Masachika, but I must ask you to stop what you're doing."

Right when he heard yet another voice coming from his right, someone grabbed his right wrist tightly, stopping him from using his smartphone. He immediately looked down to find a very familiar girl looking up at him with her usual blank expression.

"You... Oh."

Masachika wasn't the first person who realized how the scoring worked, but it wasn't one of the hundred members sitting in the audience, either.

"I am well aware of how disrespectful this is of me, but I am doing it all for Lady Yuki's victory. I am not letting you go until this trivia show is over."

It was Yuki's partner, Ayano.

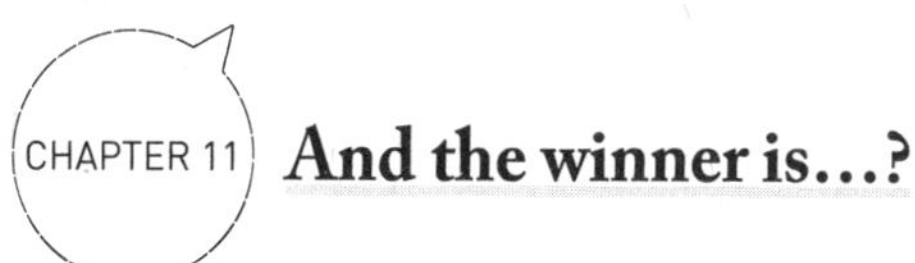

CHAPTER 11 And the winner is...?

There were a few reasons for Ayano's actions.

First, unlike Masachika, Ayano was focused on the score, so she was quick to realize that the questions' difficulty didn't match what she felt would be the general percentage of correct answers. In addition, unlike most of the students there, Ayano had never watched a trivia show before, so she never had the preconception that the general percentage usually came from the game show surveying random people in advance before the show aired. Last but not least, Ayano was both Yuki's and Masachika's maid, and she excelled at predicting what they would do next.

"Lady Yuki...? Why did you choose me to be your running partner in the election?"

Ayano had asked Yuki this question after the student council gave their speeches at the first semester's closing ceremony. It was a question she was even expecting would remove her from the position, since she was well aware that her talents were mediocre compared to the other candidates.

"You could easily find someone far more talented and popular than me. Wouldn't you prefer that?"

She wasn't being modest. She was genuinely inquiring after carefully evaluating her qualities. But in spite of the great courage and determination it took for Ayano to say that, Yuki nonchalantly replied:

"Hmm? Yeah, I guess from a popularity standpoint, I could get more votes with someone else as my partner...but that still wouldn't help me defeat my brother, would it?"

Her grin was fierce.

"There are only two people in this world who can easily read what my brother is thinking: you and me. Nobody else even comes close, and that's why you would be not only my perfect right-hand woman but also the greatest weapon against him."

That answer carved itself deep into Ayano's heart, and with those words, Ayano immediately began to put everything she had into reading Masachika's mannerisms and predicting his every movement the instant the trivia show began. She used the data she had on hand to predict what Masachika would think and do, and she also used that information to predict what conclusion he would come to as well. It was the same skill Ayano usually used to help her master Masachika, which allowed her to be two steps ahead of him and stop him in his tracks. As a result, she managed to successfully stop Masachika from contacting his friends, thus preventing those friends from manipulating the number of points Yuki could get.

"I just need to pick Yuki Suou first… Oh, it worked. Now, I just need to keep copying Alisa Kujou's answers?"

"Yes, please."

"You got it! I told my classmates about the plan, and I think they're all going to help."

"Sorry, Kuze. It's nothing personal."

"Of course, a member of the student council would never use force on weak little girls like us, right?"

The three female students wore fake smiles as they closed in on Masachika from each side while Ayano continued to hold on tightly to his right arm.

"I do not want to hurt you, so please slide your phone back into your pocket."

"Hurt me…? What exactly do you plan on doing?"

He turned his frustration with himself into a vacant smile.

Even if it's four against one…do they really think they have a chance against me?

When Masachika coldly observed the girls surrounding him, his threatening gaze wiped the smiles right off the faces of everyone but Ayano.

"If you do not do as I say..."

Ayano's expression did not change while she continued to stare him right in the eye.

"...I will kiss you."

"All right, all right. You win. My phone's going into my pocket."

He immediately slid his phone back into his pocket, then raised both hands in defeat. Ayano then forced him to turn back around and face the stage.

"Please do not try anything funny."

"Yes, ma'am," Masachika obediently agreed, his hands still in the air. Of course, he wasn't really planning on giving up. In fact, he was already coming up with a scheme to counter their attack based on an idea he got from their exchange a moment ago.

All right, that should do it... I hope. Now, the question is: How am I going to relay this information to Alya?

He organized his thoughts while staring hard at Alisa on the stage, but of course, she didn't notice.

At that time...

"That does it for round four. Now, let's check our contestants' scores. First, we have Ms. Suou with 570 points! And we have Ms. Kujou somewhat behind with 492 points! Ms. Suou is still in the lead!"

The gap's not getting any smaller...and there are only eleven questions left...

If their scores last round were actually compared, Alisa outperformed Yuki by one correct answer, but it didn't close the gap in their score at all.

At this rate, I'm going to need to answer three (?) questions correctly if I want to take the lead...but that's not going to help me if she gets every answer right, too...

Panic was slowly twisting Alisa's stomach.

...! What am I doing?! I can't waste my time thinking about this! I need to focus on the problems in front of me first!

She tried to devote her full attention to the questions before her after that, but each one was so difficult that mental fatigue was starting to take its toll.

"Now, the time has come…for round five! Your next topic will be…riddles!"

Riddles…? That sounds exhausting…

A series of numbers suddenly appeared on the screen. It was almost eerie how often your gut was right when it was something negative.

"Find the missing number in the sequence: 1, 2, 2, 1, 2, 1, 2, __, 2, 2, 2, 1. Is it 1, 2, 3, or 4? Timer starts now!"

Uh… First, you need to count all the numbers with puzzles like this! One, two… There are twelve numbers total! Is it something that there's twelve of? Like twelve months? That's it! Is it the old lunar calendar?! Mutsuki, Kisaragi… *No! That's not it! Then does it have to do with English? No, it has to be simpler than that. It's something there are twelve of… The zodiacs! It's the syllables of the Japanese names for the zodiacs!*

She began to name the Japanese zodiacs in her head.

Horse is uma… *Sheep is* hitsuji… *It's three syllables, so the answer is three!*

At the very last second, Alisa punched in her number and was almost immediately informed that she got the answer correct…but so did Yuki, meaning that nothing had changed. The panic was only getting worse.

I can't do this… Focus… I have to focus.

An image of the word *failure* was almost crystal clear in her mind, so she shook her head and squeezed her eyes shut to erase the thought. However, the moment she opened her eyes, the next question was already displayed on her tablet.

"Question number two! How many stars are on the sign near the entrance—?"

"Help."

All thought froze the instant she heard that voice coming from her side, but when she shifted her gaze in the direction of the voice, she saw Yuki faintly smirking while raising her right hand.

"The timer starts now!"

Right as the host's voice dragged Alisa back to reality, she returned her gaze to the question…

"What?" she grunted in a daze before lifting her head and peering into the distance. Near the entrance of the venue was a sign describing this attraction, but Alisa had no idea how many stars were on the board. There was no way she would, since you could *only see the back side of the sign* from the stage.

"Time's up!"

The merciless voice of the host sent her eyes back to the tablet in a fluster, but all the answers were already grayed out, unable to be selected.

"*Giggle.* Only one person may phone a friend per question, yes?"

Although overcome with mute astonishment, Alisa could still hear her rival's laughter, and when she turned to her side, Yuki was smiling at her as if she had already won the game.

"The moment I heard this rule, I knew there was going to be at least one question where you *had* to phone a friend."

She relentlessly rubbed salt into Alisa's wound. Her smile—her eyes were conveying a single fact, prompting Alisa to think back to what she had said a few minutes ago.

"Perhaps you only plan on phoning a friend if I do so first?"

That question she asked me during the break… She was trying to bait me into telling her when I planned on phoning a friend…

In her naïveté, Alisa answered her honestly, oblivious to Yuki's true intentions, and told her that she wasn't planning to phone a friend.

She's had me in the palm of her hand ever since then…

Suddenly, she felt a sting in her eyes.

"Now, Ms. Suou, are you ready for your ten seconds?"

"Yes."

Out of the corner of Alisa's blurry vision, she saw the host pick up Yuki's smartphone, tap the screen, then put Ayano on speaker.

"There are seven stars, Lady Yuki. The answer is number three."

"Thank you, Ayano."

There was no way Yuki got the answer wrong, because Ayano was standing right in front of the sign while on the phone. After sweetly thanking her partner, Yuki quietly tapped her answer on the tablet, and of course, the result was unsurprising.

"Correct! Furthermore, only twenty-six percent of people got the answer right, which gives you a total of seventy-four points!"

"What...?"

That would put her at a 152-point lead...?

The numbers dragged Alisa into despair, and her vision blurred. There was no way to win now. There was no way to make a comeback with only nine questions left. Besides, Alisa had been nothing more than a pawn on a board being manipulated by Yuki every step of the way. Struggling now wouldn't change that...

"On to question three!"

The host read the next question aloud, but Alisa couldn't hear him. Her brain couldn't process the question on the screen that her eyes were supposedly locked on, either. Her thoughts were plagued with hopelessness and resignation, which completely prevented her brain from functioning. All she could do was wait for the timer to run out. That is, until a certain word tickled her ear.

"Help!"

It was the loud declaration from her partner in the distance.

Great... Everyone's staring at me. Then again, who wouldn't after that?

Every eye in the venue speedily gathered around Masachika the instant he raised his right hand high into the air and yelled. Not only the students standing but also the ones sitting in their metal folding chair turned to look at him. Even the girls standing around him seemed startled...but it made sense when you considered they weren't expecting him to just randomly scream like that.

Regardless, this isn't against the rules.

Masachika got the idea from listening to Yuki talk about the phone-a-friend rule. In addition, he clearly remembered the host saying:

"Each candidate pair is allowed to 'phone a friend' one time. One pair being Ms. Suou and Ayano Kimishima, with the other pair being Ms. Kujou and Masachika Kuze. I know it's self-explanatory, but 'phoning a friend' means they are allowed to ask their partner for help. Therefore, if you ever want to phone a friend, you need to raise your hand and say, 'Help.' After that, you are allowed to talk to your partner on the phone for ten seconds tops."

He never said anything about the contestant being the one who has to make the call!

His eyes, which were quietly locked on the host, made his intentions clear, and although the host needed a few moments to gather his thoughts, he eventually replied:

"Well, uh... It sounds like Ms. Kujou's partner would like to phone a friend. Of course, there is no rule stating that the contestant must be the one who makes the announcement, so it's absolutely no problem at all. Now, uh... It appears that Ms. Suou has finished answering, so let us begin. Mr. Kuze, please call Ms. Kujou's smartphone for us, will you?"

Masachika waved back at the host while he whispered to Ayano to let him go.

"You heard him. This isn't against the game's rules. Obviously, you wouldn't want to do anything to make Yuki look bad in front of all these students, right? You'd ruin the game and hurt Yuki's reputation along with it."

Ayano shuddered, and her gaze wavered with bewilderment. The other three seemed to be unsure of what to do as well as they waited for their leader to reply. But before Ayano could even answer, Masachika quickly called Alisa on his phone.

"There he is! Ms. Kujou, are you ready? You only have ten seconds once I answer this phone," mentioned the host with Alisa's phone in hand, but she was sluggish to react, as if she were mentally not all there. Masachika could feel her puzzled gaze, so he confidently looked straight back into her eyes.

Don't worry. You didn't mess up. Your pride and your stubbornness weren't all for nothing. We would have never had this opportunity if you had used your phone-a-friend lifeline earlier.

And that was why Masachika already knew exactly what he was going to say. He wasn't going to do anything that would hurt his proud partner's drive for greatness, and he wasn't going to use these ten seconds to give her a hint to answer the trivia question before her.

"Your ten seconds start…now!"

The host tapped the answer button on Alisa's phone, connecting them. What Masachika needed to give her in these ten seconds was…

"Alya! From this question on, wait until the last second before you punch your answer in!"

…a strategy to overcome the enemy's scheme…and the encouragement she needed to go on!

"You deserve to become the student council president, Alya! I promise you that! And that's why you can't give up!"

The ten seconds were over. Other than a select few, most of the audience exchanged bewildered glances, as if they couldn't comprehend how that was supposed to help Alisa answer the question, but their questions would almost immediately be answered.

"Interesting…"

The voice came from the stage. It was Alisa's…rival's voice.

"I thought something was strange after the previous question… but it all makes sense now."

After her long introductory remark, all eyes shifted from Masachika to Yuki, who surveyed the audience briefly, then asked in a deciding voice:

"Can everyone in the audience see our answers?"

The commotion that erupted in the audience was all the proof she needed. She calmly smiled and added:

"The general percentage of correct answers is being calculated from your answers in real time. That would explain why the percentage is given after the correct answer is announced, and it would also explain how the previous question had so many wrong answers. Furthermore, it probably goes without saying that the previous question would have not even worked unless you were here with us at this venue." Yuki giggled and explained the hidden rule of this game while a great deal of people in the audience who hadn't realized it listened attentively to her in astonishment and excitement.

"In other words, each member of this audience has the power to manipulate the outcome and decide how many points each of us deserves. I can now see what the host meant when he said there would be elements related to the election. What an interesting rule," she exclaimed, glancing at the host. She then stood out of her chair, placed a hand on her chest, and suggested with the utmost sincerity:

"However, I want to beat Alya fair and square. Therefore, while I really appreciate that some of you may try to manipulate the scores in order to help me, I ask that you please stop. I do not need any help. All I ask is that you believe in me and quietly watch over our match."

Yuki's wish to fight one-on-one evoked a gasp of admiration among the crowd. Countless people at that moment were spellbound by what appeared to be a noble-minded gesture...but Masachika scowled.

Tsk! She's good. She's real good. Anyone who was planning on manipulating the score to hurt Alya lost their chance the moment I called her and gave her that advice, so what does Yuki do? She exposes the entire system and needlessly tells people to not cheat, which makes her seem both confidently capable of winning and noble-minded. Looks like she was trying to win back those who were charmed by Alya's passionate speech during their break.

Her scheme seemed to work perfectly. Those who were hoping to see Alisa make a comeback now seemed to be only excited to see the best woman win.

"I would like to ask everyone who is playing to not look at our answers and only answer based on what you think. Would that be possible?"

Yuki's innocent, adorable request had everyone nodding before covering part of their smartphone's screen with their finger, a handkerchief, or anything else they could get their hands on. It was a clear display of neutrality. In the span of one minute, Yuki had managed to convince an entire crowd to follow her and change the rules.

"Ngh…! Uh… Do you think we could continue?"

"Yes, of course. I apologize for the interruption," replied Yuki with a bow to the host before gracefully settling herself back into her seat. The host forced himself to smile back and replied:

"It is no problem at all. Now, Ms. Kujou, are you ready to answer? Your ten seconds starts now!"

Alisa was given another ten seconds to answer after her call had ended, and even though Masachika didn't give her a single clue that she could use to answer this question…she was confident in her answer nonetheless. After taking two seconds to choose her answer, she calmly said:

"Thank you, Masachika."

Her gratefulness could be heard throughout the entire venue while the radiant sparkles returned to her azure eyes. Masachika knew the moment she gazed into his eyes that she had awakened from her trance.

"I would like to thank you as well, Yuki, for wanting to do the right thing. Now I can beat you fair and square."

"*Giggle.* You took the words right out of my mouth."

Their competitive gazes locked, which excited the crowd even more.

"The correct answer was…number four! Good job, contestants! You both got it right!"

Their aggressiveness and unwillingness to back down had the

audience cheering even more loudly. Everyone had completely forgotten that the host had warned them to be silent during the show, but being quiet had already lost all meaning, regardless.

"Relax, Ayano. I'm not scheming anything anymore." Masachika shrugged and glanced to his side at Ayano, who seemed shaken.

"The rest is in Alya's hands. And you just need to believe in Yuki."

He looked away from his unsure childhood friend and focused on what was happening onstage. After all, he wasn't lying, so there was no need for him to do anything else. He had already done everything he could and said everything he needed to say.

Even now, people Ayano had contacted to help Yuki win were gathering at the venue, but nothing they did would benefit Yuki anymore. If anything, Masachika was ready to welcome them.

"That does it for round five! We have six questions left, but before we continue, let's look at the scores. Ms. Suou has…776 points! And for Ms. Kujou…680 points! Although Ms. Suou is still in the lead by almost a hundred points, the following questions are the most difficult ones yet, so they will most likely be worth a lot of points. In other words, Ms. Kujou still has a chance to make a comeback! Anyway, is everyone ready for round six? Your final topic is…brain teasers!"

The host ended up being right. Multiple questions were worth sixty or more points, but after a while, both Yuki and Alisa started making mistakes. Nevertheless, Alisa still didn't give up and succeeded in getting three of the questions right, as opposed to Yuki, who only got two, bringing Alisa one step closer to taking the lead.

"Incredible! What a close game this is turning out to be! Now that round six is over, there is only one more question left in this thrilling battle! The current scores are…Ms. Suou, 904 points! Ms. Kujou, 880 points! There is only a measly twenty-four-point difference between them now!"

The audience was on the edge of their seats, attentively watching the extremely close game, but in the midst of their peak excitement was Masachika, breathing a sigh of relief.

"That's Alya for you. Incredible."

Ayano watched him quizzically as he put his phone away and clapped softly.

"Isn't it a little too early to start celebrating? Lady Yuki is still in the lead."

It was a reasonable question, but Masachika replied with the utmost confidence:

"No, it's over. Alya already won."

Masachika glanced to his side, noticing that Ayano had returned his conviction with a baffled stare, so he added:

"You've never seen one of these trivia shows before, right? On one hand, that was how you managed to realize before anyone else that the percentage of correct answers was being calculated from the audience's answers in real time. On the other hand…it's also why you aren't familiar with the cliché showdowns in the end."

"Cliché showdowns?"

"Yeah, most of the older, well-known ones always make the last showdown a question that's worth enough points so that the losing contestant can make a big comeback."

Ayano briefly wavered, but she immediately looked straight back into Masachika's eyes and replied, undaunted:

"A comeback won't be possible when Lady Yuki answers the last question correctly. I believe in her."

"Believing in her isn't going to help because with all these friends you invited, the last question is going to be worth over twenty-four points."

"…? How does that change what I said?"

But Masachika didn't reply as his eyes shifted back to the stage, prompting Ayano to face forward to look at the stage as well. Originally, the scoring system greatly benefited whoever had the most people in the audience on their side. All you had to do was figure out how the system worked, then you could abuse it. Put simply, it wasn't fair. Therefore, it would only be right for the person who had fewer people on their side to get a chance to score a ton of points. But what if that one opportunity was the last question of the game? And what would that question even be? A hint to what it could be was already out there and had been there before the trivia show even began.

"Who do you think is a better fit for student council president?"

Yuki probably would have been able to figure it out if she knew this question existed.

But it was too late for her. Their approval rating had already been set in stone.

"Now, let us move on to the final question! Ta-daa!"

The host held out his hand toward the monitor in an exaggerated manner as the final question was displayed on the screen.

"Do you believe you have what it takes to become student council president?! Yes or no?! Your timer starts…now!"

It was such a bizarre final question that it created a commotion among the crowd, but when Alisa swiftly looked up in surprise, Masachika peered right into her eyes, then faintly yet firmly nodded.

To victory, Alya
"К Победе, Аля!"

But obviously, there was no way she could hear those soft words of his. Alisa smiled in a somewhat troubled manner but seemed genuinely happy as she placed a finger on the tablet's screen.

"Time's up! Both of our contestants have answered! But first, let's discuss how the final question is scored!"

Everyone's eyes were locked on the host while he spread his arms out wide to the audience.

"As you all know, each one of you in the audience was asked in the very beginning who they thought was better suited to become the next student council president: Ms. Suou or Ms. Kujou. Put simply, the survey's answers' percentages—your approval ratings—will influence your scores! In other words, the number of points for a correct answer differs between contestants!"

The moment Yuki heard that, her lips curled into a wry smirk like she had figured it all out. She then shot her brother a meaningful glance as if to say, "You little punk."

"Sorry, Yuki," muttered Masachika, grinning right back at her.

"The correct answer for the final question is obviously yes. Someone who isn't confident that they can be student council president doesn't have any right to claim any points! And whichever contestant got the answer right will receive their points using the formula one hundred minus approval rating equals points!"

In other words, this was essentially an act of charity to help out the contestant with fewer supporters. It was a special rule to make a major comeback possible, since the fewer supporters you had, the more points you got. After the host revealed the truth behind the entire project, he moved on to announce the contestants' scores.

"Both of our contestants answered yes! So after calculating their approval rating, our contestants' scores come out to be—"

Pledge

"That was the most intense trivia show I've ever seen. Our noble princess got close, but…"

"Nah, man. That was some BS. She got way more answers right, so she deserved to win. Plus, she figured out how those percentages worked in the middle of the show. She may have technically lost because of that last question, but she basically won."

"The only reason she got more answers right was because Alisa got every pop culture question wrong. Other than that, Alisa got more answers right on basically every topic, so if we're judging them by how knowledgeable they are, then Alisa wins."

"Ayano deserves credit for figuring out how the percentages were calculated! You guys probably don't know this, but she was actually the first to figure it out! Pretty awesome, right?"

"Seriously?! But you know who's legit badass? Kuze, for using that phone-a-friend lifeline! I low-key couldn't even understand what he was trying to say, but looking back, he sounded like he knew what the last question was gonna be."

"I feel ya, man. Same vibes. I'm still shook."

"To tell the truth, I was most touched by Alisa's eloquent speech. Seeing her be so courageous in the face of adversity made me a fan."

"Oh my. Then what about Ms. Suou? She was so brave for not taking advantage of the rules and for fighting fair and square. That was very respectful."

"Yes… After thinking about it, it's hard to decide who really won."

"Yeah, those were some bizarre rules, but it was so much fun!"

Exhilarated voices could be heard in the background while Masachika and Alisa sat in metal folding chairs behind the stage. There was not another soul in sight, since every other worker was busy preparing for the next attraction. The excitement still hadn't worn off from the match while they sat side by side without saying a word.

"...I wanted to prove that I was good enough to be your partner," Alisa eventually muttered. Masachika stayed quiet and listened. She continued to face forward and added:

"A lot of people depend on you...and a lot of people accept and respect you. And they talk about you and Yuki...like you're the ideal pair..."

She paused for a moment—the next time she spoke would be with more force. She would speak her mind boldly, making her competitiveness and determination no secret.

"That's why I wanted you to see just how capable I was. I wanted to prove that I was more than a prop who needed you to hold me up. I wanted to show that I could beat Yuki all by myself and that I was good enough to be your partner. I wanted to be acknowledged..."

Her voice trailed off at the end, and her brows furrowed as she gazed into Masachika's eyes.

"But...I failed. I would have lost if it weren't for you," she whispered in a self-deprecating manner as her stare drifted toward the ground. Although her expression was hidden behind her silver hair, her fists were clenched on her lap, which was more than enough to convey how she was feeling.

She's like a brilliantly shining star.

Masachika was envious of how she could honestly acknowledge how helpless she was and be so frustrated by it. It was this noble nature of hers that he felt needed to be protected at all costs...but at the same time, it hit him like a truck because he realized that—

Someday, Alya's not going to need me anymore...

Countless people were going to be drawn to Alisa one day. Her single-minded, proud way of living was going to move countless people who would gather around her and support her. But even when she became the center of it all, she would continue to move forward, never looking back…and someone like Masachika, who still couldn't let go of the past, wasn't going to be able to keep up with her.

If…

If he agreed with what Alisa claimed and said something cheap like, "Yeah, you're probably right, but don't worry. I'm going to continue being right there for you, every step of the way," then maybe she would continue to depend on him from now on. Maybe she would take Masachika's hand, smile, and tell him that she was counting on him.

But he couldn't do that to her. There was no way he could say something that would slow someone down just so the two of them could walk at the same pace.

Right now, what I need to do is…

Masachika quietly stood up, spun around so that he was standing right in front of her, and got on his knee…like a knight about to pledge his loyalty to the princess.

"Alya, you were never losing to begin with."

Alisa looked up to find him kneeling before her, and her eyes widened in wonderment. As he gazed deeply into her eyes, Masachika placed a gentle hand on her tightly clenched fists.

"The pride and willpower that you showed onstage was very attractive to a lot of people, and now you have countless followers who are going to support you, no matter what. And that's why you were never losing to begin with."

There was no reason to embellish his words or put on a show. All he needed to do was speak honestly from the heart.

"All I did was go head-to-head with Ayano as a rival striving for the position of student council vice president, and it revealed a path to victory. But you already found something even more valuable than that. You alone were the one who captivated that audience. Your success came from your hard work, and that's why there's no reason to feel frustrated with yourself."

She began to tremble while her fists clenched tightly around Masachika's hand.

"Really?"

"Hmm?"

"Did I really earn everyone's respect and acceptance?"

It must have been stressing her out for so long. She had been worrying and fighting this battle alone for a while, and it was Masachika's inexperience that forced her to do that.

"Yes, really. You have my word," he assured as if he were trying to make up for his mistakes, but it still wasn't enough to rid Alisa of her sorrows.

"How can you be so sure?"

"Because…"

Only when he paused for a moment to think did he realize his mistake. He promised himself that he wasn't going to embellish his words, so he decided to reply only with honesty and only from the heart.

"Because…your performance onstage captivated me as well."

Alisa looked stunned, but Masachika continued as if he wanted to be sure that what he was saying reached her heart.

"You have no idea how cool you were when you said you were going to beat Yuki fair and square. It made me genuinely proud to be your partner."

He smiled but with a hint of sorrow.

"And that's why you need to keep being bold as you move forward. I'll get rid of anyone who holds you back or slows you down."

Even if that person is me, he added in his head.

"…Thank you," she whispered, smiling like she wanted to cry as she took Masachika's hand and placed it against her forehead.

"I'm really glad you're my partner."

His heart throbbed painfully, knowing she meant that from the bottom of her heart, but he fought through the pain and maintained his composure. Alisa then gently lowered his hand back to her lap and smiled affectionately like a blooming flower, prompting Masachika to smile in return. They peacefully gazed into each other's eyes for the next few moments…until one of the school festival committee workers returned to the area behind the stage.

"...! Huh?!"

The individual saw one person kneeling before another as they held hands and gazed into each other's eyes, which caused him to take a step back in utter shock. He blinked curiously for a few seconds before dragging his other foot back as well, then he began to scratch his cheek in a bashful and bewildered manner.

"Uh... Did I just walk in on a proposal?"

"N-no! He was just taking my pulse..."

"Come on, Alya. That's the best you could come up with?" joked Masachika. Nevertheless, their schoolmate smiled stiffly while continuing to retreat.

"Oh, okay. Well, enjoy yourselves..."

"H-hey!"

Alisa immediately jumped out of her seat, but there was no way she could simply chase him around the stage.

"...!!"

She groaned, struggling to not just chase him down while Masachika uncomfortably smirked at her.

"A proposal, huh? Wow... I mean, we're not even old enough to get married, right?"

But Masachika's comment was immediately met with Alisa's discontent, foul glare.

"We might be too young to get married...but we could still get engaged, right?"

"Come on—don't give me a serious answer. It was a ridiculous thing for him to say."

"Oh? What, am I not good enough for you?"

A devilish smirk instantly formed on her lips, making Masachika's breath catch. He eventually made a sweeping statement in an attempt to avoid the question.

"No, it's not that... It's just...freshmen in high school getting engaged? That's not even realistic."

"Really? Because I wouldn't mind it if they were my one true love."

"...?"

Ни за что!

He raised an eyebrow at her unexpected remark before provocatively grinning as if he could already taste his sweet revenge.

"It almost sounds like you're indirectly asking me to propose to you. Should I be a real man right now and ask for your hand in marriage?"

But Alisa confidently lifted her chin as if to belittle his smug counterattack.

"You're an idiot." She grinned, fidgeting with her hair with her left hand.

Afterword

Hey, Sunsunsun here.

I know I stopped at a cliffhanger at the end of Volume 4, and I know I made you wait for over half a year, but I'm back. Perhaps this is punishment, because the afterword this time is almost ten pages. Again. I know what you're thinking. What do you mean, "again"? Well, you must not have read the side stories in Volume 4.5, because if you did, you would know. Once again, there is not much of a point to reading anything I'm going to say from here on out, so if you're not *extremely* interested in whatever I'm going to ramble about, please close this book now.

Anyway, this is rough. Two afterwords in a row that are about ten pages long. I was able to squeeze out over ten pages pretty easily last time because I was weirdly excited for some reason...but I can hardly remember anything I even wrote. No joke. Of course, it'd be easy for me to check, but I'm afraid I wrote something embarrassing that I'm going to end up remembering in the shower for years to come, so I'm not going to attempt to check. Right now, I'm my ordinary self: not overly excited and not in any mood to pump out more than ten pages in the blink of an eye.

Of course, I don't have to force myself to write these obscenely long afterwords. I could just let the publisher cram advertisements into the book at the end and be done with it, but that just doesn't feel right. There's something unsightly about seeing a ton of ads at the end of a novel, and I don't mean to brag, but *Alya Sometimes Hides Her Feelings in Russian* has become a huge success. So if you put an advertisement at the end, it would surely be effective, right? Don't you think it'd be a little strange if I just started letting people post their advertisements at the end of my novels for free? If you want to start cluttering my books, then you better start coughing up some dough! Pay up, or get out!

...And yet here I am, writing an afterword that makes me absolutely no money, no matter how long it is. Feels almost contradictory. Feels almost like a cart-before-the-horse kind of thing. For example...

....

....

...I can't come up with a good example. Eh. Whatever. I guess I shouldn't have been trying to come up with something while pretending to watch ads on Magazine Pocket. Oh, this isn't a joke, either. I'm currently writing this on November 5th, 2022, and right now, watching up to three online advertisements gives readers access to a treasure box. (Opening these gives readers either points or a ticket.) Now I've opened all my treasure boxes, and I'm currently swiping through a comic that also gives me points. By the way, the comic I'm currently reading is... Hold on. Who drew this beautiful, cute girl looking at me like I'm garbage? Th-this comic...! It's...! This is Saho Tenamachi's artwork...!

This is *Alya Sometimes Hides Her Feelings in Russian*! In comic form!

Okay, I lied. I know—I'm a loser. Even I felt grossed out. Of course, Alya in the comics is extremely cute, and I do get chills seeing her look at me like I'm garbage, but I'm not actually quickly swiping through the comic right now. After all, I already read it the instant it came out. I mean, I even got to see the rough draft and proofread version of the comic before it got published, to boot.

But you all know this because I made an announcement in the last afterword. Wait. Did I? Now I'm starting to doubt myself… Oh, wait. Here it is. Yep. I did. Thank goodness. It even says on the cover's belt that the serialized comic was starting in October, so yeah. It's on Magazine Pocket right now. Every time a new issue comes out, I'm so impressed by how well it's done. I really mean that from the bottom of my heart.

Sometimes you see light novels get turned into comics, and you're like, "They don't even respect the source material. They're just doing whatever they want with this thing!" You may even wonder, "Is the author of the source material fine with this?" Nevertheless, I am seriously satisfied with how the comics are turning out for *Alya Sometimes Hides Her Feelings in Russian*. Saho Tenamachi believes that the best way to turn something into a comic is to follow the source material in a way that would make the original author happy, so I know I can trust her to make it good. Sometimes I do give her a few opinions and actually have her help me from time to time as well. Anyway, every day I'm reminded of how lucky I am to have someone like her handling the comics.

You can read *Alya Sometimes Hides Her Feelings in Russian* every other Saturday if you download the Magazine Pocket app. And as I mentioned earlier, if you watch the ads and read enough comics that award points, you'll have enough points to read the newest chapters every release, so please check it out if you can!

…Tsk. I know I mentioned earlier that the afterword was essentially going to be garbage with no substance, but that was actually a very important announcement. In other words, there was at least one important thing mentioned here.

Now that I think about it, is it even okay for me to be writing an advertisement for a comic app made by a different company entirely? I'll have to ask the editor. I wrote a lot about Saho Tenamachi as well, so I'll need to get her approval first, too. The schedule's already tight, so if I give the editor any more work, blood's going to shoot out of his nose, and he's going to have to go into overdrive and transform into his second form… I kind of want to see that, though.

He is actually really busy from what I heard. After all, he is apparently the editor for a Sneaker Bunko award-winning series for the first time in twelve years. I can't even imagine the heavy responsibility. He talked about his enthusiasm for taking on such a big responsibility on *note* (the website), and it sounded intense. Reading about him passionately writing his entire life story with its ups and downs until he finally become the editor for an award-winning series really moved me. I really wish I could write about my life like that and move people…and yet this is what I choose to write. Ha-ha!

…Hold up. Maybe it's not too late. Maybe I could start talking about something serious. Maybe I could bring up an exciting tale from my life that could touch the readers' hearts. Well, there's no time like the present! Fortunately, I still have plenty of pages left to use! All right! Let's do this! Hee-hee! Ah! Ahn! Mn! Ooof! Yeehaw! All right. Ready? I'm now wearing my big-boy serious face. *Doo-a-doo-aloo.* That's the sound of the *shakuhachi* (a bamboo flute) in the background. Following that, we have *BANG, BANG, BANG*… Uh… What sound is that? Wood clappers? Uh… Let's ask the internet. "Kabuki," "Intro," "banging sound…" Yeah, those are wooden clappers in the beginning. I was right. I'm so smart. Anyway, my apologies. I'm going to put on my real serious face now. Allow me to explain how Sunsunsun started on Shousetsuka ni Narou (Let's Become a Novelist website) and worked his way to getting *Alya Sometimes Hides Her Feelings in Russian* published.

My first step to become a novelist started in the research lab in college. I know it sounds ridiculous already, but hear me out. I was obsessed with Shousetsuka ni Narou when I was in college, and the research lab I was a part of allowed us to use the place relatively freely as long as we were producing results. It was a wonderful lab. The kind of place where you could ask the professor if you could watch YouTube in the classroom, and he'd be like, "Eh, why not? I mean, I'm watching it right now." Plus, the break room had so much booze that it got to the point that there were rumors that you had to be drunk to get inside. Of course, the fact that I was always in the break room was proof the rumors weren't true. By the way, you can find *Alya Sometimes Hides Her Feelings in Russian* hidden among the academic journals now in the break room. I bet there are rumors that you have to be a drunk nerd to be allowed inside the break room nowadays. Yeah, I know this is ridiculous, but let me finish.

If you're studying the sciences in college or are a graduate who was a student in science and engineering, then you probably already get this, but many experiments have a lot of downtime. The research I was doing took at least ten hours to complete every time I conducted an experiment, but over half of that was just me waiting. Of course, you could use that wait time to do other experiments, read essays or someone's thesis, or take another class, but even after doing all that, there was still a lot of wait time.

I'm sure a lot of you sharp ones can see where I'm going with this, and you'd be correct. I used that free time to start writing novels. The first thing I wrote was a short story that was only a little over twenty-thousand characters. I started it one day just to test out how it'd feel, and before long, the story started to take form. Once it became a real story, I showed an older student working in the lab with me. I believe he was a doctoral student two years ahead of me, but he was my only nerdy friend in the lab back then, and he was also a writer who wished to become a novelist someday. Anyway, after he read it, he told me it was good and recommended that I post it online somewhere, so I decided to upload it to Shousetsuka ni Narou. For the first time, I was a poster on that site instead of just a reader.

What happened after that was a huge surprise. It got a lot more traction than I ever could have imagined, and it got me really into loving to write. I posted novel after novel after that. To tell the truth, when I started writing this series, I already had a vague dream of having it novelized one day. I wanted professionals in the business to read my novels and enjoy them more than I wanted to be a novelist. I wanted my writings to live on without me in the form of novels one day. That was my dream. It was a wish to leave something behind while I was alive that showed that I was here. I existed. I'm sure that's something everyone feels at least once in their life. I never really had any huge dreams like making bank selling my work or having it turned into an anime. I just wanted to leave behind a reminder for after I'm long gone, that an author named Sunsunsun once lived in this world. It was a vague dream of mine, but one I gave up on relatively quickly.

And that's because, surprisingly, I'm not the kind of person who can sit down and write extremely long novels. I'm not being modest. I'm being serious. Whenever the story gets too long, I start getting the urge to add so many different storylines and details that things get out of hand. The story becomes a mess. Plus, I got bored with sticking to the same thing for too long, so the longer something gets, the harder it becomes to maintain quality. It got to the point that when I read the serialized stories I wrote, I realized the writing was amateur and not fit to be made into a book.

But that failure helped me realize that I was good at creating short stories. *"I want to write about situations like this." "I want to write characters like that."* The ideas just kept popping into my head, so I decided to use these ideas to tackle short stories, and I immediately felt at home. I started calling myself a short-story writer, and I continued to produce numerous short stories after that. Before long, I had thousands of people "favoriting" my account, and my stories started making the rankings for best short stories. I eventually even made it to eighteenth place out of the top three hundred short-story rankings for a while. Up until then, most of them didn't crack the top one hundred, and I only had one that made it into the top fifty...but you know what that story was? *Alya Sometimes Hides Her Feelings in Russian.* And a month after I posted it in the middle of June 2020, I received a message asking if I was interested in novelizing the story.

"What?"

That was the first word that popped into my head. I couldn't believe it. After that, I noticed the message was sent by an editor for Sneaker Bunko, and my head almost exploded. Technically, it wasn't exactly an offer to novelize the short story. It was an offer to try to turn this short story into a longer story. But I was like, "No way… There's no way I can pull this off." I was a short-distance runner who only performed somewhat well in contests for amateurs, and I was basically being told I was going to have to run a marathon with the pros. And it was a professional editor for the legendary Sneaker Bunko, of all companies, who saw potential in me. It was an honor, and I was thrilled, but I had my reservations. Nevertheless, I decided to at least hear him out first.

The first person I spoke to was none other than Miyakawa, the editor I have now. The first thing he told me was that the title, *Alya Sometimes Hides Her Feelings in Russian*, was perfect, and the premise that the protagonist could understand Russian but Alya didn't know was an amazing concept to build off of. He then passionately talked about what he loved about the short story, told me he saw huge potential in it, and asked me to work together with him to novelize it. I was touched by his passion and told him I would love that.

The first promise we made was to start writing the plot out, and that was how my first remote meeting with Miyakawa concluded. The path to turning this story into a book had suddenly revealed itself right before my eyes. My vague dream, which I had already given up on, seemed like it could very possibly come true. The opportunity came unexpectedly and quickly. After that, I deeply exhaled, then said:

"All right! Time to start a new short story!"

I wish I was joking. But this is what I really said. This is nonfiction. I'm sure you could check my Shousetsuka ni Narou account and see for yourself, but I continued to post short stories for a while after that. Ridiculous, right? I can't believe there are people in this world who can hear Miyakawa speak so passionately about something they put their heart into and feel nothing. I know. Rip me apart, guys.

But first, I have an excuse. A small one, but an excuse. I was all about writing short stories back then. That was my life. Plus, I had heard tales of people getting offers that never actually worked out, and the deal fell through… It was like, "Do I want to work on something that's six thousand characters that will definitely be posted and read, or do I want to work on something that's twice as long that may never even be seen by anyone?" Plus, back then I wasn't the kind of person who liked trying out new things, either. Yeah, I know that doesn't excuse what I did. I can feel novelists and aspiring novelists starting to dislike me already. But you know how you sometimes hear stories like "I went with my friend to the audition to help them out, but I actually got the part"? Well, that's me. The chance just fell into my lap. The world can be fair at times but extremely unfair as well.

I didn't have the drive, and yet I somehow managed to finish writing the first novel for *Alya Sometimes Hides Her Feelings in Russian*, and it was all thanks to Miyakawa. He took a kid like me—who you could hit and still wouldn't do what I was told—and he continued to hit me with love and passion until I finished the story. I used to be like, "*There's no way I can write over one hundred thousand characters without hearing the readers' feedback.*" It was a naive, weak way to think, but Miyakawa was always there to give me his detailed thoughts on every story. Even when I was writing this volume, Volume 5, I sent him a message saying, "*There aren't any fan-service scenes with Alya yet. Do you think we need to remove some clothes so we can have a nice illustration for the first few pages of the novel?*" And he immediately replied, "*Do it for the people. Do it for the world.*" The instant I read that, I genuinely thought to myself, *Man, I'm so lucky to work with a guy like that.*

Looking back, I can really see how fortunate I was to be surrounded by great people. Of course, my editor, Miyakawa, is one of those people, but I am also very grateful for having the illustrator,

Momoco, and Saho Tenamachi as well. There are so many people who have helped me get *Alya Sometimes Hides Her Feelings in Russian* out there. I am grateful for having parents who completely supported my passion to be a part-time writer as well. *Alya Sometimes Hides Her Feelings in Russian* would have never made it this far without the help of countless others. (Did that comment help me win back some people?) Hmm… Strange… I actually took this afterword seriously for a change, but I feel like it actually made people think less of me? Maybe it's better that some authors just keep their mouths shut and focus on writing stories. Besides, it's really not like me to actually put effort into the afterword, especially after mentioning how pointless this afterword was going to be in the very beginning. I should probably rewrite the beginning and mention that nothing will be gained from reading this afterword. Oh well.

Anyway, I'm out of pages, it looks like. Hmm… Yeah, I'm really not made for writing serious stories. Plus, longer isn't better when it comes to afterwords. If anything, these should be short but sweet. You can't maintain the quality when you write this much, but you can really show what you're made of with shorter afterwords. Yep. I really am only meant to write short stories. The foreshadowing finally came together. All right, that's enough of this.

I rambled so long that we're out of pages, so I think it's time for me to move on to the special thanks. I want to thank the great editor Miyakawa, Momoco for always meeting my detailed requests, Kinta for joining in this time as a guest illustrator and making Alya look not only cool but extremely beautiful as well, Tei Ogata for also joining as a guest illustrator with his extremely tasteful illustration of Masha, everyone else involved in the production of this novel, and of course, you, the reader. Thank you very much! I am looking forward to seeing you again in Volume 6. Until then.

P.S. Hey, you. Yeah, you. The guy who thinks I'm not the real Sunsunsun for being serious in the afterword for a change. You're smarter than you look. Meet me behind the gym.

Alya, I look forward
to continuing to
work with you! :)